April in Paris in June

To Gretchen,
Happy reading!

[signature]

JESSICA CLEM BARNARD

Table of Contents

Prologue

Paris, France 1999
The End of the Beginning.

Paris lives up to the hype. Honestly, it's about the only thing that does.

And even by Paris standards, the Eiffel Tower is a bit of a panty dropper. The metal scaffolding is delicate yet strong. The arcs and curves are graceful. It's probably a little taller than you imagined. It actually looks like the pictures, which anyone who's ever tried online dating can tell you is the ultimate compliment.

No surprise that on a beautiful June evening back in 1999, with gentle breezes and a golden-hour glow, the place crawls with starry-eyed tourists. As the sun begins to set, they are struck with a sudden pang of romantic longing. The singles gaze out over the city's quaint twists and turns with a newfound certainty that somewhere love waits for them—how could it be otherwise in such a perfect place? The coupled, haloed by the warm light, remember the intoxicating rush of their first meeting while life's little disappointments temporarily fade into the background.

One pair—somewhere between single and coupled—turns to each other. April Andersen literally knocked Paul

Stone off his feet just yesterday, and this moment has been building ever since. Paul brushes his fingers to April's cheek in a question, she meets his eyes in answer. He leans in and finds her mouth. She winds her hands around his neck. He parts his lips, she responds. Surrounded by throngs of people, they kiss atop the Eiffel Tower at sunset like they are completely alone. Cliché wrapped in cliché, but it's so damn romantic you could cry.

How very French, thinks one of their fellow tourists, who has just finished sighing and looking out over the city, imagining where her true love could be. Unnoticed by Paul and April lost in their perfect kiss, she snaps a photo.

Chapter 1

2019

April

Today is going to be one of those sweet, stupid days, damn it.

April Andersen blinks grumpily as she awakes to a perfect May morning. A sunbeam drips across her quilt like melted butter. The starlings and sparrows and jays of the neighborhood chirp manically like some bird Greek chorus: *Kiss! Kiss! Kiss!*

April still thinks about that kiss a few times a year, mostly on these glorious late spring days that hint at summer. As much as she tries not to, it has a way of sneaking up on her as New England comes back to life after a long, dark winter. Twenty years later, it feels like a dream. An over-the-top dream, even for someone like her whose first gear is over-the-top: Paris, sunset, the Eiffel Tower, a cute Canadian guy she never saw again. If someone else told her that story, April would roll her eyes even harder than her pre-teen daughter Liza.

But maybe, thinks April, kicking off her starburst pattern quilt and luxuriating in the warm sun on her bare legs, she can give in just for a minute—the press of lips, the rumble of the crowd, the unfamiliar feeling of just being herself without overthinking. Just one more minute, and then pull back before the inevitable edge of shame and loss creeps in. Hey, it was just the first of many life lessons on keeping her inner chaotic girl under wraps.

Sunlight dances over the nine yellow stripes on the opposite wall, paint samples ranging from Baby Buttercup to Goldfish Parade. She keeps meaning to just pick one and paint the whole room, but each is perfect in its own way. So for now, she will stretch luxuriantly, slip on that purple around-the-house caftan, shake out her wavy bronze hair, and wander to the kitchen to make coffee. Liza is at her dad's, so April can stomp around all she wants.

Downstairs, the part of the house that outsiders see has that airy, bland HGTV look expected by clients who visit her home office. The requisite open kitchen so your dirty dishes are visible from the couch; the greige wall color that would look so great if only it were cotton candy pink. As April tells her home staging clients, potential buyers need to picture themselves living here. And then adds silently, to herself, *That's why I get rid of all your personal touches so buyers can imagine there is no past, only a future where they can move in with a blank slate and finally be happy.*

April lets her mind wander back to Paris, plugging in the cheap Mr. Coffee she always comes back to after flirtations with French presses and moka pots. Sometimes she remembers the warm hand cupping her cheek, the way the crowd pressed them together, the feeling that they were alone among hundreds of people. She remembers other things, too—his broad shoulders and gravelly voice, and hiding from the rain with his hungry eyes locked in hers.

April catches herself holding her mug in both hands and gazing out the window dreamily like some dumb bitch in a Folgers commercial. These daydreams always end in a painful stab of regret at how she ran away. It was the right thing to do, especially for him, she tells herself for the thousandth time. So what if it had set up the pattern of running away that she'd been caught in ever since: from her marriage to Danny, from a relationship with her father, from her art. Everyone has their flaws, and hers is just a very special knack for being altogether too needy, too messy, all around too much, and then hiding behind her navy pantsuit before anyone catches on. Her best friend Selma warns her that one of these days April is going to paint herself taupe and disappear into one of her staged homes, but hopefully she still has a few good years left.

Speaking of which, it's time to lock up the silly kiss memories in a little box, throw on that pantsuit, and get to work.

Paul

Paul Stone wakes up five minutes before his clock radio alarm, as always. He lies in bed, in the house he grew up in, waiting for the radio to blast 98.6 FM Classic Rock, as always. It's his birthday, but it's just like any other day.

And just like any other day, he thinks about that kiss.

Paul tries to ration the memory, maybe use it as a reward for balancing the books at Stone Dry Cleaning or completing his run along the Assiniboine River on these still-freezing May days. But today is his birthday, damn it. If he has to turn forty-two and sit through all the birthday hoopla his sister planned, he can spend a few minutes replaying what he sometimes worries was the most romantic moment of his life.

Paul closes his eyes to run through the familiar sequence: raking a hand through April's hair with its faint, smoky smell, the other hand tangling with her fingers. A glance at her wide, happy mouth before locking eyes and leaning in. And then a first kiss like nothing before or since, full of sweetness and desire but also a shuddering intimacy, like he could know everything about her through the touch of her lips.

Well, clearly not everything.

The alarm snaps on— "Abracadabra" by the Steve Miller Band—and startles the crap out of Paul, as always. He knows it's a weird ritual, to lie there and wait for his alarm to jolt him like a clown popping out of a jack-in-the-box, but he needs the shot of adrenaline. At least he can say he feels *something* each morning.

Paul grits his teeth and drags himself out of bed and over to the window. Spring comes late in Winnipeg, and it's a chilly gray morning with just a few damp stalks of forsythia for color. His younger brother Tommy is supposed to open

Stone Dry Cleaning so Paul can sleep in on his birthday, but it's hard to shake the ingrained routine. Wake up at 5:55 AM, make the bed, do twenty-five push-ups while his dog Muffin watches with concern, and off to the bathroom on autopilot.

He shouldn't have even been in Paris back then, Paul reminds himself as he splashes water on his face. The whole thing was so out of character that he should just be grateful for a few crumbs of nice memories. At twenty-two, he'd seen the window closing. His mother already struggled to talk clearly when she was tired and only used plastic cups and plates since her grip had gotten unreliable. The doctor said it would only get worse.

"You're going to Paris? By yourself?" she had asked, a note of fear creeping into her voice. But she was still able to make it up the stairs then and manage the twelve-year-old twins with some help from Mrs. Kovalenko next door, and Paul knew even then this was his last chance. "Yep," he nodded, and went back to packing.

Paul squeezes the toothpaste too hard and brushes his teeth like he can scrub away the next part of the memory from the inside.

After that golden evening, after April slipped away, Paul was shattered. He imagined never going home, staying in Paris and every evening waiting in the same spot on the Eiffel Tower in case April came back. But his plane ticket was nonrefundable, so he told himself that remembering the perfect moment would make what came next almost bearable. He nearly even believed it. As his mother slowly lost the ability to walk, then talk, then swallow, and finally breathe, and Paul took over parenting twin whirlwinds Tommy and Teresa, Paris seemed more and more like something that happened to another person. The sting of losing April folded into his other disappointments and losses, just another part of the background noise in his life.

Paul checks his reflection in the mirror. Forty-two looks a lot like forty-one, a couple more grays in his dark hair. He's had a middle-aged man's strong nose and impatient eyebrows since he was a teenager—at least he's growing into it now. Sometimes one of the elderly customers at the cleaner's calls him Eddie, his dad's name.

And speaking of Stone Dry Cleaning, there's about a 30% chance that Tommy forgets to open, or oversleeps, or gets distracted flirting with some girl in line at Tim Hortons, so Paul might as well stick to his usual program in case he's needed. Paul is the kind of person who helps other people, and the less he needs for himself, the better.

Chapter 2

April

The house reeks of despair. In her line of work, April sees enough of these to smell the stench of disappointment underneath the Spring Linen Yankee Candle. On the surface, it's just another 3 bed/2 bath Cape with low ceilings and a decently renovated kitchen, but in her bones, April feels the family's regrets and grudges so strongly that even the children's drawings on the fridge look sad and ominous.

This is why people hire her. The Miller home staging project. A separating couple needs to sell their house quickly and ask April (president, CEO, and sole employee of AA Home Staging) to sweep away the lingering traces of their unhappy family life. They trust her to disguise the ways in which their home absorbed the marital conflicts and reflected them back through strange shadows, tricks of the light, and most of all that oppressive—if metaphorical— reek.

The thing is, April knows how to fix this. The answer is to send half the furniture to storage, disguise the rest with white slipcovers, and put a huge wooden bowl of green apples in the center of the kitchen island. That is always the answer. Conveying hopefulness and optimism at her job is easy, almost a reflex at this point. Too bad she feels it less and less outside of work these days.

"When is it going on the market?" April asks as she surveys the furniture (expensive but uncomfortable) and jots down notes in a Moleskine notebook. Her client, Joe Miller, is tall and a little stooped, as though the energy in the house is pressing down on his shoulders. Usually, it's the wife who meets with April, and the first part of the consultation requires some delicacy to imply that while she is certainly *capable* of staging her own home, wouldn't it be easier to allow April to take that off her plate?

"As soon as possible," Joe says, pinching the bridge of his nose. "I know it's short notice, but our realtor Sandy says that you're the best home stager she knows."

April smiles. She is the best home stager she knows as well. She can take a chaotic family home and distract from the lack of closets and the high-traffic street with a giant wall clock and a potted ficus. She knows how to warm up a sterile condo with a row of perfectly fluffed throw pillows along the couch. Most importantly, she knows what buyers *really* want underneath the neutral paint colors. She understands the desire for a blank canvas, and the hopefulness that drives people to offer above asking price for the dream of a fresh start. Ever since she was fourteen and suddenly the woman of the house, she's carried that impulse to make things around her pretty so all sadness might stay below the surface. Even if her own tastes run to bright colors and flea market treasures, she understands how an artfully draped beige afghan and a stack of books chosen for the color of their spines can trigger that desire in a person, to finally have the life they hope for.

"Sandy's too nice," April says, but she can't help adding, "Though I'm not going to deny it."

Joe Miller gives a short bark of a laugh. It sounds slightly painful, maybe through lack of use. He's actually kind of cute,

April realizes. He probably just needs a few good laughs to get rid of that lingering air of sorrow, plus maybe a few good meals, a few good blow jobs...

Stop, she tells herself firmly. This is wildly unprofessional. It's not this poor man's fault that you are still in a post-divorce dry spell, and that you woke up in a sunbeam remembering being twenty. But April still strolls into the kitchen, giving Joe a chance to follow her and maybe check out her ass. When she reaches the kitchen island, she gives a little spin and leans back, hands on the countertop and her chest thrust out. "The first step is always decluttering. I recommend renting a storage unit." She really doesn't mean it to sound like a come-on, but desperate times, yada yada.

Joe Miller looks a little startled but then meets her eyes. "And then what?" he asks, his voice suddenly deeper and more resonant.

April sighs inwardly. As much as she wants to paint one wall orange or make that colorful living room rug into a joyful focal point, the answer is always the same. Declutter, depersonalize. Put the family vacation photos in a drawer. White furniture, neutral accents. It's hard to make any of that sound flirtatious.

But it doesn't mean she can't try.

"Maybe you could..." she purrs, and Joe Miller leans in slightly. "Move the couch from against the wall so it anchors the living room." She glances down meaningfully at his spindly arms, as if he might pick it up single-handedly. "A stack of those big arty books that no one reads on the coffee table, with photos of Frank Lloyd Wright houses, or...Paris in the spring." Where the hell had that come from? April's allotted time for thinking about Paris is over—she's at work now saving the saddest house and flirting with the saddest man she's seen in a while. Don't think of warm breezes, far-off city sounds, warm lips and strong shoulders.

April smiles brightly and focuses on Joe Miller's slightly gaping mouth. "Have you ever considered painting your front door? People often forget that home staging begins with curb appeal. Green is always inviting, or maybe red? It's a lucky color in many cultures, makes you wonder why in America we connect it with Satan, or anger, or lust." Joe Miller flinches at that last word, and April realizes she's doing that thing where she lets her inside thoughts into the outside. She's also doing that thing where she covers up her embarrassment at talking too much by talking more. She tries to steer the proverbial ship back towards the house.

"Obviously the kid's drawings have to come down from the fridge. How do kids make so much art, and what the hell are you supposed to do with it all? My daughter Liza—she's twelve now, but when she was in preschool, she used to go through the trash to make sure her drawings weren't in there, so then I had to stuff them way down deep after she went to bed." That last part doesn't sound great when she hears it out loud. April glances over at Joe Miller who is gazing at the artwork with a newly stricken expression.

"And Joe? The wedding photos need to come down." April gestures to the large, sepia-toned photo of Joe Miller with slightly more hair and a toothy grin dancing with his future ex-wife. "Rule number one, buyers don't like to be reminded of the people currently living in their prospective home. Especially one like this where the whole place has that sudden and angry divorce feeling all through it. No one wants to think they could be next. But really, it's bound to happen to most of us, right? When Danny Martini and I got divorced and sold our house—yes, that's his real name, I know it sounds like an *Ocean's Eleven* character—I tried burning sage. It was amicable, like they say, but even an amicable divorce can really stink up the place."

Joe Miller brushes his fingers against the wedding photo frame. Seeing his almost-handsome younger self and his slightly faded current version is unsettling enough for April to finally trail off. While she watches, his shoulders stoop even more, and he sniffles loudly. April has a terrible feeling that he's about to cry.

"It's really over," Joe says softly. April isn't sure if he's talking to her, but silence makes her uneasy, especially in this sad house.

"Maybe...a door is closing, but a window is opening?" she says and tries to smile encouragingly. Not her real smile—a wide grin that shows too many teeth and borders on kooky—but her work smile. "Maybe it's a new beginning?"

Joe turns to face her. "No," he says. "It didn't hit me until now. I guess I thought maybe it would still work out. But Emily left me, I'm only going to see my girls every other weekend. And you're here like some kind of...decorator vampire to suck the life out of our home so some young couple will buy it, because they think it could never happen to them." His voice gets louder as he grabs the photo off the wall and throws it on the couch where it bounces gently on the cushions: a small, safe protest against the raging unfairness of life.

April makes a note to tell her best friend Selma about 'decorator vampire'—it pretty elegantly captures what she'd said to herself multiple times. It's kind of sexy, even... much better than the glorified maid-slash-therapist she sometimes feels like.

Joe is looking at her now, breathing hard, eyes bright. What does it mean that she's a little turned on by this version of her client, passionate and a little angry, raging against the homogenization of his home? Selma would say that it means April needs either therapy or a new vibrator, or probably both. But Selma isn't there.

April straightens her shoulders, wishing she was wearing something sexy and flowing instead of Ann Taylor's finest office separates. "Look, I know it sucks. Life is really fucking hard sometimes, and divorce makes you crazy, even if it was your idea and you know it's the right thing. When it happened to me, I could have really used a divorce buddy, someone to bring over a bottle of wine and keep me from falling back in bed with my ex. Maybe I could help you out?"

In April's mind, that had been a joke, but somehow her rusty flirting muscles get stuck in gear and somehow it all comes out with a purr instead of a friendly wink. Joe Miller not only looks horrified but literally takes a step back, gasps, and clutches his chest like he is reaching for his pearls. April has clearly—spectacularly, even—misread the room. She really is her mother's daughter, she thinks, as her client glares at her with disgust. Somehow, she just keeps digging in deeper when anyone else can see it's time to back off, until feelings are hurt, and everything just generally turns to shit.

"Are you propositioning me?" chokes Joe. "When I just told you my heart is broken?"

"Well, you didn't exactly say…" starts April, but at Joe's sputters she holds her hands up in surrender.

"I'm sorry. Clearly, I misinterpreted things." Usually, work is her space to be contained and professional, the April of clean white slipcovers. She never tries crap like this at work.

"Obviously I'll have to tell my wife everything that happened between us." Joe looks almost smug at that idea. "You're a lot, you know. Anyone ever told you that?"

Only all the fucking time. April wants to laugh, or cry, or throw the Miller wedding photo for real. Sometimes she really hates her job.

But it's a good job, she scolds herself. The problem is you.

"I'm very sorry, Joe," she says crisply. "Thank you for meeting with me today. I'll write up a plan and email it to you. I'll get you a quick sale."

He nods formally, and April takes that as her cue to beat a hasty exit, biting her tongue to keep from saying another word.

She hasn't always been like this. She hasn't always tried and failed so damn hard to be a normal person. Once upon a time she wore orange corduroy pants with a maroon suede jacket in the autumn. She bought furniture at flea markets and spent days sanding it down and adding bright blue glass knobs. She didn't straighten her hair or wear pumps, and she certainly didn't encourage people to paint their walls Eggshell. She'd been warm and exuberant, and love found its way to her. She had perfect kisses on the Eiffel Tower at sunset.

Oh. That again.

April gets in her car and reapplies her Totally Taupe lipstick in the rear-view mirror before driving away. When you're twenty-one, love and romance just happen. You can be careless with it, just walk away if the mood strikes. Now, twenty years and one failed marriage later, April knows less about love than ever.

Paul

Paul doesn't want to open his birthday presents.

He keeps busy instead, clearing the table and rinsing the dinner plates while the rest of the small group chats and laughs, but his younger sister Teresa catches him. Like Paul she's dark-haired and sturdy with Resting Serious Face, but unlike Paul she can make others bend to her will. With a withering look, Teresa directs him into the head chair at her dining table. She momentarily disappears into the kitchen and returns with a birthday cake glowing with a startling number of candles, leading the group in an enthusiastic but off-key "Happy Birthday."

It's a lot, being the center of attention when Paul prefers to blend into the background. He's lucky, though, that they all still get together for him, even as everyone else dates and marries and has kids and okay, maybe goes to jail, but at least they do *something*. Paul peers over the blinding cake at what's left of his family: the twins, Tommy and Teresa, of course—Teresa with their dad's brown hair and brown eyes, Tommy tall and fair like Mom had been. Teresa's round-faced son Matty, and in recent years Teresa's husband Griff. Yes, he's very lucky. Then why does he feel like an outsider with his face pressed up to the window, watching another stoic guy confront a birthday candle bonfire?

The cake is a fire hazard, and everyone is staring at him. Paul makes a wish and blows out the candles.

Teresa immediately picks off the candles and puts them on a plate. Ever since she got rid of Matty's deadbeat dad and married Griff, she's appointed herself the family matriarch. Thanksgiving, birthdays, the Canada Day barbecue—these are all her territory now. Paul hasn't inherited their mother's talent for entertaining, but he liked hosting because it means keeping busy, not sitting there while everyone sings at him. Paul isn't used to Teresa being such a grown-up, either, or having a life so separate from his. Griff's a pretty goofy guy, but he is nice to Teresa and has legally adopted Matty. Paul likes him, but he doesn't really know him. He's trying to give their little family some space, even though he pretty much co-parented with Teresa until she met Griff. Probably the last thing Griff wants is Paul hanging around while he bonds with his new son.

Finally done denuding the cake, Teresa cuts slices and hands them around. "This is good, Tree," Paul says, even though it isn't really. It's an overly sweet red velvet cake from the grocery store, thickly frosted with fluffy hydrogenated oils. Paul doesn't like red velvet cake—he doesn't have much of a sweet tooth at all— but he'd made a big fuss over one at a birthday a while back, when Teresa was a shy, scared single mom and he wanted her to feel like at least she'd done something right. Now the cake appears every year, and it's easiest to keep pretending it's his favorite.

"What'd you wish for, anyway?" asks his brother Tommy.

"Don't tell him!" pipes Matty. "Then it won't come true!" Matty is eight years old and a big bruiser of a kid, but with tender concern for earthworms, dandelions, and his family.

"That's absolutely right, baby," says Teresa, taking Paul's half-eaten cake without asking if he's done. "Now, let's open some presents."

Right. The presents. He can't put it off any longer.

Griff taps his index fingers on the table in a pseudo-drumroll. Matty excitedly fetches a small gift bag, and Paul cringes inwardly. He knows what it is. He always knows what it was, and to put on a fake smile for Matty's trusting face leaves a bitter taste in his mouth.

"I picked them out myself," says Matty proudly.

Paul reaches into the tissue paper and pulls out...socks. A garish pair of novelty socks, this time printed all over with a half-peeled banana wearing red sunglasses.

"Hey, thanks, buddy!" says Paul, trying to give his nephew the enthusiastic response he deserves.

"It's because you like socks! And bananas!"

Paul doesn't really like either of those things. But like with the red velvet cake, he'd probably overdone it when about ten years ago, Tommy, who hadn't gotten him a birthday present in years, handed him a paper bag containing a pair of Canadian flag socks. Back then, Tommy was still trying to make his way through university, when he wasn't too hung over to go to class.

"Now open Uncle Tommy's!" says Matty. At least someone was excited about Paul turning 42. He tries not to think about how much he misses Matty and Teresa living with him as he dabs the frosting off Matty's cheek with the red bandanna he always has stashed in his pocket.

Paul is startled to see that Tommy's gift is beautifully wrapped in thick, gilded paper with many, many curled gold and white ribbons. He's used to any gift from Tommy, assuming he even showed up, to be still in the shopping bag.

He's less startled to open it and find socks.

These ones had a bunch of sharks carrying pool cues tucked under their fins against a Kelly-green background.

"Uh, pool sharks, you get it?" chuckles Tommy, awkwardly pulling his dark blonde hair.

Paul doesn't play pool or have strong views on sharks, but he gets it. He gets that he is the novelty sock guy now. It's not their fault that Paul's interests have always been keeping the family dry cleaning business going and failing to keep his siblings out of trouble. He doesn't blame them—if anything it's his fault. He's ten years older than Tommy and Teresa and pretty much raised them since their mother died when he was twenty-two. Maybe he's overcompensated with trying to be a parental figure when he should have just stuck with being the best big brother he could be. So maybe dad presents are his destiny.

Life was definitely easier when Tommy and Teresa still needed him. Rides to the movies changed to being available for late night pick-ups when someone (usually Tommy) drank too much. Then Teresa had a lousy boyfriend, and Tommy drank too much. Then Teresa had another lousy boyfriend, and Tommy still drank too much. Then Teresa left her lousy boyfriend but decided to have the baby on her own, and Tommy got another DUI and had his driver's license suspended. For a while big brother Paul was the center of their lives, helping Teresa with baby Matty and driving Tommy to and from work and meetings with his parole officer.

Things are different now. Teresa has Griff, and Tommy apparently hasn't had a drink in nearly two years. So he says. Even Paul, always on the alert for a slurred word or a stumble, hasn't noticed anything, though he is still watching.

Griff hands him one more small package.

"I saw these and thought of you, my man. Happy birthday."

SpongeBob SquarePants socks this time. Paul has no idea why these made Griff think of him, and he doesn't want to know.

Teresa hands him an envelope. "It's not socks," she says reassuringly. "It's a gift card to that new Italian restaurant where Griff and I went on our anniversary. They make Caesar salad tableside, and the tiramisu is to die for. You could bring someone!"

If there's anything that proves that his family knows nothing about him, even more than SpongeBob socks, it's a gift card to a date restaurant. Because Paul has not been on a date since...well...maybe it's better not to calculate that number. Between raising the twins, helping with Matty, running the business, and keeping an eye on Tommy, Paul hasn't had time for much else until recently. And now he just doesn't know where to start, and his confusing relationship with Claire—affair, really—last year left him more lost than ever. Everyone talks about the various apps he has to download, so he can swipe through dozens of women and make a split-second decision about whether he wants to meet them. That is as appealing as manning the Stone Dry Cleaning press machine in August while wearing a wool sweater. And if that's his analogy, no wonder he's single.

April was his road less traveled, to quote that old poem stuck in his brain since high school. On the Eiffel Tower, Paul's life divided into two paths, the one he currently follows with the daily duties of work and family, and the one where he's a different person, a romantic guy with confidence that love is out there, and so it is. The problem is that one of the paths had dead ended so abruptly that he became stuck.

Teresa hands him a sandwich baggie filled with birthday candles. "Remember what Mom used to say—you have to sleep with them under your pillow tonight or your wish won't come true." She kisses his cheek. "Happy birthday, big brother."

Paul tries to scoff, but he slips them in his pocket. Every year, in one form or another, his birthday wish comes back to that other path. Who would he be if he'd fought the dead end, cut through the bushes, and forced his way through? Or even committed to his well-traveled road instead of always being aware of April on some parallel plane? Is she happy, does she remember him, will she come back one day as suddenly as she appeared?

This year is different. Twenty years of thinking about April is enough. He'll just have to accept that the sweetest moment of his life was quickly followed by one of the worst. Time to move on and leave the dead end for good. It's either that or be right back here next year choking down red velvet cake and trying to smile at silly socks.

Time for a new wish, Paul thinks. His fingers brush the baggie of birthday candles in his pocket. Time to look ahead on the path more traveled and find someone who needs him, maybe even someone to love.

Paris, France 1999

Paul had a bad habit of stopping in the middle of the sidewalk when a sight struck him as particularly Parisian. A perfect *tarte aux fruits* in the bakery window or a surprise glimpse of the Eiffel Tower between buildings, and he was just a kid from Manitoba rooted to the pavement, stunned by the charm of it all. That's what happened on the morning that April wiped him out with her backpack.

Paul was walking, map in hand, supposedly heading for the Pont Marie along the Seine, home of the famous used book kiosks. Really, he was meandering, drinking in the scene of uniformed school children, the elegant, rail-thin older women, the flower sellers, and generally going to that "Wow, Paris. I can't believe I'm in Paris" headspace again. He had done it. He was brave enough to take the trip he'd always dreamed of. Or maybe selfish enough to leave his sick mother and his rowdy twin siblings back at home while he blew through his savings and tried to have a few last weeks of feeling young. Paul stopped dead in his tracks as dreaminess mixed with guilt.

The intrusive sound of American-accented English barely registered in his thoughts: "Selma, this is the wrong way, we should have taken a right back there." Until suddenly, a tremendous weight crashed into his right side and knocked him to the ground.

Paul lay sprawled on the sidewalk, trying to figure out what had happened. Did a lamppost appear out of nowhere? Or maybe an escaped rhino from the *Parc Zoologique*? He felt strangely peaceful there on the sidewalk, looking up at the apartments with their wrought iron balconies and the soft blue sky above. His guidebook claimed that Paris was the City of Light because of the early adaptation of gas streetlamps, but to Paul it described the soft, romantic glow that bathed the city—tender and wistful in the rain; golden and hopeful in the sun. He liked it down there on the ground, where the battling emotions of guilt and excitement melted into a pleasant daze.

Paul's peaceful thoughts were interrupted by a flurry of long limbs and bronze waves of hair tied with a bright yellow scarf standing over him. A red backpack loomed behind the blur of gold and amber.

"Claudette, you fucking bitch!" a voice hissed in exasperation, while gray eyes like morning rain clouds glared. "Goddamn it...I mean, *pardon, monsieur.*" The hair, the eyes, the voice were all coming together into the form of a young woman. A very intense young woman. The air around her seemed to vibrate, and looking at her Paul tasted honey in the back of his throat.

"Am I Claudette?" Paul asked. Anything was possible. He must have been whacked over the head with a blunt instrument, perhaps a frying pan or maybe just the sudden force of his own longing for this whirl of bronze and gray and yellow.

"You speak English!" she responded, gracefully crouching to stare at him from so close that her face blurred. She was beautiful. He knew she was beautiful, and he couldn't even see all of her, just little flashes that his brain struggled to piece together: chipped purple nail polish, a glint of silver in her nose, the smell of clove cigarettes and sunshine. "Thank God. I think my French has gotten worse since we got here. Claudette's what I call my harlot of a backpack. It makes me hate her less. She weighs 5000 pounds, and it's all my fault. I don't know how to pack." She shrugged her shoulders but the giant red monster on her back hardly budged.

She tried to slide down the straps and groaned. "Damn! Selma, help me, I'm stuck. This bitch is slowly killing me."

A small, fierce brunette stepped into Paul's line of sight. She tugged at the evil backpack while Yellow Scarf tried to stay steady, but in an explosion of momentum, Claudette slid off and fell on the friend like a small refrigerator. Yellow Scarf went right down with them. The three of them awkwardly sprawled for a moment, until Yellow Scarf cut through the silence with a sharp, "Fuck this!" She rolled her giant backpack off her friend onto the ground with a resounding thunk. Without her burden, she stood in one fluid movement and held out her hand. Silvery bangles jangled.

"Let me help you up. I'm April."

"April in Paris," murmured Paul before he could stop himself. It sounded like an Audrey Hepburn movie, like a madcap adventure. The honey taste lingered.

The dark-haired girl—Selma—also stood, sizing up Paul with canny, golden-brown eyes.

"Right, except it's June," Selma said firmly, clearly warning him off from any thoughts about what April in Paris in June had to do with him. Paul wanted to try to stand up, and he very much wanted to take April's hand, but Selma's sharp stare made him cautious.

"He's fine," said Selma to April, not taking her eyes off Paul. "Don't linger. He'll take it as an invitation."

"An invitation to what?" asked April, with maybe a hint of curiosity. Paul still couldn't find words, which was probably for the best because he was full of strange thoughts. He closed his eyes against the bright sun and saw this April eating lemon cake with her fingers in an outdoor cafe.

"To follow us, of course," answered the dark little warrior. "A pair of young, gorgeous, hapless American tourists. Accosted by a suspicious man on the street in broad daylight. With clear signs of eventual intent to rape and murder."

Paul's eyes flew open, and words finally came. "I'm not going to...I would never..." Describing how he just wanted to watch April lick lemon glaze off her fingers wouldn't help his case that he was a Very Normal Person. "I mean, I'm Canadian, for Christ's sake!"

The two young women looked at him and then at each other, their eyes widening with delight. "He's Canadian," murmured April. "For Christ's sake," murmured Selma, and they started to giggle. Without April looking at him, Paul could finally take her all in—lanky, frizzy-haired, faintly freckled and completely beautiful.

"You, my Canadian friend, are coming with us." April held out her hand again, and Selma added hers. They pulled him up easily. "We are lost, and Selma has to pee, and I have no idea what to do with this fucking backpack."

Wow, Paris. It meant something different this time, though. He wasn't an outsider frozen to the spot, gawking at people living their lives. This was why he was in Paris—this blur of gold and yellow, the feeling of possibility, the taste of honey on his lips.

Chapter 3

April

"So back up," says Selma. "You made a pass at your client? When did we start doing that? I have misgivings."

Even though their weekly Facetime was more like bi-weekly these days, April had launched into the story of her day without much intro, counting on Selma to keep up like she always does, though lately she often seems half a step behind.

"That's because your clients are dogs," grumbles April. Selma is a sought-after pet photographer in Brooklyn, her permanent scowl melting away for any dog, cat, or cockatoo that enters her studio. "And anyway, it wasn't exactly a pass. It was more of a proposition." April cringes again thinking of Joe Miller's shocked glare—she's broken her own rule about being messy at work, the place she usually manages at least the facade of control.

"Okay, Chickadee," nods Selma, clearly humoring April. "Though I bet the borzoi I shot yesterday had three times the sex appeal of your sad dad." Selma's eyes drift away from the phone camera, and April suspects she's checking her laptop. She waits for Selma's attention to come back, but the silence drags on, and April is annoyed. Lately, these moments happen more and more. Every fourth text from April goes unanswered and Selma's attention drifts when they do manage to speak.

"Sorry to keep you if you have more important things to do," April snaps and immediately regrets her bitchy tone. Selma is so much cooler than her, with her Brooklyn loft and Japanese designer clothes, not to mention her merciless bullshit detection radar and her willingness to call anyone out, including April. In fact, April's been waiting this whole call for Selma to ask her what the hell is going on, but all she gets is a mild questioning look.

"Oh, sorry, Chickadee, zoned out for a sec there."

"That's okay, it was stupid. Listen, don't worry about it, I'm just being a disaster as usual. Let's talk later, and I'll try not to seduce any clients in the meantime." April blows a pair of air kisses at her phone.

Selma smiles, but she looks tired behind her fashionably severe glasses, her smooth dark hair too long for her usual sleek lob. Maybe she's just working too much.

"I'm not saying to *not* seduce your clients. Maybe just not that one," says Selma, pulling her dog Collins into her lap and scratching his head. She's wearing an asymmetrical wrap that either cost hundreds of yen in Shibuya or ten dollars in the H&M kids department. "And April? Don't call my best friend a disaster. Not on my watch."

April is a disaster, though, and Selma doesn't know the half of it. If she was telling the truth, April's story would have begun not with throwing herself at Joe Miller, but with that sunbeam playing across her quilt that morning, or if she was going to be brutally honest, much, much farther back. April opens her mouth to say, "Remember that time when we were in Paris?" or maybe "Have you ever noticed how I get a little distracted on nice spring days?" but what comes out is, "Thanks, babe. Get some rest. Talk soon."

Today is just a blip, thinks April. Best not to read too much into it. Maybe it will rain tomorrow, and this hazy longing for something she'd let slip through her fingers will be washed away.

* * *

April is pretty, damn it. Sometimes she thinks she is prettier now than in her twenties. She gets her eyebrows professionally plucked, for one thing, and wears good bras that fit. She keeps her bronze waves just past her shoulders now and thank God she got rid of that nose ring before most of the people currently in her life ever saw it.

Still, though, while she isn't horrified by what she sees, it's all a little...flat? Especially if she's facing her ex-husband Danny Martini, the most infuriatingly good-natured ex-husband a gal can have. She armors herself with two swipes of fuchsia lipstick and hops in the car to collect her Liza.

Danny and Liza are in the parking lot in front of his condo complex, washing his car together. It's a happy scene, and April watches Danny give Liza a teasing spray with the hose, and Liza gives Danny a bubble beard with a scoop of sudsy foam. Liza is lucky to have a nice, fun dad, April tells herself as she feels the familiar clench in her jaw.

Why did Danny Martini make her so agitated still? Three years ago, they surprised all their friends by announcing they were divorcing, and then went through the process so amicably that even the mediator asked if they were sure. They split custody of Liza, attend parent-teacher conferences together, and he still sends her roses on her birthday. Even though April hates cut roses.

For starters, it's pretty infuriating how good Danny looks in his gym shorts and old t-shirt, rendered clingy

28

from Liza's splashing. For another, he shouldn't be so happy to see her. Can't he at least have a trace of pain in his eyes, and be haunted about how three years ago April asked him for a divorce after suspecting him of having an affair (he wasn't) and then realizing she didn't even care? Can't he even pretend that he's pining a little? And can't he live in one of those depressing apartment complexes where newly separated men congregate in under furnished rental units instead of finding this cute place with a balcony and a golf course view?

Danny gives her an enthusiastic wave and pretends to splash some soap bubbles in her general direction.

"Mom!" calls Liza. "I'm going to give you a big hug!" Her leggings and t-shirt are wet and streaked with dirt as she runs towards April. April spreads her arms wide. Hugs from her long-legged preteen are getting rarer, so she's going to take them as they come even if it means getting damp.

"Hi, baby," she murmurs into Liza's hair, trying to get a sniff. She pulls back and holds her daughter by the shoulders. "My God, I think you grew an inch since yesterday morning." April reached close to her full height of 5'10" by thirteen, but it's alarming to see it in one's own daughter.

Liza runs inside to grab her things, leaving April and Danny alone. Great. Danny still has a dab of bubbles on his chin and it's unsettlingly intimate, like watching him shave back when they were married. He catches her looking and grins. "Hope you took advantage of a night to yourself," he says. "Maybe had a hot date?"

Danny says stuff like that, and he genuinely means it. There isn't a trace of sarcasm or even prying in his tone. Which only annoys April more. If Danny ever truly loved her, then how could he casually ask if she's dating anyone?

"I had a pretty quiet night. Talked to Selma, watched some Netflix."

Danny gives her a look, and April knows a pep talk about "getting back out there" is coming. Another confirmation that her ex-husband, the one she thought would give her the life she imagined, has moved on—in fact he probably never metaphorically moved *in*.

April thinks back to meeting Danny Martini at her cousin Sara's wedding when she was twenty-seven. Dating after college was disappointing. She was already weary of awkward blind dates, of one-sided flirting, of mediocre looking guys explaining to her that they weren't looking for anything serious, as if she would even want something serious with their dandruffy selves. When Danny Martini asked her to dance and made her laugh, it seemed like maybe he was her reward for all those Saturday nights of forcing herself to go out.

So when he sent her red roses, she thanked him and didn't mention that roses made her skin crawl. When he encouraged her to focus on the growing field of home staging instead of creative interior design, she told herself he just wanted her to be successful. When she dropped hints that she'd love a vintage engagement ring, maybe with a sapphire, and he presented her with a big, boring cushion-cut diamond on a platinum band, she told herself she was being shallow. But every time she looked at that ring, she had a pang that she was marrying a man who didn't really know her and never would.

She needs to get out of there before she says something sharp, or God forbid cries. April calls for Liza and drags them both to the car before Danny can say anything else.

Liza is silent for the first few minutes of the drive, staring out the window at the clear blue sky. April notices that she always needs a little time to adjust from one parent to another.

30

Finally, when they're almost home, Liza speaks. "I heard you through the window, telling dad you didn't do anything last night. That's kind of sad. Why don't you have a boyfriend?" she asks, more curious than accusing. "Or a girlfriend, 'cause that would be fine, too. Emma P's mother has a girlfriend now. She lent Emma her suede jacket."

Even Liz Planck found someone? Damn, April is more pathetic than she even thought.

"I just haven't met the right person yet," answers April, because that's the kind of vague, non-threatening response mothers are supposed to give to personal questions. Though as April says it, she knows it's not quite true. She knew what it was like to have a man look at her like he truly saw her, like he knew everything about her and still wanted to be with her. It had just been a moment, and she had been so young, but it was one of those things you never forgot, even if you tried.

"Want to stop for ice cream?" asks April with forced enthusiasm. She doesn't want to talk about her sad, sad love life any more today.

Paul

Paul has a nemesis.

Sure it's completely one-sided, and his nemesis probably doesn't give him a second thought, but 'nemesis' has a nice ring to it. Makes him feel more like the hero in the story than a boring guy with an annoying neighbor. Grounds him when he starts thinking about Paris and sunsets and the taste of honey, which he absolutely isn't doing any more.

"Muffin!" Paul calls, ignoring the sidelong glares from his sworn enemy Sid Mohapatra. Sid is trimming his already perfect hedges, surely part of a well-constructed plot to shame Paul for his haphazard front yard. Paul keeps things tidy, but it's obvious he didn't inherit his mother's green thumb, especially when Sid spends hours each day fussing with each azalea branch and blade of grass. He also enjoys glowering at Paul's little dog Muffin, as if she's about to hop the fence and pee on Sid's pristine rhododendrons.

To Paul, Muffin has every right to pee on those rhododendrons. She'd been there before Sid, after all. After Mrs. Kovalenko broke her hip and had to move to a rehab facility, she'd been so distraught about her little dog that Paul offered to take Muffin, with a promise to visit every weekend. When Mrs. Kovalenko passed away before ever returning home, the arrangement became permanent.

"Muffin!" Paul calls again.

Sid gives him a curt nod. "Hello, Paul," he says coolly. "I got the name of that dog obedience school I was telling you about from my sister. Her Bichon Frisé is a complete gentleman now."

"Thanks, Sid, but I think we're okay," says Paul, as other, more colorful responses flood his brain. Fortunately, Muffin graces him with a glance over her shoulder and saunters over to the screen door.

"Time to go to work," he tells her.

Muffin wanders into the kitchen for a drink of water, taking a moment to look around disdainfully. Even she notices how out-of-date the kitchen is, with its matching mustard yellow counters, walls, and appliances. Paul doesn't know where to start with bringing things up to the current century. Last time he was at Target to buy a pack of underwear, he walked by the home decor section and got confused by the sheer number of candles and a big wooden bowl containing what looked like balls of woven straw.

His mother's house looks pretty much the same as it had when he, Tommy, and Teresa were growing up, except it's much quieter and emptier. Teresa and Matty lived there until Teresa and Griff got married. Tommy stuck around longer, up until he and Paul agreed living and working together wasn't helping their already rocky relationship. Everyone seemed relieved when Paul said he was getting a dog for company. The same people tried to hide their surprise when it was fluffy little Muffin.

"I guess I was expecting a bulldog? Kind of strong and compact and with a serious expression, just like you?" says Teresa before adding hastily, "But it was really nice of you to take Mrs. Kovalenko's dog. She always gave me and Tommy the best apple *solozhenik* when she babysat. I just thought you'd want to choose your own."

"Muffin needed a home," Paul tells her simply. That's all there is to it.

Paul carries Muffin out to his car and settles her in the back seat. Sid is still trimming his front hedges with old-fashioned clippers that look like big scissors. Paul ignores his smirk at seeing his gruff neighbor carrying his dainty dog, as if it doesn't happen every morning.

Paul can drive to Stone Dry Cleaning with his eyes closed. He grew up helping at the counter or running errands after school and on weekends. Almost every day of his life had involved making the trip from Aberdeen Place to the business, a seven-minute drive for early morning openings, a nine minute trip home if he hit after-school traffic.

Paul is surprised to walk in and see Tommy behind the counter inspecting the dirty shirts and tossing them in a laundry cart. Tommy registers his expression and nods. "Jaden's sick again. Joanie asked me to cover for her while she takes him to the doctor."

"Sure," says Paul. He brings Muffin to the back office, where she has a bed and a few toys, and comes back out to the counter. Tommy continues with the shirts, quickly checking for stains before stapling a number onto the shirt tag. He chews on his bottom lip while he works, just like when he was a little kid helping out. Paul's gut twists a little thinking of those days when Tommy was still shorter than him, standing attentively at Paul's elbow with yellow "STAIN" stickers attached to each finger, ready to place where Paul pointed.

Paul means to say, "Thanks for the shark socks" but what comes out is, "Make sure you're checking the cuffs, that's where most of the stains are."

Tommy doesn't look up. "I always check the cuffs," he says. Pause.

"Quiet so far?" asks Paul. He looks around for something to do with his hands, but the counter is tidy with everything in place: pens in the cup, a fresh receipt roll in the register.

"A little bit of a rush around 8. People getting an early start on their Saturday errands, you know? But quiet since then." Tommy's about to add something but stops.

"What?" says Paul.

"It's nothing. It's just that…" Tommy straightens up and looks down at Paul. "Business is slow," he says, like he's breaking some bad news to Paul instead of stating the obvious.

Paul feels a familiar wash of irritation. "I know it's down. It's an industry-wide trend. It's all you Millennials wearing stretchy pants to the office. 'Pajama culture.' That's what *Dry Cleaning Today* calls it. Business is down for everyone. It's not because we're doing anything wrong."

"Well, we're not doing anything *right* either," snaps Tommy, folding his arms in front of his chest. He's been taller than Paul since he was 15, and it's especially annoying when Paul wants to be the one with authority.

"What's that supposed to mean?" asks Paul, unable to hide his irritation now.

"It means that we could make some kind of effort to attract new customers," says Tommy. He sounds more excited than angry now, and Paul watches the stickers on Tommy's fingers wiggle as he gestures to the gray tile floor and worn counter left from their father's time. "We could change over to environmentally-friendly cleaning, so more of my so-called Millennial friends will consider sending their clothes here."

Paul chokes back his retort—too expensive, too complicated, too hard to retrain the staff—and lets Tommy continue. Tommy's excitement builds.

"We could offer delivery. Maybe even get a contract with one of those new tech companies downtown, so people can just bring in their stuff to work and we pick it up from there. Or what if we had a Stone Cleaners app?"

That's too much. "What the hell do we need that for?" grumbles Paul. "Come on! Do you think Mrs. Marconi is going to download an app to bring in her good church dress? Or old Mr. Chang and the same three shirts that he drops off every week? They come here because we're nice and friendly, and we remember their names, and because they've come here for thirty years. I'm not going to turn this place upside down hoping some young tech guy will think of us when he wants to get a suit cleaned for his grandmother's funeral, and then never wear it again. Got it?"

Paul knows he sounded like a cranky old jerk. He knows it, but he's powerless to do anything about it. Why does Tommy always push him in new directions when Paul barely trusts him to mark the stains on the shirt cuffs?

Tommy just looks at him not with anger, or disappointment, but with resignation.

"I have to do the payroll," mutters Paul and heads back to the office. He sits down in front of the old desktop computer which hums and creaks as it comes to life. Muffin stirs from her nap, stretches, and hops up on his lap. He strokes her silky fur, feeling all his anger drain away.

What is he going to do about Tommy?

Tommy was eighteen when he got his first DUI. Paul tried to ground him, to take away his car keys, to act like the father Tommy couldn't remember, but everything he did backfired spectacularly. Tommy got another DUI and lost his license for a year. Two years later he got probation for leaving the scene of an accident. A few months after that, he ended up in jail for thirty days after violating his probation in a drunken bar fight.

Paul had been totally in over his head. At the same time, Teresa was pregnant and finally realizing what a loser and a bully her boyfriend was. Paul was trying to set up a crib in Teresa's room and take her to doctor's appointments and remind Tommy to meet with his parole officer. When Tommy went back to jail a few years later, for driving with a suspended license and crashing into the front of a convenience store, sending one poor lady to the hospital with a broken leg, Paul visited every week, bringing books and change for the vending machines and anything else that was allowed, but mostly they just sat in silence.

Tommy was his guy, his shadow, for so many years. But then Paul failed. He wasn't a father, and he was a crap big brother, and he couldn't save Tommy from himself.

When Tommy got out of jail the last time, he moved back into the family home with Paul. He went to AA meetings and spent his weekends with Teresa and Matty or shut up in his room. His probation required him to hold down a job, but no one wanted to hire someone with his criminal record. Working at Stone Dry Cleaning was the only option, but Paul dreaded allowing Tommy into the stores, only to have the rug pulled out from underneath him again when Tommy had a few drinks and forgot to come into work or borrowed a few bucks from the cash register.

To Paul's surprise, Tommy shows up for work every morning. He's pleasant to the customers and well-liked by the staff. Paul keeps waiting for the other shoe to drop, but Tommy goes to his AA meetings, shows up for work, and stays sober.

Paul knows he should be glad that Tommy's interested in the business and has ideas to improve it. He knows that the business needs help, but he just isn't ready to trust Tommy yet. His younger brother has been sober a few weeks here, even a month there. This two-year stretch is by far his record.

But it never lasted, and it always hurt so much when Paul noticed the little signs of Tommy drinking again—the smell of mouthwash, the evasiveness, the feeling that his sweet little brother was taken over by someone angry and untrustworthy.

Paul sighs as the computer wheezes to life and opens QuickBooks to start payroll. All the love he has for Tommy is still there, underneath the anger and disappointment, and he's holding onto it painfully with nowhere for it to go. Sometimes it feels like anger and disappointment are the only things keeping him going. If he released them, all he'd have to think about is what he'd missed and would never get back. Paris, sunset, waves of bronze hair. And he is done with that.

Paris, France 1999

April hoped this guy didn't get the wrong idea. Sure, knocking him over on the street like that was peak rom com, but he wasn't the Paris native or Australian backpacker she pictured for her first vacation fling. She didn't want him to leave, though. The morning had been a string of disasters, and she was still cringing at losing her temper back at the hostel. Something about his dark, watchful eyes made her heartbeat slow down, and gradually she realized what a beautiful June day it was, full of warm sun and delicious bakery smells. This Paul person might get their day back on track.

They kept walking silently, three abreast on the busy sidewalk with Paul frequently moving out of formation to dodge other pedestrians with an *excusez-moi*. After a close call with a chic mother pushing a stroller, he finally spoke. "So, if you're lost, maybe you should tell me where you want to go instead of just walking?" His voice was unexpectedly deep, with a hint of a rasp. "Or maybe you two are trying to kidnap me, and I'm the...how did you put it? Gorgeous, hapless tourist in danger."

April looked him over, absolutely not lingering on his broad shoulders or slightly crooked nose. "You aren't hapless. Look at your sensible walking shoes and your normal-size day pack. I bet you have a guidebook in there. I bet you have a pen, just in case somebody needs one."

Paul's brown eyes flickered for a moment. Was April flirting with him? Not flirting, she decided, but stretching her flirting muscles in case they bumped into that Australian backpacker.

"It's a pencil but sure," replied Paul tartly. "Not all of us can be as thorough packers as you." He glanced meaningfully at the hump of Claudette the Backpack looming over April. "Bet you've got a couple pens in there."

Selma halted in the middle of the sidewalk. "If by pens you mean a hair dryer without a plug adapter plus the collected works of Agatha Christie, then sure. We're going to the Louvre."

"The Louvre," repeated Paul. "Forgive me if I thought you'd be heading somewhere a little more...off the beaten path?"

Selma looked at him challengingly. It wasn't meant to be unkind, April knew—Selma was just suspicious of all people and accepting of all animals until proven otherwise.

"Whatever," Selma said. "I want to take a picture of the tourists taking pictures of the *Mona Lisa*."

"Sure," said Paul, "But it's almost noon and the lines will be really long already. We...I mean, you could go to the Rodin Museum instead," he offered. "It's quieter, and it has *The Thinker* statue and rose gardens."

April tried to think of something funny or clever to say but hearing the word roses, even so far away in Paris, made her stomach do that cold clenching thing. "I..." she looked at Paul, who stood perfectly with a glint in his eye, like he was waiting for more (practice) flirtatious banter. "I don't like roses," was what finally came out of her mouth.

That was an understatement. Ever since that day when she was fourteen, when her mother told her that she'd done all she could for April and it was time for her to finally be free, roses made her feel cold and trembly, and the sweet smell made her retch. Guys never understood that one.

"Okay," said Paul, not missing a beat. He reached into his backpack, took out a map, glanced at it for a few seconds, and began walking towards the corner. "We'll go to the Louvre, then," he called over his shoulder. "But they won't let you bring Mademoiselle Claudette inside."

April looked at Selma and raised her eyebrows. Selma scowled back, and they jogged to catch up.

"Most guys ask why I don't like roses," said April after they'd crossed to the next street and fallen into a brisk pace.

"Do you want to tell me?" Paul asked. He kept walking, interested but not seeming entitled to any response or explanation.

"Not really," said April frankly.

"Okay then," said Paul. He looked at the map, frowned, and gestured towards the upcoming crosswalk.

"Do you want to know why I'm carrying a giant backpack?" asked April. She wanted to hear his raspy voice again, maybe see another glint in those dark eyes. She liked walking beside Paul, letting her body fall into rhythm with his. He wasn't that tall, maybe an inch or so shorter than her, but April secretly liked short guys. Short and confident with great posture and a little bit of a swagger really did it for her, even if most of her girlfriends assumed she wouldn't look at a guy under six feet.

"Right now, I'm more concerned with solving the problem. They have luggage lockers at the Gare du Nord. We can leave your backpack in one of those, and then we can walk to the Louvre. It's not too far."

"I got into an argument with the woman running the hostel," said April. "She said that we made too much noise after curfew last night, so she was moving us up to this weird attic room. I said it wasn't fair and stormed out, and I didn't realize until I was outside that I still had Claudette on, and I was too embarrassed to go back in." April hoped this story sounded cute in the telling, with none of the panic and embarrassment she'd felt at maybe getting kicked out of the hostel.

"Did she still save the room for you?" Paul seemed neither enchanted nor disgusted.

"Oh, yeah, Selma moved her stuff up there and everything while I cowered outside."

"Then you're home in a coach, like my mom used to say."

Something loosens in April's chest. This stupid day was going to be okay after all, and she was ready for an adventure. She was young, and pretty, and in France, damn it, and the world owed her something. This guy—no, this *man*—with his watchful eyes and gravelly voice was going to help her find it.

Or maybe, said a small voice in the back of her mind, he *was* it.

Chapter 4

April

It isn't that April *likes* sharing custody but reconnecting with her daughter after a short time apart meant she's always seeing her through fresh eyes. Back home, Liza gradually transitions from precocious wise teen to cuddly little girl, ignoring the spring sunshine and warbling birds to reread her Percy Jackson books with her head on April's lap.

Liza yawns and stretches, and April ruffles her hair. Back when she was twelve, had she ever had this kind of relaxed afternoon where she wasn't watching, observing, waiting for something to go wrong? The memories of her childhood barely feel real, especially since she rarely speaks to the one other person who shares them. Even though it's irritating and yet predictable, like a champagne hangover, she picks up the phone.

"Hi, Dad," she says in that tight, chipper voice used only for him. "How are you?"

Hank Andersen lives in a condo up on the North Shore of Massachusetts. He likes walking on the beach with his girlfriend Marie. He likes meeting his friends at Dunkin' Donuts on Saturday morning to argue about politics, even though they all hold the same opinions. He doesn't like tears, laughter, or talking about the past.

"Is this April? Doing fine here." There is a pause which April itches to fill but she holds back, waiting to see if he says any more. Finally he continues. "Marie just went out to Shaw's to get some ground lamb. She's making *kofta* and potatoes."

"Wow, sounds delicious," says April brightly.

"I'll tell her to email you the recipe," he says. April isn't much of a cook, and she doesn't eat red meat, but her father never remembers that. He doesn't know that much about her at all. He stopped paying attention when she was fourteen, when everything April did reminded him of his absent wife.

Another awkward pause. With anyone else, April would launch into a colorful monologue about her day, about work, about something funny Liza said. She knows from experience, though, when she does that with Hank, what he sees is April's mother all over again, trying to get his attention with increasingly wilder antics.

Her father clears his throat. "To what do I owe the pleasure?"

"I just wanted to hear your voice, Dad. I'm sitting here with Liza."

"Ah. Tell her I said hello."

April almost asks, "Don't you want to tell her yourself?" But she doesn't want Liza to overhear if the answer is no. Or not no, something vague like, "Maybe later." In some ways that's worse, not to inspire dislike but just indifference.

"Marie's back and she needs some help with the grocery bags. I'll let you go."

"Okay! Bye, Dad! Talk to you soon!" April's face feels brittle with forced smiles.

Liza lifts her chin to look at April upside down from her place on her lap. "What did Grandpa say?" she asks.

"Oh, that everything's fine, and Marie is making that Armenian lamb dish tonight."

"Poor little lambies," says Liza absent-mindedly, returning to her book. April smiles. For all his flaws—his many, many flaws—her ex-husband Danny adores Liza, and even more importantly is *interested* in her. Liza will never know what it's like to grow up practically invisible. April's mother hadn't been able to exist that way in her own home, like a plant without sunlight. Neither of her parents were bad people, just so mismatched that they just about destroyed each other.

"Baaah," bleats April plaintively and pokes her daughter in the ribs while Liza keeps her eyes on her book and tries not to smile. "I'm hungry. Let me up so I can make us some angel hair with that Trader Joe's pesto."

After dinner, while April and Liza watch *Project Runway* and discuss dessert, Selma texts. *Are you home? Are you sitting down?*

Why??? asks April. Hopefully it's something juicy, like Selma booked a photo shoot with a celebrity's dog or has some good gossip about one of their art school classmates—something normal and familiar, like before their current weirdness.

Trust me, answers Selma. *I'm going to send you a link & you are going to die laughing.*

JUST SEND IT demands April.

There's a pause. April pictures Selma on the couch in her Brooklyn apartment with her dog Collins curled by her side. She's clearly hovering her finger over the send button, gleefully making April wait.

And there it is. April taps the link and opens a Facebook post with a photo. It's an old picture, the clothes and hairstyles maybe from the late 90s. Lots of people, lots of bodies. Wait, where is this? She reads the caption: "Help me find them! Going thru old vacation photos. Paris, 1999. Who is this cute couple kissing on the Eiffel Tower? I have thought about them over the years! So in love, so French. Must know where they are now. Hope they are still together!"

April's heart pounds so hard she can hear it. She scrolls back up to the photo.

Holy mother of God. Now she sees it. Just off to the left, in a bubble of space apart from the crowd, next to the tower's metal scaffolding. There she is. And Paul.

April's finger traces the image. Her long, wavy hair and Paul's short, dark hair. His hands, the way one tenderly brushes her cheek and the other firmly grasps her waist. For a moment she's back there, her body anchored against his in a sea of people, feeling like they had all the time in the world when really it was slipping away terrifyingly fast.

Her phone rings, startling her. It's Selma.

"Oh my God, that's you, isn't it? And that guy, the Canadian? Can you believe it?"

"How did you find it?" April's voice comes out in a choked whisper. Seeing the moment that she has held in the back of her mind for so many years in a photograph is both beautiful and a little too raw. All this time, while she slipped back to remembering the small details of clothing and scents and surroundings, there had been an actual picture.

"Melissa Valentine is one of my hate-follows. She's an annoying mommy influencer with a huge audience. Very wholesome, somewhat creepy Evangelical vibes. All the comments are like, 'So romantic, I bet they are happily married with ten children now, just like me!' It's hilarious."

"What should I do?" asks April, a note of panic rising in her voice. "Selm, I don't want these people looking for me!"

She doesn't want anyone scrutinizing this tender moment and knowing that she's failed at love since then. She doesn't want to be confronted with her younger self, who was so confident that everything she deserved in life would easily fall in her lap.

Selma finally senses that April isn't finding the whole thing as funny as she is. "April, sweetie? It's okay. I'm probably the only person in the world who recognized you in the photo, and that's just because I was there."

"But...what if Paul sees it?"

"Right, was that his name? Don't worry, babe, he's never going to see it. Unless he's an Evangelical? Do they have those in Canada? Never mind, it's just some bored moms telling themselves that love is real, and you both lived happily ever after, just to give themselves the strength to make it through another day of smiling while they pretend that getting married and having kids didn't ruin their lives."

"Jesus, Selma," says April. "You know I have a kid, right?"

"I have nothing against moms, Chickadee. I don't hate them more than I hate everyone. And your daughter is the light of my life, but I have no idea how you manage to be both a mother and a human being with a little remora dependent on you for everything."

"It's like I always tell you, you don't think you're going to survive the first year but then...hey, why are we talking about your issues? I'm the one whose life is about to be fucked!"

"April," says Selma calmly, "You're spinning out here. What's going on?"

"I don't know!" wails April miserably. She can feel Selma's canny, knowing look bore right through her like she's in the room.

"Does it have something to do with how you haven't mentioned this guy's name since we left Paris twenty years ago, but you have clearly thought about him without mentioning it to your best friend?"

April sighs. "Maybe?"

"Then, Chickadee," says Selma, "we have a very intriguing situation. And I, for one, am here for it."

Paul

Paul hides out in the office until lunchtime, supposedly doing the company payroll but really just feeling embarrassed. Somehow, the more pulled together Tommy gets, the less patience Paul has with him. It's like after years of trying not to push his troubled, alcoholic little brother away with anger and harsh words, Paul can't keep it together for the sober, serious guy who shows up on time each morning.

After a few hours, though, Paul is hungry, and Muffin needs to pee. So what if he acted like an asshole. Tommy's probably used to it by now.

Tommy's still at the front counter, talking to a young woman in thick-framed glasses and one of those hipster jumpsuits that looked like a mechanic's uniform. When Paul walks in, they both give each other a quick glance, and she grabs her plastic-draped dresses off the rack and hurries out the door with a wave.

"Who's that?" asks Paul. She's about thirty years younger and ten times cooler than their usual clientele.

"Simone. She's a new regular. We had a long talk the first time she came in about what bullshit it is that women's clothes cost more to clean than men's. So now she always makes sure to tell me that she's dropping off her *brother's* dry cleaning."

"Her brother wears a lot of floral dresses?" asks Paul.

"Hey, I don't judge," smirks Tommy. "I think she likes me. She was asking for my phone number when you came in."

"She didn't have to run away like that," says Paul defensively. "I don't have a problem with cross-dressing imaginary brothers. And you know why ladies' stuff costs more. Their shirts don't fit right in the buck press and need to be done by hand. It's not a conspiracy theory or anything."

"But it's a way we could set ourselves apart," says Tommy, getting excited again. "What if we just offered the same prices for all shirts, no matter what, and made up in volume what we lose in mark-up on the women's stuff? Or if we had Ladies' Night, with discounts and music. And a glass of prosecco! Damn, that would be huge."

"I don't think our business license lets us give out free booze," says Paul before he can help himself. Tommy's face returns to blank and neutral again, and Paul was immediately sorry that he couldn't share in the brainstorming. When was the last thing he'd tried something new? Anything at all? A new route to walk Muffin, a new brand of peanut butter, even a new television show, let alone a new promotion for the business.

"There's that new Thai place over on Sycamore Street," says Paul before he can second-guess himself. "Let me take you to lunch."

"I'm sorry," grins Tommy, "Who are you and what have you done with my big brother? Don't tell me you didn't bring a turkey sandwich and an oats and honey granola bar with you? And what about the store?"

"Caridad gets in at 12:30. We'll go then."

Tommy nods, and Paul takes Muffin outside. His turkey sandwich will keep another day.

**

The restaurant is busy, but the server leads them to the last table towards the back.

"I didn't realize so many people had time to eat a sit-down lunch in a restaurant," mutters Paul.

"You're in for a big surprise, bro. There's this thing called Saturday night, too, where people go out and order drinks and food, and sometimes even listen to music." He eyes Paul mischievously. "Or meet up with a date."

"Never heard of it," says Paul, opening his menu.

The server comes by to take their order. Paul sticks with his usual Thai order of red curry with chicken. There's been enough spontaneity for one day.

They stay on neutral topics while they wait—their nephew Matty, the local hockey team (Paul is a Jets fan, and Tommy played hockey pretty seriously in high school.) The food comes out quickly, smelling especially spicy and aromatic. Paul feels a rare contentment to be there with his brother, not arguing, and eating good food.

Tommy had placed his phone on the table when they sat down. He turned it facedown when Paul gave him a look, but now it's vibrating dramatically every few seconds.

"Sorry," says Tommy, picking it up. Paul huffs in annoyance mostly out of habit and keeps on eating. He watches as Tommy's face slowly turns from surprised to quizzical to smiling broadly.

"Hey man," says Tommy finally, "I never knew you went to Paris."

Paul feels like a bird's eye chili is caught in his throat. "What?" he coughs.

Tommy turns his phone around. A picture. Paul sees bronze waves of hair and knows immediately.

"Where did you get that?" he demands. Tommy looks at him quizzically, confused by his quiet but deadly serious tone.

"Teresa. She saw it on Facebook, and she thinks it's you. It's an old photo some lady took in Paris back in the nineties, and now she wants to track down the young lovers."

51

Paul can't speak. Of all the ways he dreamed of seeing April again, this is definitely not one of them.

Tommy glances at Paul, then his phone, then back at Paul. "Oh, shit! It is you, isn't it! You can only see your profile, but I remember that lame Van Morrison t-shirt. I bet you still have it, huh? And your hair's kind of long in front like. Mom said it made you look like Hugh Grant. News flash: it didn't."

Paul can't form words. Finally, he manages to grab the phone out of Tommy's hand to get a good look.

April.

The golden evening light bathed her hair in rich color. From this angle, Paul sees her silver nose ring and a few of the light brown freckles on her cheek. He sees the way he's touching her, like she is precious, like she is *his*. And he sees the way she touched him back. So it was real. He hasn't been making it up all these years.

"Are you going to tell me who she is?" asks Tommy. "Some French mademoiselle? Seriously, though, when did you go to Paris?"

Paul puts down the picture. It hurts to look for too long.

"Just after I graduated from university," he managed to say. "Right before Mom got really sick. That's probably why you don't remember. Plus you had your head up your own ass like a twelve-year-old kid is supposed to."

"Right," said Tommy. They sat in silence for a moment, Tommy clearly waiting for Paul to elaborate. Finally, he picked up the phone. "Well, since you don't seem to want to talk about it, I guess I'll just delete the picture, and we can move on…"

"Wait!" yelled Paul, startling them both. "I mean, send it to me first, okay?"

"Sure, man," said Tommy. "I look forward to learning more about this mystery woman. And why seeing this picture after all these years is making you even more uptight than usual."

Paul looked down at his half-eaten curry. He'd just made a pact that he was going to forget about April and sealed it with the sacred blowing out of birthday candles. It was just like her, to pop up again when he was finally trying to move on. Looking at the picture, he could remember her lively wide grin and her joyful laugh with a new clarity that cut right through him. As much as he thought about April over the years, seeing her, seeing *them*, was tossing his little world upside down, and he didn't like it one bit.

Paris, France 1999

Paul had already been to the Louvre.

Of course he had. In fact, it was the first thing he did on his first full day in Paris, after breakfast at his youth hostel (included in the cost of the night's stay) where they served baguette with butter and jam along with milky coffee in bowls.

He didn't mention it to the girls, though. He liked guiding April and Selma through the streets while they followed unquestioningly, first to dump April's ridiculous backpack in a luggage locker at the train station. Then they veered a few blocks west until they spotted the distinctive glass pyramid. Paul knew where to stand in line to buy tickets, the morning sun already reflecting off the glass and heating up the plaza and the tourists. Paul hadn't budgeted for two trips to the Louvre and a nagging voice reminded him he was going to have to sacrifice down the road, but then April smiled at him, and he couldn't think beyond the present moment.

She was kind of a mess, this April. Her story about storming out of her hostel should have been a red flag, but the way she told it had somehow touched him: her voice uneven, trying a little too hard to entertain him. And her smile. April had a wide, expressive mouth, with one slightly crooked canine tooth that put Paul in mind of a sexy jack o'lantern.

It was still early enough that the ticket line wasn't too long, and soon they were descending the escalators beneath the pyramid. As Paul stepped off, he automatically held out a hand to April behind him, like he would with his mother or the twins. April took it, a cool hand with long fingers and three silver rings, making Paul feel sweaty and clumsy by comparison. The beginning of a hot flush rose up his neck, and he froze, willing it from traveling up to his face. The escalator, though, did not freeze, and as he gripped April's hand tighter it deposited her right into his arms. Too late, he took a step backwards, knocking them both off balance and spilling them onto the ground one more time. This time, Paul's view of the blue sky above was refracted through the pyramid's glass panels, the weight on his chest already familiar. His warm hand still felt cool silver rings.

Selma hopped off the escalator and stepped over them.

"Not to alarm you, chickadees, but you're about to get trampled by a Japanese tour group," she said. Paul looked up at the escalator to see an onslaught of people pouring down towards them. He scrambled to his feet, pulling April with him, and stepped to the side, letting go of her hand a moment too late. She was dazed and pink, the yellow scarf almost falling from her hair. The glass panels and blue sky reflected in her gray eyes.

Selma looked from April to Paul, then back to April. "Oh, noooo…" she muttered to herself. She gave Paul a weary glare and then went up on her tiptoes to peck April on the cheek. Paul heard her sternly whisper, "Not part of the plan" before she waved to them both. "Meet me at the *Mona Lisa*, chickadees!"

They watched her disappear into the crowd before turning back to each other, a little awkward and shy.

"We have to stop running into each other like this," said April finally.

"I guess we'll always have Paris," said Paul, and was rewarded with the full sexy jack o'lantern.

"I want to show you something," he said.

**

When they reached the bottom of the staircase, April gasped, just like Paul hoped she would.

"What is it?" she whispered, like they were in church, even though the noisy crowd swirled around them. The massive, graceful sculpture loomed from the top of the stairs.

"The Winged Victory of Samothrace," said Paul. April was in profile beside him, sharp chin, snub nose, curls escaping from the yellow scarf. "The first time I saw her, I felt like someone kicked me in the stomach. She was so beautiful." He looked at April as he spoke, realizing he'd had the same feeling twice in just a few days.

The statue didn't have a head, or arms, but she still burst with life, wings unfurling and draped garments catching the wind. One foot stepped forward with commanding presence.

"What do you think she looked like?" asked April. "Her face, I mean."

"It doesn't matter," said Paul. "You wouldn't dare make eye contact anyway."

"Being headless suddenly seems like a very legit choice," said April, and Paul snorted before he could catch himself. April looked pleased and leaned in to talk softly in his ear.

"When I was 8," she said, "I played the angel in one of those church Christmas pageants, where the kids wear their dad's bathrobe and there's a doll wrapped in a towel that's supposed to be Jesus. Classic American childhood rite of passage." April kept her eyes on the statue like she was watching a beautiful sunrise. "The Bible says that the shepherds were 'sore afraid' of the angel—not 'so' but 'sore'— and I loved that, the way these older boys would get on their knees and bow down to me."

Paul could picture it, small April with the same wild hair dramatically gesturing at the audience. "You must have looked like her. Winged April."

"I felt like that. Brave and commanding." She looked at Paul with a wry smile that didn't match her dreamy gray eyes. "I think I've been trying to get that feeling back ever since."

Paul wanted to take her hand and hold it to his chest. He imagined the pulse of his heartbeat against her hand, somehow sending her the courage she'd had when she was 8.

"Should we go up the stairs for a closer look?" he asked.

"Let's stay here for one more minute. I like the anticipation."

Paul nodded. He'd never thought of anticipation as a pleasure—the future was too uncertain, people got sick—but April made it sound delicious. Something wonderful was happening, and his hand slipped easily into April's as they stood at the bottom of the stairs, waiting for the next moment to unfold.

Chapter 5

April

April can't sit still.

After talking to Selma, she paces around her house. She wishes she was one of those people who deals with nervous energy by cleaning—or with stress by forgetting to eat, but that's never going to happen. What she really wants is a cigarette, though she hasn't smoked in twenty years. April remembers buying a pack of Gauloises in Paris and trying to smoke them with chic detachment in an outdoor cafe but having a coughing fit once she realized that the French cigarettes were so much stronger than the Marlboro Lights she occasionally indulged in at college.

Damn it, why does everything make her think of Paris? And of being twenty-one and so certain that love was waiting for her? And of Paul, who looked at her from the first moment like he understood all her weirdness, and insecurity, and liked her despite it? Maybe even because of it. What if he sees the photo? April cringes at the thought. What are the odds that Paul has a wife, sister, mother, or nosy coworker who follows the mommy influencer Melissa Valentine?

April gives up. She collapses on the couch with a dramatic sigh, next to where Liza watches *Rupaul's Drag Race* with rapt attention, and picks up her phone.

It's just a picture, she tells herself. Think of it as a stock photo that a client would save to a Pinterest board called "Romance Inspo." A young couple—not a couple, exactly, but for the purposes of objective observation—pressed together in front of a bronze telescope. Maybe they'd been looking through it, trying to find the places they'd been together earlier that day. April can practically feel a strong hand on the small of her back, a deep, calm voice in her ear. She doesn't particularly like heights, always feels like she might spontaneously fall off, but that voice and that hand kept her rooted to the steel structure. And if she still felt unsteady, she could grab onto those shoulders...

"Mom? Mom! Earth to Mom!" Liza is saying. April startles and looks over. The show is on a commercial break, and Liza nudges her with some shockingly cold toes. "What are you looking at?"

"Nothing," April automatically replies, but Liza is already maneuvering herself under April's arm to look at her phone screen, managing to poke her with sharp elbows several times in the process.

"Who's that girl? Her hair looks like yours in that picture of you and Selma at college. And who's that guy? Mom, is that you kissing a boy? That's not Dad, is it? Oh my God. I'm freaking out a little."

"Honey, don't freak out." April sighs. There isn't much use hiding the truth, and anyway, what's the point? "That's me, from a really long time ago. Like, twenty years. And a guy I met when Selma and I went to Paris after college. We went to the Eiffel Tower, and it was romantic, and, well, *that* happened."

"Okay…" hesitates Liza, clearly trying to take in the idea of her mother being young and spontaneous. "So why are you looking at it like that?"

"Like what?"

"Like you want to crawl inside it or something. It's weird."

April lays the phone face down on the couch, hesitates for two seconds, and flips it back over.

"Someone posted it on Facebook. We didn't know she took the picture, but now she wants to find us and see what happened since then."

"So what happened?" asks Liza. "Is that guy my real father or something?"

April tries not to meet sarcasm with sarcasm—the ultimate test of the modern parent. "I don't know what happened to him. We...lost track of each other right after that."

"How do you lose track of somebody?" asks Liza. "Didn't you get his number, or just find his Insta, or, like, his Facebook since you're both old, and slide into his DMs like a normal person?"

"Hah, I'm even older than you think. We didn't have any of that stuff. My college gave me an email address my senior year, but I didn't really use it for anything, and it stopped working the day after I graduated. The only phone number I had was Grandpa Hank's, and no way I was going to have guys calling there. Believe it or not, there was a time when you could lose touch with someone and just never see them again."

Liza looks at her skeptically, and April realizes her daughter will never lose touch with anyone in her entire life unless she makes a conscious effort to do it. Every girl she shares a bunk with at summer camp, everyone from the school play or the softball team will always be in her orbit. April isn't sure if that sounds wonderful or terrible. Surely you need to prune out some of your old acquaintances every few years. Otherwise, you just stay the same person forever.

And there is no way April is the same person as that skinny, long-haired girl in Paris. She'd worked hard to keep that needy girl under wraps.

Liza looks at her with wide eyes. "So, Mom, this is like, a big deal," she says intensely. "If you didn't think you would ever see this guy again, and it turns out there's a photo you never knew existed, and someone posted it now while you're very, very single…"

"Just 'single' tells the story, sweetie."

"But don't you think the universe is trying to tell you something? I mean, just this morning Dad asked me if you were dating, and then I told you it was okay if you had a boyfriend, and *then* this picture gets posted. So many signs, Mom!"

April smiles at Liza's growing excitement. The last time she thought the universe was telling her something, she ended up married to Danny.

Liza continues, "So with all these signs, that must mean that this guy is also single, and that he never stopped thinking of you, and he wishes all the time that you'd had a cell phone in 1999 so he could have texted you later. But he understands that the time wasn't right then, but it is now. It's your time! Mom, you have to find him!"

"That's not always how it works, baby," says April, kissing her daughter's forehead. "Now bedtime for you. And don't stay up reading under the covers."

"Okay," says Liza. "But we are not done talking about this!"

April watches Liza take the stairs two at a time. Then she picks up the phone and looks at the picture again.

Maybe it is her time. *Their* time. Maybe Paul had thought about her over the years, and Melissa Valentine's minions will track him down. More likely, though, he's married to someone quiet and capable like he is, and they have a brood of polite Canadian sons, and they go on healthy family hikes even in winter and drink cocoa around the fire. The idea of Paul seeing her now, seeing what a mess she's made of things, and after what she'd done to him...no. It can't happen. She left him in Paris for a reason. It is not *their* time, it never has been, and it never will be.

Before she can second-guess herself, April taps out a comment on the Facebook post. *Hey, that's me, back when I went to Paris with my best friend after college. Can't really remember the guy though. Sorry! I wish I had a great love story for you and your readers.*

April turns off her phone. She feels a little sick, but it's better this way.

Paul

"*Au revoir, mon frère!*" calls Tommy as Paul bolts out Stone Dry Cleaning at 3:30 sharp to meet Teresa at Matty's softball game. Paul tries to think of a witty response but gives him the middle finger instead, which quickly transforms into a nose scratch as an elderly customer wanders in. He and Tommy don't dare look at each other or they'll laugh.

Teresa waits for him in the bleachers, wearing white jeans and a red t-shirt to coordinate with the Puffins' team uniform. She gives Paul a quick hug, and they settle in the front row so Muffin can lie down in the grass by their feet.

"Ugh," she says, "I just got a haircut, and I think it's too short. Do you like it?"

Paul noticed her hair first thing. It's very short in back, a little longer in front, and striped with some new honey-colored pieces standing out from the dark brown. It looks the same as most of the other women's hair around the ball field. His wild little sister got a mom haircut.

"You look great," he says truthfully. Maybe it isn't the best haircut in the world, but she looks happy and like she belongs in the sea of doting softball parents. She isn't that rebellious teenager with dark rings of eyeliner and a nervous habit of twisting her many rings.

"Are you sure?" Teresa asks, her fingers brushing the shorn back. "I'm not used to all this air on my neck."

"You look like a million bucks, Tree," says Paul. He thinks about what their sweet, pragmatic mother would have said to her daughter and adds, "Plus it looks nice and cool for the summer."

Teresa looks pleased and pokes him in the ribs. "How is it that you don't have a girlfriend, Mr. Smooth Talker?" This is familiar territory, his younger sister hinting at him to find a new life now that she doesn't need him so much. No doubt she'll bring up the Eiffel Tower photo next, and Paul is equal parts afraid that she will and that she won't.

"Where's Matty?" he asks. He can't talk about it just yet.

Teresa points across the field where Matty is warming up with his team, and they both wave wildly. Matty gives them a quick nod, unlike his usual happy two-handed wave.

"Matty's so nervous," sighs Teresa. "He's in a slump. Hasn't had a hit in three games."

Paul hasn't been to a game in a few weeks, he realizes with a pang. He used to come to all Matty's Little League games and even coached his Peewee Hockey team, but since Teresa and Griff got married last year he's backed off.

"Maybe he'll get one today," says Paul. "Slumps can't last forever." He regrets his words as soon as he hears them, and Teresa takes the bait.

"Apparently not," Teresa grins. "I forgot you went to Paris."

The game starts. Paul watches Matty's team assemble in the outfield. "New cleats?" he asks.

"Yes, he already outgrew the ones from the beginning of the season, if you can believe it," says Teresa, momentarily distracted. "But no, we're not talking about Matty's feet right now. I saw that photo, and now I want you to tell me everything."

"How did you see it, anyway?" asks Paul.

"Oh, I have about five stupid mommy accounts that I check on every morning." says Teresa placidly. "They're so stupid, it keeps me from feeling bad about all the cutesy shit I didn't do when Matty was a baby because I was barely keeping it together. The hate wakes me up, like caffeine."

"Makes perfect sense," nods Paul, feeling a pang of guilt that he hadn't made things easier when Matty was a baby. He'd changed diapers and paced the floor with a squalling newborn, but he isn't Matty's dad, or Teresa's dad—he's just the placeholder.

The crack of the bat, a tiny boy on the opposite team tagged out at first for a third out. Teresa and Paul automatically cheer while Matty's team skips, marches, and runs from the outfield.

Teresa continues, "Melissa Valentine gets under my skin. She calls her husband Doctor Love, you know, because Valentine and because he's a chiropractor, and it makes me want to throw things. So, of course I always check her first. She was doing her thing, humblebragging about going to Paris when she was in high school, when most of her readers are like me, they've never been and probably never will, right? I barely even looked at the picture. But for some reason it stuck in my head, and I went back to it at lunch and thought, that guy looks familiar. He looks a little bit like my romantically challenged brother Paul." She whistles startlingly loudly as the first Puffin goes up to bat and gives Paul the same side-eye she's been giving him since she was a teenager. "Though if it was Paul, he would have said something to his only sister about some pretty girl he kissed on the freakin' Eiffel Tower."

He should tell her. Maybe he should have told her a long time ago, and not tried to be an authority figure who had his shit together. He leans back, his elbows on the bench behind him.

"Yeah, it's me," he says, checking on Matty out in left field. He's a stocky kid, and his uniform shirt is a little too small, occasionally exposing a slice of his belly when he lifts his mitt. "I went to Paris right after I graduated from university. I met a pretty American girl. We had some fun for a day or so, which apparently was captured on film. I came home. Mom got sicker. I never saw the girl again."

"Well, damn," says Teresa. "Maybe there's hope for you after all. Did you ever try to find her?"

"Sort of. About ten years ago, when all of a sudden everyone was on Facebook and stuff. April Anderson. There were a ton of them, and none of them were her."

Paul doesn't mention how typing her name into his computer felt as private as a search for obscure fetish porn, and how he'd methodically clicked on dozens of April Andersons, hoping to see something familiar. One of them had even been an "In Remembrance" site, which clenched his heart for a second. That time he was relieved it wasn't his April.

"That's it?" says Teresa, snapping him out of his daydream. "A Facebook search ten years ago? You have to make an effort, Paul. Look, I know I get on your case about finding someone, but I just want you to be happy."

"I'm not unhappy," says Paul.

"Not good enough," says Teresa. "Hey, I know you still see me and Tommy as bratty teenagers, or twenty-something fuck-ups." The blonde mom next to them gasps, and Teresa glares at her, a flash of her younger self. "Oh, hi, Cheryl. Too bad your Frankie missed that pop up. Anyway, I was just having a private conversation with my brother." She turns back to Paul. "You missed out on a lot. You took care of Mom, then you took care of us, and you took care of the business."

Paul looks down at his feet. He's used to Teresa being bossy, but they don't talk about the past. "That was nothing," he said. "Anyone would have done that."

"Look at me," says Teresa, and Paul does, Teresa's brown eyes unsettlingly like their mother's. "It was not nothing. You made it so I could leave Matty's dad and now we have Griff. You made it so Tommy had a place to come home to when he was on parole. But life goes on, and you're just staying in place. You can't just tread water for the rest of your...Oh my God! RUN, MATTY, RUN!"

While they'd been so deep in their conversation, Matty came up to bat and hit a grounder towards first. He chugs to the base for an expected easy out, but the Tigers' fielder fumbles while scooping up the ball in his too-big mitt. Matty rounds the base and keeps going. Paul and Teresa jump to their feet. "C'mon, Matty!" yells Paul.

The fielder pauses to pull up his pants and then flings the ball to second base but massively overshoots. The shortstop and the third baseman both go for it, crashing into each other, and fall over, lying stunned in the dirt while the ball rolls out of reach. Matty keeps running. Now the pitcher, a tiny freckled kid with spooky intense concentration on the mound, goes after it but trips on his untied shoelace, landing on top of the third baseman.

Paul and Teresa clutch each other and jump up and down, never taking their eyes off sturdy, determined Matty, who is going for third now without a moment's hesitation. "Go go GO!" calls Paul. Teresa's mouth hangs open, but no words come out. Matty lumbers past third base as the catcher scrambles for the ball but trips over the shortstop still sprawled on the ground, adding to the pile up of boys. As Matty rounds home plate, Paul and Teresa gape at each other in stunned silence until Teresa grabs him and hugs him tight.

"It's a sign," she whispers intensely. "Matty broke his slump and got a home run. Now it's your turn. Find your girl. Make up for lost time. Maybe have some goddamn fun for once."

Paul holds on just as tightly, watching over her shoulder as Matty is surrounded by his teammates, getting hugs and pats on the back while the parents cheer. The world kept turning and everyone kept moving forward, except for him. His birthday wish was for a new beginning, to be needed and useful to someone. Instead he got the opposite, with all signs pointing back to April. Moving towards the past was at least still moving, though, and Paul and Teresa run to Matty.

**

Paul turns down Teresa's offer for a celebratory pizza outing and drives home, feeds Muffin, and makes himself a peanut butter sandwich. One of the light bulbs in the kitchen burnt out weeks ago, and he hasn't replaced it yet.

What is he supposed to do now? What do you do when someone is searching for you in a viral photo? He takes out his phone and opens Facebook again, taking his time to really absorb the picture. He looks so damn young, younger than he ever remembered feeling. Also so confident, like he was meant to hold this girl in his arms.

The picture had been shared 101,235 times, which Paul thinks is probably a lot. And comments, hundreds of them. After a moment's hesitation he scrolls down and starts to read.

OMG, that's the most romantic thing ever. My DH says we will go to Paris for our 10th anniversary next year. I want him to kiss me like that!

If that's not true love right there I don't know what is. What God has joined let no man put asunder. Matthew 19:6.

While I can't approve of PDA I hope you find them. If anyone can do it, Melissa can!

The comments are pretty repetitive, all in a similar vein, but he can't stop reading, amazed that so many people saw the picture and are interested enough to say something.

I can't even, this is so pure. Love is a gift that blesses those who witness it.

He likes that. *Love is a gift.* He pictures presenting his love in a small, beautifully wrapped package, pressing it into someone's hand and saying, *I made this just for you.*

But the next comment stops him in his tracks. *Hey, that's me, back when I went to Paris with my best friend after college.*

Paul's heart races and his gut twists in a way that he isn't sure is pleasant or not. A tiny profile photo, but he can still make out the bronze hair, less wildly wavy now, and wide grin.

April Andersen, it says. Not Anderson. Of course. She's been out there all this time while he's been in one place, treading water and sometimes barely keeping his head above the surface. April Andersen is real.

He keeps reading. *Can't really remember the guy though. Sorry! I wish I had a great love story for you and your readers.*

Oh. Of all the scenarios he's pictured, somehow this one never occurred to him, that he is cheerfully and vaguely remembered with no pangs of curiosity or regret. Maybe he isn't very memorable—he is quiet, more average than tall, more polite than charming—but seeing it spelled out for 101,235 people really stings.

Paul wants to throw his phone out the window, though his inner voice reminds him that there is something called the cloud and destroying his phone won't make the picture disappear. So he presses on the wound and reads the responses to April. *What is wrong with you? How can you join your soul in a perfect kiss and forget?* and *I bet you are a shriveled up old maid now.* They only get worse from there: *You deserve to be alone forever.*

These angry messages directed at his April snaps something to attention in Paul. Maybe she doesn't remember him, but thinking of her over the years, especially during the tough times, had forced him to remember that love and happiness were possible. Even when his mother could no longer speak, or Tommy was back in jail, he had the memory of April, her gray eyes reflecting the sunset, with Paris spread below at their feet. It isn't much, but it isn't nothing. Love is a gift.

Maybe April needs him one last time.

Before he quite knows what he's doing, Paul types a reply. *I'm the guy in the picture. My sister saw it and told me. Please go easy on April. I'm not really the kind of guy you remember. But I remember how brave and kind and smart she was. And beautiful. I'm sure she still is. It's my most perfect memory. I hope everyone who sees the picture remembers that sometimes good things happen to regular people.*

Paul powers down his phone and sticks it in a kitchen drawer. He wants to be alone with his thoughts. April needs him, and he's answered the call. Surely that deserved a little dream, back to the Eiffel Tower, to the cooling evening air and April's warm mouth. This is the last time.

Who is he fooling? Unless April needs him again.

Paris, France 1999

April draped her hand invitingly on the park bench and quickly snatched it back like a goddamn lunatic. She wanted Paul to hold her hand again, but she didn't want to want it.

They had stayed at the Louvre until April was dizzy and disoriented from the combination of hunger and the knowledge that she was surrounded by so many masterpieces that even if she gave each one just an appreciative glance, they would still be there for days. So she and Paul collected Selma, bought baguettes with ham and brie, and found a small, shady park to eat and recover. When Selma announced she was heading back to the hostel for a nap, April felt rooted to the spot, conscious of Paul's strong-looking fingers curled around a bottle of water, holding it firmly, yet tenderly.

Oh my God, she snapped at herself. Get a grip! You did not come to Paris to spend all of your time with a kind and sincere Canadian guy who looks like your best friend's older brother home from college for the summer, and you never realized before how broad his shoulders were...Oh my God, April, just shut up already!

"Why did you come to Paris by yourself? Didn't want to compete with any bros for the ladies?" She tried to sound flirtatious, like she would have with any of the guys back at college, but from Paul's slight flinch and set to his jaw, she realized she'd made him uncomfortable.

Instead of backing off, April did what she always did and took things up a notch. Somehow it seemed easier than acknowledging Paul's discomfort. If she pretended she hadn't noticed, he could keep his dignity, and she could pretend she wasn't observing him so closely.

"Or maybe…" she blabbed, "You're the responsible, nice guy, and this is your, as the Amish say, rumspringa? You go a little crazy, pick up American girls on the street, soften them up with sculptural masterpieces, and then fuck their brains out?"

For someone with lovely olive skin that no doubt tanned beautifully, Paul could certainly blush. The redness traveled up his neck, through his cheeks, and all the way to the tips of his ears. April realized she was making an ass of herself but was still unable to admit how utterly invested she was by apologizing. She certainly didn't want to brush her fingers against Paul's cheek and feel the heat for herself, or drift down to those shoulders under his worn t-shirt…. Damn damn damn! April felt heat in her cheeks, her own blush rising. She looked down into the small purse she wore slung across her body and pulled out the Swiss army knife she'd bought for the trip, feeling every inch the cool girl.

"I need to cut up this apple," she said, opening the blade as she attempted to hide behind her hair. "My dentist doesn't like me biting into hard things…" Jesus, could she not just shut her mouth? But to stop talking now would be to give Paul a chance to tell her that it was time for him to go, and that he hoped he never saw her again. "Because of my veneers," she continued to babble. "I have peg laterals. That's when the incisor tooth is underdeveloped and looks like a little fang… *God damn it!*"

Her shaky, nervous hands had cut off a crooked piece of apple as well as sliced her finger. Blood poured out. April felt a stab of panic, and the sudden urge to run away and cry.

"Hey," said Paul in a gentle voice. "Look at me, not at your hand."

April tore her eyes away from the red stream already dripping down her hand. Paul's face was calm. His dark eyes stayed locked on hers as he reached into his pocket and pulled out a red bandana, the kind that cowboys wore in the old movies her dad liked.

"It's clean," he said, and wrapped it around her finger. "Just keep breathing, okay? In one-two-three, out one-two-three."

April felt her hand rising and realized that Paul was carefully lifting it above her head. "What..." she started to say and drifted off. Whatever he was doing was surely fine.

"Just holding your hand above your heart. It'll help stop the bleeding. Keep looking at me. Keep breathing."

They sat side by side on the bench, holding hands in mid-air.

Paul was holding her hand, April realized. She sure had a strange way of getting what she wanted.

Her breathing slowed to match his. Her eyes stayed locked on his dark ones, and she felt flooded with calm. Except for a tiny part of her that was beginning to feel a little tingly.

This wasn't supposed to happen. She was in so much trouble.

Chapter 6

April

It's my most perfect memory.

April can't help grabbing her phone and opening Facebook the minute she wakes up, but now she wants to pull the covers over her head and spontaneously combust. Paul's words are a knife in her heart. No, that's too dignified. Reading his words is like laying a loud, stinking fart in a conference room and laughing along with everyone while inside you want to die. It's like making a joke about someone's mother only to learn she was murdered yesterday, and then getting your period on an airplane while wearing a white jumpsuit.

April didn't expect the angry responses from Melissa Valentine's minions, but she probably should have. She knows how internet outrage works—there's a new villain every day, and for God's sake, you don't want it to be you. Well, it's probably her turn to be famous for fifteen seconds.

April sighs and flings the covers back, feeling the sun on her bare legs. April Andersen, successful home stager, has a busy day ahead. She doesn't have time to lower herself to respond to the angry moms out there. She especially doesn't have time to reread, *I remember how brave and smart and kind she was.* And definitely not, *I hope everyone who sees the picture remembers that sometimes good things happen to regular people*. She doesn't have time to wonder who the stocky little boy in Paul's profile picture is, and to wish he had more of an online footprint. She certainly doesn't have time to google "Paul Stone Canada," and if she did, she doesn't have time to sift through the 137,000 results.

No, April will put on her gray blazer with sensible flats, slap on some nude lipstick and neutral eyeshadow, finish the look with gold stud earrings, and meet Juan Pablo and the truck at the Miller house. She's going to put inoffensive furniture in predictable places, so a man who dislikes her can get a lot of money for his house. Because that's what grown ups do.

And yet...April doesn't turn off the notifications on her phone. She needs the pings, like intermittent pinpricks, to remind her that today is different, that something has happened.

May is a glorious month in New England. March is surprise blizzard season; April, her birth month and namesake, is vastly overrated, full of wet days with an unexpectedly bone-chilling cold. May is lilacs and warm afternoons, with the glories of summer visible on the horizon. April is surely ready to face the world on a day like today, or at least Joe Miller and his sad house.

Juan Pablo is already at the house when April arrives. He picked up the items on her list from her storage unit and brought his cousin Oscar to help unload. April grabs a box of ornamental books (never read) and carries it to the front door. It's locked, and no one answers the doorbell, so she leaves the box on the front steps and comes back for a second box of knick knacks (symmetrical faux silver vases for the mantel, potted succulents, a large wooden fork to hang in the kitchen.)

"Better leave the chairs in the truck for now, guys," she tells Juan Pablo and Oscar. "I'll text the owner and let him know we're here."

Just then, Joe's beige Nissan Sentra pulls in front of the house. He steps out, clearly alarmed to see her. Maybe he forgot she was coming today, though how could he when the realtor's open house is tomorrow. He looks good, though. Less stooped and gray. Maybe he managed to get laid by a less offensive person than herself.

"Oh, it's you," he says flatly. "Didn't you get Sandy's message?"

April's phone had pinged on and off all morning, each buzz a well-deserved stab in her conscience, but she stopped checking messages hours ago.

"Hello, Joe. Lovely to see you again. I'm afraid I'm on message overload today, so Sandy's might have slipped through the cracks. I'm glad you're here. If you can let us in, the guys and I will start unloading."

"That won't be necessary," says Joe, smugly crossing his arms.

"I don't understand. Was the open house postponed?"

"No," he says. "It's just that we no longer require your services. My wife Emily is going to do it herself." He pauses and looks at April meaningfully. "Emily is a big fan of Melissa Valentine, you know. A very big fan. And we prefer to work with someone who shares our values."

April's mouth is suddenly as dry as a saltine. Even Joe Miller knows about...whatever this situation is? He is clearly enjoying making her the scapegoat of his so-called *values* which apparently include wasting the time of working single mothers. April silently counts to three and forces a pleasant smile.

"I supposed you saw the photo of me that Melissa Valentine took. It was very long ago and taken without my permission. I'm not sure how this has anything to do with my work for you."

Joe narrows his eyes and looks down at her like he's a foot taller instead of a few inches. "Seeing that picture of you reminded Emily of our honeymoon in Venice and how in love we were," he says. "It made her want to give me another chance. We're going to move and make a fresh start. She realizes she's been unfulfilled since the kids were born so she's starting her own business. Life coaching and home decoration."

April tries very hard not to roll her eyes at that one. She's beginning to think that Joe really deserves his Emily.

Joe stares her down. "How could you enter my home and tell me what I should do to make everything look perfect, and then offer your body to me? Emily was very upset. I should have known that you had a twisted past, kissing a man like that in public and then forgetting him. I don't usually use such strong language, but you have a careless heart. Now, I would like you to leave."

Juan Pablo, sensing that something is wrong, comes to her side. "Everything okay?" he asks, giving Joe a cautionary glare.

"Fine, thank you. Mr. Miller has canceled our contract. Can you and Oscar take everything back to storage?"

April turns to slink away, but her phone pings again in her purse, another pin prick of misery. This is her life now, a constant stream of reminders that by trying to move on, she's only dug a deeper hole for herself. Well, she might be a stupid, messy bitch, but at least she hadn't woken up that morning and decided to be a fucking life coach, whatever that was. April spins around on her sensible flats and stomps back towards Joe, jutting out her chin and pointing her index finger at his chest. How dare he say those things to her that only she's allowed to say to herself?

"I do *not* have a careless heart," says April. Joe steps back, and she feels a wonderful thrill, like when she'd been the angel in the Christmas pageant and made the shepherds cower. "I have a heart that has been disappointed and embarrassed, but I am not a bad person. I talk too much, and I make mistakes, but I keep trying. You know what? I even hope that you and Emily live happily ever after in this house. Because I do not have a careless heart, Joe Miller. After I got divorced, at first, I was afraid...I was petrified." The Joe and Emily Millers of the world can all go to hell, along with Melissa Valentine. "But did I crumble? Did I lay down and die? Oh no, not I!" April wonders where she's heard these words before, but it doesn't matter. They roll deliciously off her tongue as Joe shrinks back. "I *will* survive," says April triumphantly and flounces to her car as gracefully as possible. The Winged Victory is back.

But now what? April can't go home. It's too quiet there, with Liza in school. Nothing to blunt the now-constant pinging of her phone or to boost her rapidly crashing adrenalin rush. Instead she finds herself pulling into the parking lot at Round and Round, the eclectic thrift store run by the local Humane Society. She hasn't been here in at least a year, but somehow the idea of browsing through racks and racks of clothes loosely arranged by color sounds like the only bearable option.

The smell of the store—not the new fabric smell or curated scent of a mall store but like detergent and old books and life itself—immediately soothes April. She heads directly to the jumble of scarves in a large basket, next to a rack of blazers. She has dozens of scarves at home that she never wears, but the colors and patterns swirled together give her something to focus on, besides Joe Miller, Melissa Valentine, and Paul. If Paul has any hurt feelings from her stupid lie about not remembering him, surely he's already moved on and accepted that his "most perfect memory" is best forgotten. He's probably on a healthy hike through the Canadian Rockies with his strapping sons and sensible wife right now.

April picks up a delicate chiffon scarf, swirled with pink and orange and yellow like a sunset on acid. She drapes it around her neck and looks at herself in the narrow full-length mirror tacked to the wall. The colors are jarring against her gray black jacket. She releases her hair from its ponytail and shakes it out, setting the waves and curls free. That's a little better. The vivid colors clash perfectly with her gold and bronze (and yes, well, the occasional gray) curls.

April remembers the cheerful yellow Goodwill scarf she brought with her to Paris in an attempt to dress up the cut-off jeans and t-shirts she wore every day. Parisian women, though, had elegantly folded squares of Hermès silk knotted artfully in countless, subtly different variations. After she left Paris in such a rush, April lost her yellow one and didn't look for it.

She'd felt so brave in Paris, so open, and so ready for adventure. But she'd also been naive, and careless, and confident that the world owed her something. She'd been a polyester yellow scarf that thought it was a Hermès.

God damn it. April rips off the scarf and throws it back in the basket. Maybe she's a cheap scarf, but she doesn't deserve this shit. All those bitches blowing up her phone can go to hell. What no one understands is that everything she's done to Paul, even her stupid Facebook message, was for his own good. If April was going to break his heart, then better to do it sooner rather than later.

But somehow Paul doesn't hate her. April remembers the way he looked at her, from the very first moment she knocked him over on the street: like even her messiest quirks delighted him. Maybe she should write to him. It's a tempting thought, to just tell him that she does remember him, that she remembers everything. Or maybe she should just go to Melissa Valentine's Facebook page and tell everyone to back the fuck off.

April storms out of the store and sits in her car. The weather is annoyingly lovely, with clear spring skies, abundant blossoms, and fresh green leaves. April wishes for a thunderstorm to match her mood.

April takes out her phone. It's time to face the music and see what exactly she's dealing with. She has 104 Facebook notifications, 97 new emails, and a string of unanswered texts, including several from Stacy the realtor canceling the Miller job.

She starts with the emails. There's one email from her father's girlfriend's daughter Angie. She hopes that April was okay with "letting the world know about her past." She won't tell Hank and her mother about the photo because she wanted to "protect them from this scandal."

After that, April deletes without reading. One message catches her eye, though, from gabriel@heart2heart.com, with the subject "Need a do-over?" Her finger clicks it open before her brain can say no, she's doing just fine, thank you, gabriel@ heart2heart.com.

Hi April, says the message. *I hope this reaches you, since your inbox must be out of control. I am head of PR for an exciting new dating app, Heart2Heart, which helps newly single adults in their prime get a second (or third, we don't judge!) chance at love. I was moved by your and Paul's story. I am offering you both the exciting opportunity to return to*

Paris and recreate your viral photo with a kiss on the Eiffel Tower for a Heart2Heart ad campaign. We would cover your airfare and hotel. We believe that your story will awaken the romantic spirit in our mature clientele and show them that it's never too late for love! Please call me at the number below to speak further. Cheers, Gabriel Ramirez.

Mature clientele indeed. How old is this Gabriel Ramirez?

Onto Facebook. Since Paul's post last night, everyone's echoing each other about what a cold-hearted succubus April is. Paul has countless responses telling him to forget about April, that there are better women out there, and would he like to meet their single sister in Provo who likes baking and water skiing.

Farther down she sees what she'd been dreading: *I think I found her. Check AA Home Design on Instagram. You know what to do.* She switches over to Instagram where there's already a flood of comments on her bland little photos. *Do not hire this woman!* And *April Andrewsom is a homewrecker.* Some are chilling, like *We will come for you April and anyone who hires you.*

No. This is absolutely not allowed. She built AA Home Designs from the ground up. It's her refuge, her professional world where she is competent and collected. And where she earns money to give Liza a nice home. For the first time since this whole disaster began, April is scared. People can call her a stupid slut until the cows come home, but if they come for her business, she'll fight like hell.

There's only one way out of this, and it's only a little less terrifying than the trolls. April calls Gabriel Ramirez at Heart2Heart.

"Hello?" Gabriel picks up right away, sounding bored and annoyed that someone is calling the phone that is no doubt attached to his hand 24-7 for texting and selfies.

"This is April Andersen. I got your email. I want to go to Paris." Saying the words makes her less rattled. It's the obvious solution. By recreating that kiss on the Eiffel Tower for an ad campaign, she will take control of the narrative. She'll prove to Melissa Valentine's minions that she isn't evil, make sure she doesn't lose more clients, and really stick it to Marie's Angie. There's the small matter of seeing Paul again, but she'll deal with that later.

There's a pause on the other end of the line. "Wow, okay," Gabriel finally says. "I wasn't expecting that. I'm going to be straightforward with you—I sent that email before I saw all the comments on that lady's Facebook page. And before I realized that you are not very popular with women of your own age right now." Gabriel's voice is smooth and professional with a touch of uptalk betraying that he's probably a young person in his first job at a tenuous internet start-up.

"You really didn't do your homework, then," snaps April. "I have your offer in writing, and I'm accepting."

"I'm just becoming acquainted with this demographic," Gabriel retorts. "I didn't realize that your fellow white middle-aged suburban mothers were such bitches."

April's mouth almost twitches into a smile. Oh, it feels good to be angry at someone who can take it and dish it out as well.

"Well, then you clearly need me," hisses April, "Because if there is one thing you should know about white middle-aged suburban mothers it is that we are total bitches, because of the countless things men do each and every day to piss us off. Especially when you offer us a trip to Paris and then take it back."

Gabriel pauses again. "You keep talking about Paris, but you haven't mentioned Paul. The whole proposition is contingent on him accepting as well, and I haven't heard from him. And after you told the world that you couldn't remember his name, I'd be surprised if he wants anything to do with you."

"Then it's a good thing you are such a charmer, Gabriel Ramirez, so you can convince him to do it," says April, leaning back in her car seat. "I'm ready to get on a plane as soon as you can send me the ticket. I'm losing clients, I'm getting emails from high school randos that I would rather forget, and I'll probably never get a date again. So you are going to help me fix this. And in return you can have a nice ad for your poorly named website, and we can let people of my demographic think for a moment that maybe someone will love them again."

"Why do you think it's poorly named?" asks Gabriel with genuine interest.

"Because of the tv show. *Hart to Hart*. My parents watched it in the seventies. Robert Wagner and Stefanie Powers? They're international middle-aged spies with a hot marriage. Blatant pandering to the demographic, as you say. How old are you, anyway? Like, twenty-five?" She tries to make being twenty-five sound like a terrible insult.

"Twenty-four. And I know about the show. We're named after it. At least subliminally."

"What?" sputters April. She has a brief flash of her parents in happier times, sitting on opposite sides of the couch and watching the glamorous spy couple donning disguises and saving each other. It was probably exactly what her mother pictured marriage would be like.

"How old are you? Forty-three?" responds Gabriel crisply. "Focus groups show that Heart2Heart is associated with feelings of nostalgia, adventure, romance, though most of them can't explain why. Pandering to the demographic as you say." He pauses triumphantly. "I'll reach out to Paul again and call you back at this number if it's a go."

"You better," says April. "Have a blessed day."

She hangs up before Gabriel can reply.

Paul

"I had no idea you were such a Casanova."

Paul's neighbor and nemesis Sid Mohapatra is, as usual, fine-tuning his already perfect hedges. It's like he's been waiting there for hours for Paul and Muffin to come out, formulating the perfect mix between neighborly greeting and insult.

"And I had no idea you were a Melissa Valentine fan," retorts Paul. He's already fielded sympathetic phone calls from Tommy and Teresa, and his email inbox count is rising by the minute. His patience for Sid is even less than usual.

Sid chuckles with forced warmth, as though Paul has made a witty remark, as he sharply snips an errant leaf. Not for the first time, Paul wonders if Sid uses a carpenter's level to check the perfect lines of his hedge.

"I find it useful to follow popular figures like her on Facebook," says Sid crisply. "It helps one understand how women's minds work."

Paul freezes for a moment, distracted from his plan for a quick getaway by Sid revealing the most personal thing he's ever said in their three years of side-by-side living. Tommy was full of jokes about Paul's kissing skills, and Teresa had clucked with motherly sympathy and assured him he was too good for a stuck-up bitch like April, but neither of them has provided any useful advice on what he should do next.

"So how do women's minds work?" blurts Paul.

"What?" asks Sid, clearly startled that his neighbor is making conversation instead of slinking to his car.

"How do they work? Why do they do the things they do?" repeats Paul, realizing what a ridiculous question it is, especially between two forty-something bachelors.

Sid looks thoughtful, his usual condescending smirk relaxing away. "My studies tell me that there are no universal truths," he begins. "But as a rule, a woman wants to feel that they are with a man who sees her for who she is and cares for her despite her flaws. Perhaps even finds them endearing, part of what makes her special." Sid is lost in his own thoughts now. "A woman wants a lover who projects strength and is able to make hard decisions, and who allows her to be his ally against the world." Sid snaps out of his reverie and looks straight at Paul again. "Plus he needs to be rich and handsome. And tall." He chuckles bitterly. Sid was no taller than Paul, not particularly handsome, and Paul suspects not rich either.

"So, what does a man do, if there's a woman he can't stop thinking about, but she doesn't feel the same way?"

"My advice?" says Sid. "Get a haircut, buy some new clothes that aren't baggy all over, and wear some of those Timberlands with the thick heel. Don't look so shocked, I watch those Queer Eye guys, too. And hey!" he calls as Paul waves and heads to his car, "Prune your hydrangeas! The main thing that women want is someone who knows how to care for his plants!"

**

Paul is the first person to arrive at the dry cleaners. He unlocks the front door, turns on the lights, and helps the morning rush of regulars dropping off or trying to pick up a clean shirt for a weekend wedding or funeral. It's after 9:00 before he has a chance to sneak into the back room and turn on the kettle for tea, keeping an ear out for the bell that chimes when customers enter.

The phone rings, and Paul grabs the office extension. "Stone Dry Cleaning, Paul speaking."

"Paul Stone?" says a man's voice, sounding young and uncertain.

"Yes, this is Paul Stone. What can I do for you?" It's probably one of those cold call sales guys, pitching him a new vendor for hangers or cleaning fluids. Paul always feels a little sorry for them and tries to be polite.

"Hi, Paul. My name is Gabriel Ramirez. From Heart2Heart. com? Did you read my emails?"

"Uh, no, sorry. I'm pretty behind on email right now. What was it regarding?"

"Of course, your inbox must be at capacity. I'd like to tell you about an exciting new opportunity. At Heart2Heart, we help the newly single in their prime get a second chance at love. Or a third, we don't judge." Gabriel Ramirez gives a practiced-sounding chuckle.

"Okay?" says Paul. He's beginning to realize this is not a call about hangers.

"I'm going to cut to the chase here, Paul." Gabriel Ramirez's voice grows more confident. "I have an offer for you. We were moved by your story. You seem like the kind of everyman that our demographic will connect with. You did something wild in your early twenties, and it's become part of what defines you all these years later. Your Facebook profile says that you're single?"

"Yes," says Paul, his head swimming with questions. How has Gabriel seen his private account? Do they want to set him up with someone? Demonstrate how their service can find a match for anyone, even forgettable Paul Stone?

"We'd like to send you and April to Paris. For an ad campaign. Another kiss on the Eiffel Tower. Show that it's never too late."

Paul is stunned. Things like this didn't really happen, did they?

"Sure," he scoffs. "April would never do that. I mean, you saw what she said. She has no desire to ever see me again. She must be married, anyhow, to some tall, rich guy." Sid's advice comes back to him.

"I talked to April this morning. She wants to do this as soon as possible."

Paul's gut twists, from panic or maybe from a flash of excitement. "You talked to April," he repeats stupidly.

"Yes," says Gabriel with the exaggerated patience of a young person talking to the elderly. "April is in. With enthusiasm."

"With enthusiasm." Paul wraps his mouth around the beautiful words, thinking of April's wide smile and gray eyes, so easily joyful.

"Yes, Paul, with enthusiasm." Gabriel's patience is already wearing thin. "So, can I count you in? We'd like to schedule for the first week of June, strike before the internet has completely forgotten about you. Even that is pushing it."

That's less than two weeks away. Paul has to arrange for coverage at the dry cleaners, find someone to take care of Muffin, and make sure that his passport is still valid.

"Yes, I'm in," he says. This is the sign he's been waiting for. He can finally see April again, do over the kiss, and move on with his life, for better or for worse. "With enthusiasm."

"Great. I'm going to ignore how grim your voice sounds right now because that's what I like to hear. And Paul? If I can speak to you as one guy to another? I looked through your photos on Facebook—you should really lock that down, by the way. Anyway, you look good, man. Congratulations on keeping it tight at your age. But if I can suggest, maybe some Crest White Strips? And a haircut? Not at the Hair Cuttery or whatever, either. Go someplace where you have to make an appointment."

"Okay," says Paul. He 'll do anything Gabriel says. He's going to see April again.

"Thanks, man. I say it because I care. Talk soon." Gabriel hangs up.

The kettle hisses loudly. The doorbell chimes as a customer enters. And Paul sits there, typing "men's haircut appointment" into his phone.

Paris, France 1999

Paul felt April's heartbeat slow as he held her hand above her head, trying to stop the bleeding in her finger. What a gift that he could do this for her, his body silently leading her body to calm. His own heartbeat, though, was in danger of speeding up again as he sat on the bench, facing her, their knees touching and hands clasped in midair to form a clumsy heart shape.

"Deep breaths," he told her again, just as much for himself. Her eyes were wide and trusting, fixed on his, and for the first time since they met, she was quiet. He could see her sprinkle of freckles, the darker gray flecks in her eyes, the vulnerable curve of her bottom lip that appeared when she was still.

Tommy and Teresa were always getting cuts and scrapes, and as their mother grew more and more helpless, Paul was the one in charge of peroxide and band aids, as well as reassurance that their finger was not going to fall off. As he wiped their tears and lectured them to be more careful, though, his body never responded like this. He felt completely present, maybe for the first time in his life not having thoughts of the dry cleaners, or if it was time to get one of those chair lifts for the stairs, and how could they afford it. He was on a park bench in Paris with a girl named April, and their breath and their heartbeats were effortlessly in sync.

After a few minutes, when his arm started to prickle with pins and needles, Paul lowered April's hand to his chest and peeked under the bandana.

"I think the bleeding stopped," he said. "You should probably keep it wrapped up, though."

"Sorry about your hankie," said April softly. Her voice was a little scratchy, like she'd been silent for days instead of minutes.

"Don't worry about it. That's what it's for." Paul still held her wrapped hand to his chest.

"So a lot of girls cut themselves around you," said April, nodding wisely.

"What can I say, it's the way to my heart," said Paul, and then froze. Surely that was too much, and he'd broken the delicate connection. Sure enough, April took her hand back, twisting the bandana nervously. She was still quiet, but her wide mouth twitched, and her unguarded stillness returned to the familiar lively eyes and smile.

"Maybe I should go," she said, looking at her makeshift bandage. "I told Selma I'd meet her back at the hostel."

Paul felt a stab of panic. He didn't want her to go. She was so...so much. Funny, impossible, observant, vulnerable. He wanted to keep watching her wide mouth quirk with amusement, and her long arms gesturing expressively. She wasn't the fairy tale girl he had pictured meeting in Paris. She was messy, and maybe a little terrifying, but she made him feel alive in a way he never had before.

"Just a little longer?" he asked, brushing her uninjured hand.

"I don't know...Selma and I are..." she said, but her cool fingers tangled with his. The reassuring touch made Paul bold, or maybe just more achingly needy, and he brought his other hand to her cheek. Their eyes locked.

"Here's the thing," he said, keeping his voice steady. "I'm not ready to say goodbye to you yet."

April opened her mouth as if to say something but stopped, and the sweet curve of her bottom lip reappeared.

Paul kept talking. "So, what I'm thinking is that I'm going to keep holding your hand, April. Because I'm not sure what's happening but it feels like something worth leaning in to. We should stroll through Paris, maybe hold hands a little more, and you can tell me about how a nice girl with you ended up with a backpack like Claudette."

April smiled like the sun coming out, and Paul's mouth went dry with *wanting*. "And you can tell me what a nice Canadian not-murderer does by himself in Paris," she said.

Paul thought for a moment about kissing April. She probably wouldn't mind. But he was waiting for more than her not minding. He brushed his lips over her bandaged hand and pulled her up from the bench, stepping off the well-worn pathway of his life into something unknown, but exactly right.

PART 2

Chapter 7

April

"Two glasses of Champagne, please," says April to the flight attendant.

"Not for me, Chickadee," says Selma, burying her nose deeper into her e-reader.

"What made you think one was for you?" April says, trying to hide her disappointment. April had been thrilled when Selma agreed to cash in some airline miles and come with her to Paris. She pictured them cackling and strategizing on the plane, but that weird distance was back. Still, if Selma is with her, then this trip to reunite with a guy she barely knows to pacify the pitchfork-wielding villagers of mommyblogdom has to be a good plan.

Danny doesn't see it that way. Yesterday, when she dropped off Liza for the week, he asked disbelievingly, "You're bringing Selma? Don't you think it sends a certain...signal? About your interest and availability?"

Trust Danny to be excited for her to hook up with an old flame. He's the kind of guy who will arrange for chocolate dipped strawberries to be sent to her room, forgetting that April is allergic to strawberries.

"Danny, this is just a business arrangement. A silly publicity stunt, and I need some good publicity," said April, trying to sound crisply professional. "They asked me to recreate a moment from twenty years ago. Selma was there twenty years ago, and she should be there now."

Danny shrugged. "Okay, Lulu. Just trying to give you a guy's perspective."

April winces every time he calls her by that nickname now, from when the Calypso band on their St. John honeymoon played "Bang Bang Lulu" while they danced close on the beach. If he can still call her that so casually, did their marriage ever mean anything?

April tries to fold her long limbs into her airline seat, noticing enviously that Selma is comfortably sitting criss-cross applesauce in hers. April sips on her first glass of Champagne while Selma serenely accepts a water and swathes herself in a black wrap with a startling architectural ruffle. She looks like an exotic moth emerging from its cocoon, and April is flooded with how much she's missed her friend. When Selma goes back to reading, April blurts, "Talk to me, please. You agreed to come, but you've hardly said anything about this whole setup. Do you think I'm making a mistake?"

"Probably," says Selma evenly, but she puts her e-reader down.

"Okay," says April, her shoulders already unclenching a little with her friend's attention. "No doubt you're right. But for argument's sake...why? Why shouldn't I do this?"

"Why shouldn't you fly to Paris on a whim to see a guy you claim to have forgotten and haven't mentioned in twenty years so a picture of you two kissing can be used by some dating start-up that makes mildly depressed divorced people convinced that if they get back together with someone who knew them back when they were young, and less ugly, and still idealistic, then they would finally be happy?"

"I'm still idealistic. Sometimes," says April, taking another drink of Champagne. She doesn't quite like the idea of being the poster girl for forty-somethings giving up on the present and circling back to their younger selves.

"Of course you are. Sometimes," says Selma. She leans back in her seat and stretches out her legs, folding her hands over her stomach. She is so tiny that her feet don't touch the floor, while April's legs spill into the aisle and trip the flight attendants.

April waits for Selma to read, or maybe close her eyes for a nap, but she sits there for another minute, the muscles in her jaw silently working, until finally, she speaks again.

"Maybe," Selma begins slowly, "I have some compassion for the poor guy. Maybe I keep hearing you talk about how this is going to save your client base without asking yourself why he agreed to come. Maybe I know you well enough to know that you are pretty good at creating a diversion when you are protecting yourself. Maybe I just think this whole plan is bullshit."

April's eyes prick with tears. Or maybe it was just the damn dry airplane air. Gwyneth Paltrow probably has some kind of organic eye drops made from nuns' tears in her travel bag. Not that Gwyneth would ever find herself in this situation, crossing the Atlantic, twenty years too late, to throw herself on the mercy of a guy she'd hurt just because she realized she was falling too hard and fast. And not even being able to tell her best friend because to put it into words was terrifying.

Selma grabs April's Champagne, takes a slug, and hands it back. Her face is serious, but her eyes are warm. "I know you're scared of losing your business from those Valentine bitches harassing you. And I know you've had a rough time since Danny, who was never worthy of you in the first place. Just don't go breaking any hearts to make yourself feel better." She takes April's hand and lightly squeezes. "It's rough out there."

April squeezes back. "Thanks for coming."

"Wild horses couldn't keep me from this trainwreck," says Selma, resting her head on April's shoulder. "Plus I will always be there when you need me, blah blah blah."

They stay like that for a moment until Selma gives her fingers a final squeeze and reaches for her e-reader. "I can never sleep on planes," she says.

Selma is right, except about the part where April has to worry about breaking hearts. She'd nipped that in the bud with Paul, at least. But why had he agreed to come, she wonders as she idly peeks over Selma's shoulder.

Damn, Shane Adams sure had a hockey ass, noted his new teammate Tyler Johnson approvingly. Only hours of squats and lunges in the gym combined with even more hours on the ice produced that kind of proud, meaty swell of muscle. Tyler had to look away before the arousal in his mind spread to his...

"Selma Shapiro! What are you reading!"

Selma looks up at her with a guilty expression on her usual resting bitch face. "What, can't a mature woman enjoy an erotic m/m ice hockey romance on an international flight without getting the third degree?"

"No, she cannot! Please tell me more about how a cold-hearted cynic such as yourself started reading romance novels. About gay ice hockey players. What do you even know about hockey, for God's sake?"

"A lot more than I used to," says Selma with a twinkle in her golden-brown eyes. "Goalies are sexy and superstitious. Forwards are cocky but vulnerable underneath. And apparently every team has a big guy whose unspoken job is to fight."

"Doesn't everyone fight?" asks April. She's already quite drawn to this world of hot, volatile, horny men.

"Nah," answers Selma. "The star players don't want to get injured or get put in the penalty box, so the Enforcer fights anyone who picks on them. But underneath it all he's usually really sweet and sensitive."

"Of course he is," sighs April.

"And then, of course, there's all the fucking."

April giggles. "Of course there is." She missed this. Having Selma by her side again feels so right. She leans over and kisses the top of Selma's head. "I'm so glad you're here."

"I wouldn't miss it, Chickadee. I know I've been distant with you lately." April feels Selma's body tense next to hers as her friend jiggles her left foot and twists her silver rings. "I'm just...in a weird place right now."

April waits for more, staring straight ahead into her upright tray table.

"It's like I'm at some kind of crossroads where I become either a bitter old hag or a content old hag. My parents are dead, my Orthodox brother in Borough Park doesn't talk to me because I'm a tattooed bisexual Lilith, but I have my dogs, I have you and Liza. I never wanted to get married or have kids or leave the city, but on the other hand, what do I want carved on my gravestone? 'Here lies Selma, being abrasive and single was her brand.'" She shrugs nonchalantly, but April hears the catch in her voice.

"First of all," says April, "You already told me that when you die you want your ashes compressed into a diamond tiara for Liza, and she's really counting on that, so no more nonsense about your gravestone. Second of all," continues

April, nudging Selma with her elbow and getting a quick half smile in response. "Selma, you are the coolest woman I know." It's true. It's not just the arty job or the stylish clothes—Selma goes through life not caring about other people's opinions, which is the purest kind of cool. If a guy on the street tells her to smile, she gives him the finger. If she doesn't want to go to a baby shower or a networking cocktail party, she says no. She isn't like April, always calculating her actions by how the other person must see her.

"Maybe I used to be," says Selma. She leans back and closes her eyes. "I think I'm pregnant."

"Shit," exhales April. "I mean, congratulations?"

"Shit was closer." Selma collects her face, looking defiant.

April puts her hand on Selma's leg. "I should have figured it out when you passed on the Champagne." She has a million questions, but those can wait. Her voice is gentle. "Pregnant in Paris, huh? I bet French women wear heels until the ninth month."

"I bet they lose the baby weight in a week. Bitches."

"Hey," whispers April. "You know I'm here for you, right? We're going to figure this out."

"I know," says Selma, pulling down the window shade and readjusting her black wrap. "We're going to figure out your thing, too. Just because I'm in a conundrum doesn't mean I've forgotten about how you pined for some Canadian for twenty years and forgot to mention it."

"Wasn't *pining*," mutters April, but Selma positions the e-reader invitingly so April can see. The humming white noise of the airplane, the horny antics of men on ice skates, and the two glasses of Champagne lull her into a light doze. But when she sleeps, she dreams of golden light, dark eyes, and hands tangled in her hair.

Paul

The ten days before Paul leaves for Paris are endless, full of boring tasks and jittery anticipation. The mundane arrangements of stopping his mail, buying Euros, and fending off unwanted advice from Teresa are punctuated by texts from Gabriel elaborating the plan. Gabriel himself is coming to Paris to supervise their reunion, coordinate with the French photographers, and craft some witty and heartfelt posts about how first love is the best love. He also reminds Paul a few times not to bother the Heart2Heart admin about travel or anything, just send all questions to Gabriel directly. In fact, best not to have any contact with anyone else at the company, since some aspects of the trip were complicated to explain to the pencil pushers back in New York.

Paul runs through the details over and over while he vacuums and dusts his house, since no doubt Teresa will use her spare key and pop in a few times to make sure he hasn't left the coffee maker on. The trip has a clear itinerary, but what about afterwards? Gabriel will try to persuade more middle-aged singles that they, too, can find love, while Paul and April...well, that's the part he can't imagine. He knows what it's like to be twenty-two with April on the Eiffel Tower above the confusing, disappointing world, to feel the way her wide smile makes his heart pound so hard he can feel it in his ears. He knows what it's like to kiss her, to completely lose himself in her long arms and the exotic shampoo-and-cigarette smell of her hair. And he knows what it's like after she disappears, to feel like the promise of something ripped away, and you can't even properly grieve because it wasn't there to begin with. He knows what it's like to spend years trying not to forget April Andersen, because she's what happens when he gets carried away with wanting too much.

Paul looks around for something else to scrub, the dirtier the better. The oven will have to do, even though it's disappointingly clean from lack of use. Still, he uses his mother's old trick of coating the inside with a baking soda-vinegar paste and fills the sink with hot, soapy water for the racks.

He isn't that kid in the Van Morrison t-shirt anymore, Paul thinks as he attacks the oven racks, the water satisfyingly scalding. Though technically he still has that shirt and Jesus Christ, he's wearing it right now like he sometimes does for dirty jobs. There goes that metaphor. But he'll be damned if he spends the next twenty years thinking about April. He'll see her, get some answers, kiss her, and move on. And then he'll come back to Winnipeg, go to his nephew's baseball games, take Muffin for walks, keep dry cleaning the Sunday dresses and funeral suits of his loyal customers, and...what? Meet a nice woman who (unlike Claire) isn't already married? Spend the rest of his life not kissing the one person who has ever made him feel like liquid sunshine is running through his veins? Can he really kiss April Andersen one more time and leave it at that?

Yes. Yes, he can. Of course he can. It's the only way, he mutters to his very clean oven racks.

In the past few days, he had gotten a shockingly expensive haircut, done some sit ups, made the Stone Dry Cleaning schedule for the week, and tried not to look at the picture of him and April kissing more than five times a day. He checked out French language CDs from the library and listened to them in his car; and he stared at the men's grooming products in the drugstore but got too overwhelmed to buy anything.

That just leaves Muffin. Teresa could have taken her, if Griff wasn't so allergic to dogs. And Paul can't ask Tommy for any favors right now. There's still an undercurrent of tension between them since Paul rejected Tommy's ideas for the business, and Paul worries that asking Tommy to take Muffin would seem like a gesture signaling that he is ready to re-open the discussion.

Paul can see his neighbor Sid out of the window over the sink, framed by the frilly, dark yellow curtains. He's fine-tuning the straight edge on his hedges, as usual, and there's fresh mulch around the flowering pink bushes. Paul remembers Sid's advice about what women want, something about strength and being their ally. Honestly, it isn't the worst advice he's gotten in the last week, and Paul appreciates Sid's skepticism in contrast to everyone else's cloying enthusiasm. Next thing he knows, he heads out his front door and turns right, with Muffin under one arm and a six-pack of beer in the other, his hands still red and wrinkled from the hot water.

He faces Sid over the hedges, not even waiting for him to look up. "I got a haircut," blurts Paul.

Sid registers no surprise at his sudden appearance. "I see. It looks...shorter."

"And I'm going back to Paris. Some dating website is sending us."

Now Sid's eyes flicker with interest, and he pauses his clippers.

"I've been thinking about what you said before," continues Paul. "About what women want." Muffin yaps as if to answer, and Paul sets her down.

"A man who knows how to take care of plants?" Sid glances meaningfully at Paul's raggedy hydrangeas.

"Well, that," says Paul, ignoring Sid's familiar curtness. "But also the other stuff. Believe it or not, I don't really know what the hell I'm doing here."

Sid sighs and folds his arms, setting the hedge clippers on top of his mailbox. "Excuse me for not being shocked. About you not knowing what you are doing. I might be a bit gobsmacked that you are going to Paris."

Paul wonders if that's an insult or a compliment. Sid has never given him a compliment, and why would he start now? The possibility that his neighbor is chirping him is surprisingly comforting. At least someone might tell him if this is a terrible plan. He pulls a beer out of the six pack and hands it over the hedge, where Sid hesitantly takes it and gives it a suspicious look before popping the tab.

"Do you think I'm making a mistake?" asks Paul.

Sid takes a sip of the beer, sighs, and finally relaxes his shoulders. "I don't know why you are asking me, but I will tell you what I think. This is one of those things you have to do and live with the consequences, because staying here," he gestures to Paul's house, "j ust so you can see your weeds grow in real time, is very depressing."

"I always thought I'd be the hero of my own story," says Paul. "But it feels like I took a wrong turn somewhere and now I'm a supporting character at best. Something needs to change." He's surprised to hear the words come out of his mouth and to realize how true they are.

Sid nods like this is the most sensible thing Paul's ever said. "For me, I missed out on an earlier opportunity because I was not a very good listener. And I think my time has now passed." He looks at Paul challengingly, daring him to say something helpful.

Paul doesn't rise to the bait. For the first time, he thinks about why Sid spends every spare moment forcing his hedges into geometric perfection. It isn't to passive-aggressively shame Paul over his overgrown yard (though that might be an added benefit). It isn't to become the larger-than-life nemesis that feeds Paul with the glow of anger and annoyance. Sid Mohapatra is lonely. Just like Paul.

"Can you take care of Muffin for me?" Paul says instead. "While I'm in Paris? I'll be gone for five days. She naps a lot, and she isn't too much trouble."

Sid looks genuinely surprised, and maybe a little pleased. He steps through his gate, and with a surprising courtly grace crouches down to take Muffin's right paw in a formal greeting. "Miss Muffin, I hope I will not let you down."

"Oh, you will," says Paul, and they both laugh. Muffin looks at one and then the other with the dog version of an eye roll, waiting for the frivolous moment to pass.

When Paul and Muffin return home an hour later, after drinking a beer with Sid on his front steps, he realizes something.

He might have a friend.

**

And then he's in Paris, dropping his suitcase in the hotel room.

His room has a bathroom.

Paul isn't sure why this surprises him. Of course the hostel he stayed in twenty years ago had toilets down the hall. That one night he spent in a cheap hotel near the station, raw and stunned from April slipping through his fingers, he had a room with a sink and a bidet right across from the bed. He pissed in the bidet that morning, hung over and unable to face the line for the toilet.

But now he has a chance to do it again, this time in a stylish hotel in the 16th Arrondissement. His room at the Hotel Voltaire is small and charming. The eaves are slightly pitched on one side to evoke an artistic garret, but the colors are warm, and the double bed covered with a white spread and deeply fluffy pillows. Narrow glass doors open onto a wrought iron balcony just large enough for one, and if he goes up on his toes, he can see the top of the Eiffel Tower just across the Seine, poking over the neighboring building.

So what if the bathroom is about the size of an airplane lavatory? So what if it's a bit warm in his room on a pleasant June afternoon because Parisians don't approve of air conditioning? And so what if it reminds him of the last time he was in a hotel room? Hotel Voltaire has a different aura than the Days Inn in Winnipeg— hell, it might as well be on a different planet— but entering a quiet, neutral space brings back those meetings with Claire. Claire was a petite, confident real estate agent who Paul had contacted about putting his house on the market. She click-clacked through the downstairs on her high heels, looking respectfully at the linoleum floors and the shabby furniture.

"This is a real family home," she says. "You must have grown up here." Paul's frustration over how to make the house into something suiting an adult male like himself faded some. Claire smiled with her red-lipsticked mouth and tucked her shiny brown hair behind her ear and promised to send him some comps. Paul wasn't that surprised when Claire offered to meet him at O'Shea's to go over them instead of just emailing, and even less surprised when she suggested they go to the motel across the street. When he offered his house, she just said, "I prefer not to mix business with pleasure."

Paul doesn't like dating— the small talk, the awkwardness, the sympathetic looks when he mentions his dead parents— but it turns out he didn't like *not* dating either. Claire texted him a room number once a week or so, and he drove over. She wore lingerie for him, the black lace stuff like women on soap operas, and he appreciated her effort maybe more than the actual aesthetics of the scratchy, delicate fabric with its impossible hooks and hidden snaps. And she seemed to appreciate his effort on one of the room's two queen beds, which made him feel good. For a while. Until Claire refused his offer for dinner, or a movie. He noticed that she packed the lingerie in her bag and put on everyday underwear and a bra.

After the fifth or sixth time, he followed her home. There were chalk drawings on the driveway and a scooter on its side in the grass. A man opened the door as she approached, and two children ran out to hug her.

Paul felt sick. And stupid.

"You knew I was married," she said matter-of-factly when he called her to end things. She should have been right. If he was a normal guy, not one who secretly saw himself as the frog waiting to be turned into a prince by love, he would have understood the arrangement. As it was, he felt incredibly stupid.

"You need to sell that house," said Claire. "You're going to be a moody teen forever if you stay there. I'm happy to handle your listing, even if you don't want to meet socially anymore."

Well, she was right about one thing. But Paul deleted her number and kept the house. He planted a hydrangea in front. He bought a lounge chair. He kept trying to figure out the secret, the magic code to changing his life without making any waves, without having to give away their mother's china or cause Tommy and Teresa to have more discussions behind his back.

Maybe now, though, in this quirky hotel room, he's ready to become the main character of his life. Sid is right, coming to Paris was the only option. Either he'll see April again and realize he's built a whole fantasy out of nothing, or he'll get his heart stomped on once and for all, but things will be different.

Paul splashes water on his face in the tiny washroom, kicks off his shoes, and spreads out on the crisp bedspread. He can't see the Eiffel Tower lying down, but knowing it's there just across the river makes him relax for the first time since Tommy showed him the picture. The pieces are all there. Now he just has to wait and see if they still fit together.

Chapter 8

April

"Does Paris have Duane Reade?" asks Selma. They lie side by side on April's cool white bed at the Hotel Voltaire. April is tearing through *Fire on the Ice*, catching up on Troy and Shane's secret locker room romance while Selma dozes off her jet lag.

"Duane Reade? Is that New York for Walgreen's? Do you need to get some shampoo or something?"

"I have to get a pregnancy test. I need to know one way or the other so I can get out of my own head and support you in your ridiculous situation. Plus, I want to go to Hermès and pretend I'm going to buy a Kelly bag, and I don't want to be distracted while I glare imperiously at the salespeople."

April bolts upright, suddenly itchy and anxious to get out of her little hotel room. "Let's go get a test right now," she says. "It'll get my mind off of...everything. The note from Gabriel said I— and you, of course— should meet him in the hotel bar at 17:00. I'm not sure when that is but it sounds very far away, and we're in *Paris*."

April doesn't know if Paul is also invited to the 17:00 rendezvous. Gabriel is super intense about the two of them not seeing each other until the orchestrated reunion, going on about however tempting or exciting it might be, he needs them to save it for the cameras. Probably Paul is even at a different hotel, so who cares if she's still in her yoga pants and coffee-stained t-shirt from the plane and her stylish messy bun is now a true messy bun. They're just running out for an errand and to soak up some atmosphere. They'll be invisible to all the stylish Parisians, just two more hopeless American tourists.

April hops off the bed, slides on her Birkenstocks and grabs the Tumi travel backpack Selma gave her as a "happy divorce" present. She doesn't want to waste time fishing out her phone and wallet and lip balm and small stash of Euros, so better bring the whole damn thing. She and Selma, who somehow looks annoyingly chic after the long trip, squish into the tiny elevator, descend to the lobby, and ask the concierge where they might find a drugstore. After a brief look of horror, the elegant young woman says, "Ah, *une pharmacie*. Take a right and walk two blocks."

There it is, just as she said, a compact but well-stocked pharmacy. April is reminded how everything in Europe is on a smaller scale than in the U.S. as she and Selma work their way single file through the narrow aisles.

"Shit," says Selma. "Where should we look? Can you check the French word for 'pregnancy test' on your phone?"

April slings her backpack off one shoulder, knocking a few toothbrushes off the shelf in the process. She gropes the back pocket before remembering. "Damn! I'm sorry, Sel, I left it charging in the room. Don't you have yours?"

"No, when you took your backpack, I just assumed you were bringing it."

"Crap. No, it's okay. We can figure this out. Pregnancy test. Test is *examen*, right? *Examen de bébé*? Just look for a small box near the tampons that says *examen de bébé*."

"Baby exam? It's not going to say *baby exam*," hisses Selma. Her black pants and sweater from the plane still look fresh, but she's uncharacteristically pink and flustered.

"Well, *you* think of something," snaps April, bending over to pick up the fallen toothbrushes. "Figure out how to say, 'Am I knocked up or not?' and go ask that guy over there." April gestures towards the young male cashier, eyes glued to his phone. Selma scowls at her so April points again, with emphasis, to say *get your ass over there*, until her hand connects with something firm and fleshy. Hoping desperately that it's not a dignified French person's nose, April spins around to check, forgetting her backpack is only on one shoulder. First comes the unmistakable sound of the bag connecting with the shelf of toothpaste boxes, and April pirouettes around again to throw her body over them and keep them from falling. This time she feels as well as hears the whap of her backpack hitting something solid, followed by the soft "umph" of a man's voice. April gives up and closes her eyes, listening to the avalanche of small boxes hitting the floor.

Maybe if she can't see anyone, then no one can see her. April is frozen, not daring to move or open her eyes. And then she hears the voice.

"April." Warm, deep, with a hint of rasp. The sound rumbles through her whole body like a far-off train, the vibrations both tingling and soothing every nerve.

She opens her eyes.

"Hello, Paul."

There he is, toothpaste piled at his feet, rubbing his left ribs and wincing, with a red, April's-finger-sized spot on his nose.

And he looks wonderful. No taller, but his shoulders are just as broad, and his black coffee eyes just as easy to get lost in. He's more solid around the middle and it suits him, emphasizing how he is like a tree that you can just wrap yourself around and hold on tight to ride out the storm.

"Are you...okay?" Paul asks. April realizes she'd been staring, and now she blushes so hard her freckles probably disappear. Trust Paul to make sure she's okay when she assaulted *him*.

"I'm amazing!" April chirps. She pictures how she must look, with her rumpled clothes and dirty hair, her incongruous expensive backpack hanging off one elbow. Everything is so terrible that all she can do is pretend that everything is absolutely normal. "You remember Selma, right? Selma and I were just buying a pregnancy test." Paul's nostrils flare as he swallows hard, reminding April that this is yet another occasion where blurting out the truth is the absolute wrong move. So, she does what she always does and just keeps talking, making sure no awkward silence has a chance to breathe and grow.

"The only problem is, we don't know how to say pregnancy test in French, and I forgot my phone."

"Yes, that's clearly the only problem here." Selma's dry voice pipes up behind her. "Hi, Paul."

Paul nods at Selma and turns those bottomless dark eyes back to April. If she lets herself, she can fall inside those eyes and never come back out. So better keep talking.

"I mean, it's probably not that hard. But we're jet-lagged, and pregnancy brain is a real thing. Kids make you stupid. I have a daughter."

Paul waits politely until April stops for a breath. "Monsieur!" he calls over to the cashier. "*Où sont les tests de grossesse?*"

Without looking up, the young man gestures towards the next aisle. "*Là bas.*"

Selma dashes over in that direction while April remains rooted to the spot. She will always be in this pharmacy, blabbing uncontrollably while Paul watches her with infinite patience.

"*Test de grossesse*? Really? Well, that's a slap in the face. Trust the French to have pretty much the same word for fat and pregnant. How did you know that, anyway? Do you buy a lot of pregnancy tests?"

If April wasn't positive that Paul's making a mental note to catch the next flight home, she'd think he has the faintest of smiles tugging at his mouth. "My sister," he says. "I bought her a few of these back in the day. Most stuff in Canada has bilingual packaging." He squats down and picks up one of the many toothpaste boxes. "I forgot my toothpaste, so thanks for this. Nice to run into you, April. Just like old times." He ruefully rubs his ribs where her backpack slammed into him. "I'm sure we'll see each other again soon." He turns around, carefully steps over the remaining toothpastes, and walks over to the cashier.

April suddenly realizes she's buried the lede and has not explained the most important part of this whole very stupid, very awkward situation. "It's for Selma! The...the *test de grossesse*! I'm not pregnant!"

Paul pays for his toothpaste with admirable efficiency and turns back to April. For a moment she thinks he'll say something else, but then he closes his mouth and gives her a strangely courtly bow, and with a flourish of his hand walks out the door.

"Assaulting him with toothpaste, interesting strategy," says Selma, sidling up to April and triumphantly waving the pregnancy test. "By the way, methinks your Paul has a hockey ass. Congratulations."

Paul

Paul doesn't remember walking from the pharmacy back to the hotel. But there he is, in the lobby, clutching his toothpaste.

Had he actually...bowed to April? Of all the ways he imagined their reunion, him acting like some kind of pretentious opera conductor was not on the list. Paul needs to get back to his room as soon as possible and bang his head against the wall for an hour or two. If he waits for the elevator, though, April might appear in the lobby, and he doesn't trust the synapses of his wrecked brain to prevent another bow. Paul sprints for a door in the corner marked *Sortie* and is rewarded with a dim, empty staircase.

April. Just saying her name is a cool, spring breeze. His body feels alive, like April is a crocus pushing through the frozen winter soil.

No, he isn't going through this again. He isn't letting April get under his skin. Spring breezes and crocuses also mean pollen, covering him in an invisible cloak of itchiness and misery. Pollen sticks to everything, sticks to his hair and his clothes, and the only way to escape it is to shut all his windows and stay inside.

But even after all this time, April is still...April. Paul recognized her the moment he walked into the pharmacy, even though those wild bronze waves were contained by a bun, and there are some faint lines around her mouth, like she's spent the last twenty years smiling. Her energy radiated through the small store, her long neck gracefully bowed towards Selma's dark head. The explosion of her spilling the toothpaste and hitting him with her backpack felt completely right. It's like he's 22 all over again, standing on the street in Paris, waiting for something wonderful to happen.

Paul has to sit on the steps for a moment to catch his breath.

April, looking tired, jet-lagged, and utterly beautiful as she made a path of destruction through the pharmacy.

April twenty years ago, disappearing and breaking his heart.

Paul flinches as the door opens, desperately hoping not to see Hurricane April blow into the staircase. Fortunately, it's a tall, handsome young man, with warm brown skin, a carefully sculpted beard, and discerning eyes.

Paul stumbles to his feet and moves aside. No doubt this guy has places to be, lovers to meet, texts to return. Instead of squeezing by Paul, though, the man pauses for a moment, taking him in.

"I'm Gabriel Ramirez," he finally says. "You've got to be Paul. Is everything okay? I saw you heading for the stairs like your hair was on fire."

So, this is Gabriel Ramirez, the man—the very young man— who convinced both he and April to uproot their lives for a whirlwind trip to Paris. In all their previous texts and conversations, Gabriel was full of take-charge energy and maybe a few too many tips for Paul on how he could improve his appearance and put his best foot forward. Having Gabriel discover him hiding in the stairwell is only a slight improvement on April finding him. He wants to disappear into the wall, but he sticks out his hand and summons his Canadian politeness.

"Hi Gabriel. Nice to meet you. Thank you for putting this all together."

Gabriel shakes Paul's hot, clammy hand with his cool, dry one. "No, thank *you* for having your perfect *Before Sunrise* moment caught on camera for me to capitalize on all these years later." Gabriel's voice is wry, but Paul feels the young man's eyes carefully checking on him. "Jet lag's a bitch, right? You need some melatonin? I usually take an Ambien when I fly international but there was this cute guy in the seat next to me, and I didn't want to drool on him."

"What was his name?" asks Paul, just to keep Gabriel talking. His sharp, intelligent energy pushes through Paul's post-April fog.

Gabriel looks at him incredulously. "I have no idea. What was I supposed to do, ask him, like some kind of creep?"

"You sat next to him for seven hours and never asked his name?" Paul always thought that young, stylish, good-looking guys like Gabriel would automatically meet equally attractive potential dates wherever they go. He isn't sure if it's reassuring or upsetting to learn that dating is hard for hot people, too.

"Of course!" Gabriel rolls his eyes to the ceiling in exasperation. "What if I said hi, and he wasn't into it, or he was straight, and then we had to sit next to each other in awkward silence for the rest of the flight. Hmmm?" Gabriel crosses his arms challengingly, daring Paul to think of a fate more terrible.

"Or maybe, he could have been your soul mate, and you missed out on your one chance at true love," says Paul. He meant it as a joke, but it comes out with grave seriousness.

Gabriel throws back his head and laughs. "Now I see why it was so easy to convince you to come to Paris. Are you excited to see April?"

Paul thinks about the messy encounter in the pharmacy. It isn't anything he feels like explaining to Gabriel, especially after the young man ordered them to keep them apart until the on-camera reunion. Better to just forget about it and move on to Gabriel's carefully choreographed plan.

"Nervous, mostly. I think. Have you met her yet?"

"No, not yet," says Gabriel. "Looking forward to it, though. She seems like...a lot."

"She's just right," snaps Paul. He hates the idea of anyone seeing April's joyful smile, easy laugh, and colorful clothes, and thinking any of it should be less. That helpless look her eyes get when she knows she should stop talking and just can't? He wouldn't even change that.

Gabriel looks at Paul appraisingly. "Sure. You're the expert there." Paul wants to protest that he isn't an expert in anything, but Gabriel continues. "Paul. My friend. While I would love to continue this conversation, maybe we could move out of this very dim and stuffy *cage d'escalier.*"

Paul is back to feeling painfully self-conscious. Here he is, in the most romantic city in the world, and he's hiding in a stairwell. And Gabriel, no doubt, would rather be in a cafe, swiping around on one of those dating apps that connects hot people quickly and painlessly, without a twenty-year build-up of pining.

So he's surprised when Gabriel gently places his quick, clever hands on Paul's shoulders. "The haircut works. Maybe just a little product to give it some height. I like what you've got going on here, Paul Stone. You are a lonely, small-town guy with great shoulders and sad eyes."

"Winnipeg is the largest city in Manitoba," protests Paul weakly.

"Exactly. So let's stick to our plan. Spend today getting a little sun, unpacking, and adjusting to Paris time. Tomorrow, we'll shoot background, some sweet little clips of you guys remembering how you met, what you were thinking during that transcendent kiss, what it means to recapture your youth and see April again. Plus something about how if Heart2Heart had been around, you could have found each other years ago, and she wouldn't have had to forget your name. Don't look so worried, I'll tell you what to say."

This is all getting very real. Paul's thoughts were full of seeing April again, not the nuts and bolts of being in a commercial.

Gabriel is still talking a mile a minute, gesturing broadly so that Paul kept glancing between his face and his hands. "I'm going to say this again because it's really important: stay away from April until the official reunion. I need that magic moment on camera. Just to warn you, April is at this hotel, too...look, I know what you're thinking, why did I do that if you can't see each other, but our travel agent is the worst, so here we are."

Paul remembers Gabriel saying he would handle the travel himself, and not to contact anyone at Heart2Heart, but he doesn't know how things work at these fancy start-ups, and anyway his brain is a mess, so he just nods like it all made perfect sense.

"Right, you get it," says Gabriel approvingly. "So one last thing...let's talk wardrobe. I'm imagining jeans—do you have any darker ones? A light blue Oxford shirt with one more button undone than you're used to, and a really sharp blazer."

Paul has never been more aware of his own ordinariness. "I don't think..." he starts.

"Relax, man," says Gabriel, guiding him up the stairs with a hand on his back. "I've got you. Underneath all this—" he gestures with one hand to his stylish jeans and handsome face— "I'm still a poor Dominican kid from Cranston, Rhode Island. I might have brought a couple things for you to try. I'm thinking you're a thirty-eight regular, but those shoulders. I die."

Paul allows himself to be led up another flight and into the hallway, just like his own floor but green carpet instead of blue. He should probably tell Gabriel he's fine, and that Gabriel should just leave him in the stairwell and go enjoy Paris. Paul isn't good at letting people help him, but he's beginning to realize he needs all the help he can get to pull this off.

Paris, France 1999

April held Paul's hand with her uninjured one, allowing him to lead her though Paris's maze of streets. She didn't know where they were going, but he said he wanted to show her something, and that was enough. Holding hands was usually just weird—an awkward mismatch of heights, grips, and hand temperatures. Right here, right now, though, their hands stuck together with a mind of their own, like magnets, and they floated around corners and down alleyways in content silence.

Soon, they reached the river.

"This is where I was coming this morning, before you, um, gently jostled me on the sidewalk," said Paul.

April took in the dozens of kiosks along the river, each one overflowing with books, prints, postcards, maps, and other treasures. It was the perfect blend of order and chaos: each one was the same size and the same green color, but also bursting at the seams with its own unique merchandise and displays.

"Amazing," she sighed.

"*Les bouquinistes*," Paul said. "The booksellers of Paris. They say the Seine is the only river to run between two bookshelves."

"Let's browse the shelves," said April, wandering towards a stall piled with ancient-looking leather-bound books. The proprietor, a tiny old man in an honest-to-goodness beret, nodded at them and returned to his newspaper. "Were you looking for anything special?" she asked.

"Just a gift for my mother, maybe a print of Notre Dame. She's never been to Paris. She can't travel at all, actually, because…" Paul turned to April, his dark eyes thoughtful. Then they crinkled up a bit at the corners, but his mouth didn't move.

April was starting to realize that Paul was an eye smiler, and the thought gave her an unexpected shiver. Imagine a man who could smile at you while his mouth was busy doing other things.

"I'll tell you what, April. What if we just don't." April gave him a puzzled look. "Don't tell our sad stories, I mean. We're young, we're in Paris, the sun is out. I don't want to think of home, or even tomorrow."

April had a set monologue she recited about herself to guys who were polite enough to ask. She's learned to joke about her taciturn dad and imply that her mother was still alive, just not in the picture, to spare anyone from being uncomfortable. What if she...didn't? She could be just April in Paris in June, walking along the Seine beside a cute guy without all the usual games.

April smiled and squeezed Paul's hand. "Okay, so what do we talk about? What's your favorite ice cream flavor?"

"Mint chocolate chip."

"I'll allow it, though the correct answer is Chunky Monkey. Favorite movie?"

"*When Harry Met Sally.*"

"Romantic, huh," said April a little more sharply than she intended. The idea of Paul eating mint chocolate chip ice cream while watching rom coms created such a vivid and tender image in her mind that she needed to move on to less salacious topics. "Favorite book?"

"*Middlemarch.*"

April stopped in her tracks and dropped his hand. "*Middlemarch.* Okay, now you're bullshitting me. I'm back thinking you're a secret murderer."

"What's wrong with *Middlemarch*?" said Paul, his forehead crinkling adorably.

"Nothing's *wrong* with it," said April. "It's just no one's ever actually read it. I mean, I spent college smoking clove cigarettes and learning to weave."

Paul had a trace of a mouth smile now, like April was a goddamn delight, not some poorly educated art school screw-up. "It's really good. Except for about fifty pages where everyone's arguing about who should be the next vicar."

"I'll take your word for it." April grumbled theatrically to herself. "Typical male. Lurks around Paris trying to pick up girls by talking about Victorian novels."

"I also know a lot about hockey. And dry cleaning."

April took his hand and started walking again. "Hockey *and* dry cleaning? Don't threaten me with a good time." She tried to purr sexily but had to suppress a giggle which turned into a loud snort. And she didn't even feel embarrassed. She'd never met anyone like Paul, so unpretentious, so interested in her, and so very, very sexy.

Chapter 9

April

"Cheers," April says, clinking her glass against Selma's.

"At least I can drink now," sighs Selma. "*L'chaim.*" She tosses back her pastis and water while April sips her Sidecar.

Hotel Voltaire has a small bar, next to the cozy breakfast room. It's dark, and quiet, and a welcome change from Paris's relentless charm. A silent, elderly bartender expertly mixes their drinks and retreats back to his corner.

"It's okay if you're a little sad," says April, trying not to inhale the unpleasantly strong licorice scent of Selma's drink.

"I failed my *test de grossesse*," Selma says solemnly, signaling the bartender for another.

"Yep. Got an F minus on the baby exam."

They had stumbled back to April's hotel room after the pharmacy, with Selma in charge of keeping a lookout for Paul. Selma peed on the stick with the bathroom door open, and April insisted on turning the test face down and setting her phone timer for the allotted minute, grateful to have something to distract her from her own flushed cheeks and racing heart. Paul. *Hello April.* The voice. The hockey ass.

The timer chimes.

Selma takes one look, throws the test in the wastebasket, and wordlessly walks out of the room. April peeks in the trash and follows, catching Selma at the elevator. She slips an arm around her tiny friend's shoulders. "Let's get drunk in Paris."

Which brings them to the least picturesque corner of the adorably quirky Hotel Voltaire, April waiting for Selma to begin her story of who was behind the suspected pregnancy, and Selma probably waiting for April to process their humiliating encounter with Paul.

Finally, halfway through her Sidecar, April cracks. "Come on, Selma, who is he? Just tell me three things about him, so I don't keep hearing all those toothpaste boxes crashing to the ground."

Selma accepts a fresh pastis and small pitcher of water from the bartender with a nod of thanks. She still looks remarkably fresh from the long flight, but April sees the dark circles and fine worry lines around her eyes.

Selma grips the pitcher unnervingly tightly and pours a splash of water into the glass, watching the Pernod turn cloudy. "His name is Ryan. He has a lab mix named Otis. And he's twenty-eight."

"Oh, shit," exhales April. Selma's love life is unconventional, and sometimes April suspects she didn't know the half of it. There have been men, there have been women, and for a time Selma lived with a man and two women in a Brooklyn loft that didn't have enough beds for four people. Nothing lasts more than a year or two, but Selma never seems particularly grief-stricken. Her fidgeting and foot-tapping now are about the strongest post-break up reaction April has ever seen.

"We're not together or anything," says Selma, drumming her fingers on the bar. She pauses and holds herself very still for a moment before looking at April intently, her jaw set. "It's not about him, you know."

"Sure, sweetie," says April lightly. She gently rubs Selma's back between her tense shoulder blades and waits patiently. She lasts about ten seconds before the silence gets too oppressive. "Do you want a baby? Because you are amazing and beautiful and strong. I would absolutely get you pregnant right here, right now, here on this bar if I could."

April hears a choked cough behind her but ignores it. If someone is going to be so rude as to eavesdrop, they can just deal with what they hear.

"I mean it," she continues. "I would knock you up so hard, and then I would rub your feet for nine months while you gestate a little human."

Another cough, followed by dramatic throat clearing. April spins around to tell whoever it is to mind their own business and sees an attractive, slender young man sticking his hand out in greeting. "Hello, I'm..." he starts before April interrupts.

"I'll stop you right there, my friend does not need your services. You are very attractive, but if anyone is getting her pregnant it's going to be me. Metaphorically speaking. I mean, I'll help her choose the donor from one of those catalogs, and maybe hold the turkey baster if she wants."

"Okay, wow," says the young man. "You are definitely April. I'm Gabriel Ramirez."

April is confused for a moment, taking in his neat beard, slim pants showing the perfect flash of ankle, and crisp windowpane shirt. Why does that name sound familiar?

"From Heart2Heart," he adds, looking her up and down. "Rough trip?"

"Holy crap, what time is it?" blurts April, suddenly remembering her plan to shower before that 17:00 meeting, though she hasn't established when exactly that is. She's supposed to have washed the stink of the plane out of her hair, scrubbed the humiliation of running into Paul so unceremoniously off her skin, and changed into a chic shift dress and MAC Ruby Woo lipstick, damn it! She cringes while Gabriel takes in her hair frizzing out of its scrunchie, her greasy skin, her coffee-stained shirt.

Well, this sucks. Gabriel is a primary part of Operation Save April, and she needs him to show the world that she is a good and very normal person. Well, work with what you have. April straightens up, smiles brightly, and takes out her scrunchie, though her hair is so dirty it magically stays in its tangled half-bun. "Great to meet you, Gabriel!" she chirps. "Thanks for setting all of this up! This is my best friend Selma, who was with me on the original trip."

Selma nods coolly. "Hi, Gabriel. So you're the demented matchmaker behind all of this. Have a seat. It's been a long and strange day. Maybe two days, since we pretty much skipped last night."

Gabriel looks back and forth between April and Selma, shrugs his shoulders, and pulls up a barstool. "April, you are all that I imagined and more. Selma, a pleasure. I'd better get a drink and try to catch up with you while we talk about what the next few days are going to bring. Negroni, *s'il vous plaît.*" He nods at the bartender.

"Have you seen Paul yet?" April blurts. She needs to know if Gabriel heard about the awkward encounter in the pharmacy. Not only does it make her look like a loser, but they also immediately broke his rule about seeing each other before the official reunion. It's not like he can call the whole thing off at this point, but she still prefers to hold onto some dignity in his eyes.

Gabriel sips his Negroni, his mouth slowly moving into a crooked grin that makes him look young and mischievous underneath the elegant exterior. "You *do* remember his name after all! Yes, I have. Paul also arrived today. As a matter of fact, we took care of some wardrobe issues this afternoon."

"Wardrobe?" repeats April. She tries to rewind her brain and remember what Paul wore in the pharmacy. Surely it wasn't that Van Morrison t-shirt from twenty years ago. She conjures up the image of Paul, standing in front of her, eyes locked on hers. God, those eyes. She can't look away even from imaginary Paul.

"Yes," continues Gabriel. "We had a nice movie montage moment. He modeled a few things. We talked."

"You *talked*?" squeaks April. She feels Selma's reassuring— or maybe it's a warning—squeeze on her thigh.

Gabriel looks at her questioningly. April tries to seem less interested.

"Just boy talk," he says. "You know. Lapel width. CrossFit. Cutest K Pop stars."

"Everyone in Blackpink," mutters Selma into her drink.

"Incorrect," says Gabriel mildly. "It's Jimin from BTS, now and forever. The skin, the shoulders, the unearthly symmetry. But back to Paul. Who is also very symmetrical."

April braces herself for Gabriel to say *and he's changed his mind about kissing you again. He told me about how you attacked him in the drugstore, and we agreed it was best if he got on the next plane back to Canada. He asked me to send his regrets...oh, who am I kidding? He couldn't get to the airport fast enough.*

But instead, she hears, "He's looking forward to seeing you. But remember what I said. It's very important to the ad campaign that you don't see each other until we officially reunite you on the Eiffel Tower. It's just like I told you in the email, which I certainly hope you read and retained: Paul will be on the upper deck, next to the brass telescope, at 19:30 on Friday." At April's panicked grimace he adds, "Let's call it 7:30. Sunset is at 9:50, so we will just be getting into golden hour. Delphine the photographer will take a few stills of him looking endearingly nervous and excited. April, you and I will come up in the elevator—"

"And Selma," interrupts April.

"Fine. Off camera," continues Gabriel. "I'm going to trust that you will have taken a shower by then, maybe even washed your hair since this is a national ad campaign. Aamir the videographer is with us, capturing your energy. You are contrite for how you didn't remember him at first, but you remember him now, and you are wistful for the girl you once were, but proud of the woman you've become."

"I'm *what*?" says April.

"Sorry, just a little Heart2Heart marketing language. Trying to keep things on brand. So the two of you lock eyes, run towards each other, and kiss just like you did twenty years ago. You are momentarily transported back to better days and are filled with hope for the future. And scene."

"I don't get it," grumbles Selma. "Why can't they see each other?"

Gabriel sighs. "Because most people are not good actors." His elegant hands move expressively. "No offense. But I may have bent some company policy in order to make things happen quickly, and I have a lot riding on this. We only have one shot at a first reunion, and I need it to be perfect. I need the kind of touching nervousness and longing and sweetness that most heterosexuals cannot perform on cue, so you are going to stay the fuck away from each other until I am able to choreograph you into the kind of perfect reunion that makes people want to download a dating app."

So Paul hasn't told Gabriel. April's heart gives a little tug. Paul is still kind, still protecting her.

Or maybe he just feels sorry for her. April Andersen, still messy and chaotic after all these years, causing scenes all over Paris. Why did he even come? Was he here to show her that he's over her and he's ready for closure on that one day that haunted her life for twenty years? Does he think he's too good for her, just because he can smile only with his eyes, and his shoulders are a touch broader at forty-two than at twenty-two? A small corner of April's brain recognizes she is not thinking logically, that she is lashing out because she's scared, but that part is quickly pushed aside by the powerful id. How dare Paul think he's better than her?

April drains the rest of her cocktail and waves to the bartender. "One of those, please," she calls, gesturing to Selma's pastis.

Selma glances at her warningly. "Are you sure, sweetie?"

"Oh, I'm sure," says April. She adds a few drops of water, swirls the pastis around until it grows cloudy and yellow, and gulps. She shudders.

"Well," says Gabriel, "Seems like this just turned into a party."

Paul

Paul is talking to Teresa when he hears the knock. Or rather, he's talking at Teresa while she tries to end the call.

"I don't see why you're leaving the bank deposit for Friday. Mom and I always did it on Wednesday so everything would clear before the weekend," he grumbles.

"Paul, I've got this, I've been doing it this way for ages. Doing the transfer on the bank's app is instantaneous. No 48 hours clearing time."

"Still seems risky to me. What about Tommy? Is he..."

Teresa cuts him off. "Opening every morning, just like on the schedule. For the love of God, please, please hang up and go eat a croissant or something."

"It's almost nine at night," says Paul.

"So drink some Champagne! Forget that Gabriel person's stupid rule and go find April! Trust that the dry cleaners will still be standing when you get home next week."

Paul thinks about that for a moment, getting a bottle of wine from the bar and figuring out which room is April's. He can show up at her door, apologize for being such a weirdo at the pharmacy, and ask if they can have a do-over of their do-over. No, that'll make him look creepy, like he wants more than to help her out of internet villain jail. What are you supposed to do when you spent half your life thinking about someone, and now she's so close but still so far away?

"I have to go, Tree. There's someone at the door. Love you." He hangs up.

It turns out April isn't so far away after all. In fact, there she is, in the same stretchy black pants and t-shirt as earlier that day, now with a neon green zip-up hoodie. Her fist is raised as though she's about to start pounding on the door again. When she sees him, she freezes in surprise, as if she didn't expect banging on his hotel room door to result in him actually opening it.

"April," he says. Again, stupidly repeating her name like he's struck dumb by how pretty she is or something.

"Hello, Paul," she says with exaggerated courtesy. "May I come in?" She steps into his room before he can say anything, brushing close enough that he catches her scent. Licorice and sweat, but in a good way.

Paul closes the door and leans back on it, needing that extra bit of support as April stares at him with the furrowed brow and pursed lips of someone about to make a very important announcement. Traces of red lipstick are smeared on the corner of her mouth, like she greedily gobbled a handful of raspberries. Paul itches to gently wipe the stain with his thumb over April's soft, cool skin. Instead, he sticks his hands in his jeans pockets and waits for her to say something. Except she just keeps opening her mouth to speak and then closing it again, and Paul isn't sure how much longer he can stand there without touching her.

"How's Selma?" he asks, searching for a topic that isn't why he can't take his eyes off her, why he remembers every second they spent together, and she didn't even remember his name. "Everything okay with, you know?"

"Great! Not pregnant!" April's face lights up, both with the news and with something to say. "Super young guy. Could have gotten messy. Plus pregnancy after forty is no joke. Not that I would know, my daughter is twelve. But you have to get the amnio, and your risk of varicose veins is very high. But maybe you know all this. I never asked if you have any children. I'm sorry about that. People without children complain that all people with kids do is talk about their kids, so if you don't have kids, you're already thinking about how I managed to use Selma not being pregnant into talking about my Liza."

"No kids," says Paul. "Never married."

"Selma's not married either. But I didn't come here to talk about her." April pauses for a moment, a little flushed under her light spray of freckles. "Can I have some water?"

Paul has a liter bottle of Evian on his nightstand. He could leave his good friend the supportive door, walk over there, find a glass, and offer her a drink. After he picks up the bottle, though, April grabs it, her cool fingers brushing his, and takes a noisy gulp. With an exaggerated "Ahhh!" she shakes her wild hair and hands the bottle back.

"Thanks. Airplanes are so dehydrating." April steps even closer and looks at him intently. Her pupils are dilated, making her soft gray eyes almost black. "There's something I need us to talk about."

Being alone in a hotel room with April, especially a disheveled and wild-eyed April, is a lot. In their brief time together, they both stayed in different hostels, sharing a room full of bunk beds with backpackers from around the world. Imagine if they'd had a room like this, with a bed, and a lock on the door. Paul's mouth goes dry at the idea. April's hair haloed against a white pillowcase. All the time in the world to explore her long limbs and delicate collarbone. He takes a noisy glug of water himself.

"Does Gabriel know that you're here?" he asks and immediately feels stupid. He's a grown man, damn it, not some teenager who can be told who he can and can't see. Especially not by a dashing millennial orchestrating some fairy tale storyline.

"No, he does not," says April, nodding self-righteously. "He has other things to worry about. Like how easy it was to

131

get the guy at the front desk to tell me your room number. Listen, I know he said we need to stay apart at all costs until the whole shebang on camera, but I have a better idea." April leans in and whispers loudly, "We should practice kissing."

The warmth in Paul's stomach spreads to the rest of his body like a shot of whiskey. Whiskey. He takes in April's flushed cheeks and disheveled hair, noticing again her potent but not unpleasant smell.

"Are you drunk?" blurts Paul. Now everything makes sense. That's why April turned up in his hotel room with hungry eyes and pink cheeks. Because she finds him so unattractive now that she has to brace herself to kiss him again by practicing in private, so she won't shudder with disgust in front of the cameras. Of course.

"No!" protests April innocently. "I mean, we had a few drinks at the bar downstairs. And then we needed to eat, so Gabriel took us to get oysters at this place he heard about across the river. And apparently you have to have Champagne with oysters. And then on the way back Selma and I stopped for gelato. She had strawberry, and I had hazelnut plus a scoop of something that looked like grass but might have been matcha. And then Gabriel gave me a melatonin gummy for later, but I was hungry, so I ate it. I think I'm just dehydrated. That's a real thing, Lindsay Lohan was hospitalized for dehydration."

She pauses for a moment, catching her breath, and looks down between her dark lashes. Her eyes catch on Paul's feet, and he's suddenly very aware of being barefoot. The strange intimacy of April's eyes on his naked feet, a part of each other's body they've never seen, makes his heart thud in his chest. April gives a little shiver, and Paul's hand automatically flies to her upper arm, rubbing gently. "Are you cold?" he asks.

She looks up, eyes locked into his, and for a moment they are both perfectly still. April looks so young like this, with her messy hair and loud sweatshirt. No doubt she usually wears silky blouses and lipstick and smells like fancy lotion.

"No. A little. I don't know," she says. Paul's hand moves up her arm until it finds a patch of bare skin where her shoulder meets her neck. His fingers gently dig into the tense muscles.

"Why do you want me to kiss you?" he asks, his voice hoarse. He's so aware of her body right now, the familiar limbs under the baggy sweatshirt, her expressive mouth uncharacteristically still. If she's revolted by him, he needs her to say it—otherwise, his body is very close to overruling his brain and pressing itself into April until he feels her all over him.

"Because," murmurs April, rolling her shoulder a little to invite his fingers to keep pressing, "It needs to look right. Gabriel has a lot riding on this, and we can't let him down."

"How should it look?" Paul's other hand apparently has a mind of its own as it settles into the curve of April's waist.

"It should look like I remember everything. Like when I saw you this morning, I felt like I was 21 again." April's voice is soft and hesitant, like it costs her something to say this.

Paul's heart is like a jackhammer. April must feel it through the few inches between them. "What do you remember?" he asks, his voice low and husky. He sounds strange to himself, assured and possibly...sexy?

"I remember the way you looked at me back then. Like you knew everything about me." April laughs weakly. "Kind of like you're looking at me right now."

That's it. How much more of this is he supposed to take? Even if she isn't attracted to him and is only acting...well, he can act, too. He'd been acting for years, damn it. Acting like a quiet, dependable guy when right now his true self is utterly wild to kiss April Andersen until she melts into his arms.

He steers her back a few steps until they hit the back of the door, not hard, but not carefully either. April makes a wonderful, breathy sound as Paul's momentum keeps him driving towards her lips. But from a few inches away, he stops.

"Is this what you really want?" he whispers, trying to keep his voice steady.

"Right, something like that would look good on camera," she says. Her eyes are dark and unfocused, and her voice has an unfamiliar quaver, but she keeps talking. "Though no doors to lean against."

Good on camera, of course. Paul feels something sour in his throat but pushes it down. He can't think beyond this moment, beyond pressing his body against April and hearing her say, *I remember.* "Lack of doors at the Eiffel Tower is a tragic design flaw," mutters Paul. April half laughs, half coughs, lightly spraying his cheek with spit.

"Crap," sighs April. "See, that's why we need practice."

"Practice makes perfect." Paul traces the tender outline of April's ear. In a few seconds he'll fall into her lips and lose himself completely. But as he moves to close those monumental, final few inches, April stiffens against him. Paul pulls back. She's suddenly gotten very pale, with a clammy sheen of sweat on her forehead.

"Oh no," she whispers. "I think I'm going to throw up."

Chapter 10

April

April opens her eyes. It's worse than she thought.

For starters, this is definitely not her hotel room. The curtains are dark red instead of blue, and the ceiling slants, like she's in a cozy garret. Plus, she is still wearing the t-shirt and yoga pants she wore for the flight to Paris, however many hours—or days—ago that was.

And then there is the man asleep in the chair.

His bare feet stretch onto an ottoman, but his upper body scrunches under a blue sweater that he's using as a tiny, sad blanket. His mouth is slightly open, and there may be a little bit of drool making its way down his chin.

Paul.

April is hit with a flood of sensations from the night before. Pastis followed by a glass of Champagne. Briny oysters sliding down her throat. Chugging a Red Bull when she felt her body shutting down from jet lag. Telling Gabriel about Joe Miller and her father's girlfriend's bitch daughter Angie, and how she's going to show all of them by having the best goddamn kiss on the goddamn Eiffel Tower, and what does Gabriel think of Paul by the way, has he said anything about her? And then lying on her bed in her own hotel room, wide awake and stomach churning from nervousness and impulsive food and drink choices, unable to think of anything but a gravelly voice saying her name. This logically led to the conclusion that she and Paul must immediately practice-kiss.

Oh, shit.

April notices the glass of water by the bed and her chartreuse sweatshirt carefully folded on the desk chair. More images come. Paul's surprised dark eyes when he opened his door. The strange intimacy of seeing him with bare feet. Paul backing her against the door with his strong arms. The unmistakable hunger in his voice saying, "Why do you want me to kiss you?" The unexpected lightness and joy overtaking her when they're about to kiss. Followed by the oysters and the pastis and the gelato and the Red Bull and the Champagne all suddenly coming together in a nauseating wave that almost knocked her down.

The next part is a little blurry, but she felt Paul holding back her hair while she retched over the toilet. A cool washcloth on her face. Hands guiding her into a bed with fresh, crisp sheets. The relief of falling into a deep, dreamless sleep.

And now this. Paul Stone yet again seeing her at her messiest. April yet again bursting into his life to cause chaos and disappointment, to prove that she is indeed this worst version of herself. She's just like her mother, leaving a path of destruction as devastating as a tornado.

Paul shifts and snorts in his chair. April tenses and holds her breath, willing him not to wake up until she figures out what on earth to say—or even better, not to say. She can sneak out of his room and pretend this never happened. Better yet, she can move to a new hotel without telling anyone and spend the next few days smoking in cafes, disguised in sunglasses and a headscarf.

Of course, that still leaves the problem of what to do about Melissa Valentine's minions and everyone else who's seen the old photo. Ever since that first email from Gabriel, she told herself over and over that the only way out of this mess was kissing Paul on the Eiffel Tower again, and she's come too far to question that plan now. Everyone will see the best part of her— the competent businesswoman, damn good mother, a dutiful daughter, and a polite co-parent. Not the secret chaos demon constantly upending the life of a good man, just like her mother.

April puts an arm behind her head as she stares up at the ceiling, trying to figure out what to do next. A sour, musky smell wafts from her armpit. Dear god, she must stink. No doubt there's a cloud of BO, alcohol, vomit, and morning breath surrounding her. Before she faces Paul or anyone else, April desperately needs a shower and a toothbrush.

She creeps out of bed as quietly as possible, picking up her sweatshirt and her slip-on sneakers. As she tiptoes towards the door, she notices a Hotel Voltaire writing pad on the desk. She glances over at Paul, imagining him waking up alone. He'll probably worry that she is okay. That's the kind of person he is, after all.

She picks up a pen. Maybe something like, "Didn't mean to force my way into your room last night and cause confusion for both of us. Also, my apologies for puking."

Instead, she writes a chipper, "Sorry about that!" She hesitates for a moment and adds, "Thank you," underlining it twice.

April slips out the door. Next time she sees Paul Stone, she will be showered, perfectly dressed, and back on script. Everything will be under control.

Paul

Paul wakes up alone. He has a stiff neck and a backache, but mostly he's just disappointed to see the empty bed. He'd hoped to wake up with April, even from across the room.

He slept in his clothes, and his mouth tastes like he's been licking the Paris sidewalk, so he hauls himself into the shower. There are still a few traces of April in the bathroom—some wavy light brown hairs on the tile, his small bottle of Advil on the bathroom counter.

Paul turns on the hot water and tries for a minute to be indignant about April turning up at his door. *Who does she think she is that she can show up after twenty years and demand that he kiss her, but just for practice?* he fumes as he scrubs shampoo on his scalp. *How dare she barge into his room, so disheveled and flushed and barely looking a day over twenty-five?* he snarls while lathering his face. *What kind of person looks at a guy's toes like she wants to suck them and then throws up while making the sweetest, most pitiful moans?* he sighs, as his soapy hand lingers over his groin.

Enough of that. He rinses off and wraps himself in a fluffy white towel. As he stumbles across the carpet in search of clean clothes, he sees the note on the desk. *Thank you!!!* and *I'm sorry.* So she hasn't just skulked out of there hoping to never see him again. Of course she hasn't. Because last night April stood in his arms and told him she remembered him. *I remember the way you looked at me.* Those words rumbled through his whole body.

Why did she pretend not to remember him, then? Doesn't she realize how that makes him feel? How can she just assume that he would drop everything to come to Paris to see some girl who had no recollection of the most magical thirty-six hours of his life...even if that's what he did without a second thought.

Last night, April rambled and joked until she stilled in his arms, his fingers working her tight shoulders. Twenty years ago on a park bench, she'd flustered herself so badly that she cut her hand. When April is uncomfortable, she talks in circles and avoids awkward silences, and clearly that hasn't changed. Paul is so charmed by it—the earnestness, the adorable panic behind her eyes when she realizes she couldn't stop talking—that he hasn't really thought what it all meant.

April is scared.

And why wouldn't she be? She's a single mother now, getting bullied online by a bunch of women who've never met her. The way she sees it, her best option is to publicly reunite with a guy she ditched without an explanation twenty years ago. No wonder she's so nervous around him. She's probably waiting for him to lash out at her like everyone else.

On that first trip to Paris, Paul felt like the hero in the story of his life, even if it was just for a day or two. This second time around, maybe he can be the hero in April's story. He doesn't have much to offer, but he can fix this mess she was in.

Paul pulls on his underwear and catches a glimpse of himself in the mirror. He looks...not too bad? He should start playing rec hockey again, but his runs plus the physical work at the dry cleaners keeps him fit. Maybe he doesn't look like a guy you pine after for twenty years, but he's okay.

When Teresa and Griff met, they were friends for almost a year before she finally agreed to go on a real date. Teresa told Paul it was because a single mother like herself couldn't take chances on men who may or may not stick around. As friends, she learned that Griff was worth her trust.

Paul and April have never been friends. They've never been lovers, either, not exactly. No wonder he can't move on, if it's so confusing what exactly he's moving on from. He and April need a fresh start. If they're friends, Paul can spend time with her, and help her, and put a simple label on this non-relationship that had gnawed at him for years.

Paul smiles. He finally knows what to do. And it starts with coffee.

Paris, France 1999

Paul slowed down in front of one of the bookseller's green stalls. Vintage postcards clipped to a string draped across the front, like socks on a clothesline. Most were old black-and-white photographs of Notre Dame or l'Arc de Triomphe with stiffly posed tourists in elegant clothes. Paul and April both stopped in front of the same one, a colorful sketch of a 1920s flapper holding a daffodil yellow parasol in front of the Eiffel Tower. Her wide grin was such a contrast to the somber Victorian ladies.

Before he knew what he was doing, Paul unclipped the card and handed the *bouquiniste* a few coins. He turned to face April, a bit more formally than he meant to, and handed her the postcard with both hands.

"It's you," he said. "April in Paris." April was the color in a sea of black and white.

April took the card from him. "Thank you," she said after a moment, her voice soft. They both stood there, facing each other. For the first time, Paul was able to just *look* at her without having to look away when she caught him. He sank into her sparkling eyes, followed the lines of her graceful neck, watched a bronze curl rustle in the breeze. She let him look without trying to fill the silence. She practically purred under his gaze.

This was what he'd dreamed of, in all those doctors' waiting rooms with his mother, in all the long afternoons at the shop plowing through his business administration textbook between customers. He needed April to understand that he was ready for this blossoming thing between them, whatever it was.

"I always thought something magical would happen to me in Paris," Paul said. He gently tucked a wild curl behind April's ear, his fingers lingering. "That probably makes me sound about ten years old, but I just had this feeling that if I could get here, everything would make sense. And here you are." He held his breath for a moment, hoping she would understand the one wild conviction he'd allowed himself.

April touched his hand, both their fingers in her hair. "I thought something would happen to me, too," she said, barely above a whisper. "Not this, though. Not something...real."

Paul needed to kiss her more than he'd ever needed anything. Just touching her ear made his fingers buzz; he had to have that tingling on his mouth and all through his body. Her lips were slightly parted, so perfect for him. April would make him come alive. He would become Paul in Paris.

He saw the exact moment where he gave himself away, when he'd needed too much. April's eyes flickered, then her mouth closed. She took her hand off his and smiled brightly, like she would at anyone. Paul snatched his hand back before she could shrug it off.

April looked down at the bright postcard. "Anyway, now all I need is a cool parasol." She laughed, silvery and pretty but also hard.

April's grin matched the girl in the picture, cheerful and two-dimensional, but it was still about the most wonderful thing Paul had ever seen. Maybe he should have kept the postcard for himself, in case he needed something to remember her by.

April

April moans happily as the shower rinses away twenty-four hours of accumulated airplane funk and nervous flop sweat. Her miraculous toothbrush peels off layers of fuzz and puke residue.

But all the soap and toothpaste in the world can't help the sickening realization that it took her less than a day to fuck up her plan to rescue herself from her last fuck up.

Paul curled up in the chair, using that blue sweater as a blanket so hot-mess April can sprawl in his comfortable bed. Young Paul bandaging April's bleeding finger in his bandanna and holding it above her head. Why is she always such a disaster around him? And why doesn't he mind?

Paul's strong hands pressing her against the door, seconds away from kissing her…

Damn it. April dries herself off roughly and pulls on the yellow caftan she packed for lounging around the room. She wraps her wet hair in a towel and checks herself in the mirror. Honestly, she looks better than she has any right to, flushed from the hot shower with a little of last night's eyeliner hanging in there.

So now what? How does she make up for acting like she thought this trip was some kind of booty call instead of a perfectly reasonable business transaction? April's head hurts. She needs coffee, toast, Advil, Gatorade, and then more coffee to make a plan, but she needs a plan before she leaves her room and risks facing Gabriel or Paul. She'll have to text Selma to bring a vat of coffee, even if it means confessing what she's done and listening to a replay of Selma's sensible advice from the airplane.

And then, as if by magic, April hears a knock. Selma must have read her mind and brought her breakfast. She flings open the door, expecting her friend's familiar cackle.

There is Paul, in a soft gray t-shirt and jeans, comb marks visible in his dark, damp hair. He holds two to-go cups and a white paper bag, and he smells like all of the best things in the world—shampoo, butter, and coffee.

"I thought you could use this." Paul smiles shyly, holding out a coffee cup. April is suddenly aware of her towel turban and loud caftan. She probably looks like an eccentric old lady in Palm Springs, the kind who seduces the pool boy. Except that old lady would have smoother moves than April, who stands there with her mouth hanging open.

"I hope you feel better this morning," says Paul. He keeps holding the cup out while April stares at it. "You were right about the front desk guy being pretty eager to give out room numbers."

Paul's polite references to last night are excruciating, but at least they push April into action.

"Thank you for this," she says, delicately taking the cup as she carefully avoids grazing their fingers together. She takes a sip. Bliss.

"Would you...like to come in?" April steps aside so he can enter without brushing his solid body against hers.

"I brought croissants," says Paul, walking past her at a courteous distance in the small room. "And I stole this from a vase downstairs," he adds sheepishly, handing her a small branch of pussy willows, the fluffy white catkins especially delicate in his strong hand.

"Ohhh," exhales April. She pops the sprig into her water glass where it looks unpretentious and brave and...tender. Not like the offering of a man who's come to finish what she'd started last night, or to announce he's backing out of the whole plan.

Just act normal, April.

Paul places the bag on a small table, and April quickly grabs a flaky croissant and takes a large bite before she can say anything stupid. The pastry is so delicate and buttery that she moans instead. A definite sex moan. She looks at Paul in alarm and sees his Adam's apple work as he swallows.

"Yum," she says brightly and takes another gigantic bite to silence herself. Plus, she's starving and it's delicious.

Paul watches her, the still complement to her antics, and then he does that eye thing. That thing where his mouth doesn't move but his black coffee eyes sparkle a little and the corners crinkle to show that deep down, he's smiling. April had forgotten that little detail, and now it hits her harder than her sparring partner the one time she tried Krav Maga.

Getting lost in Paul Stone's twinkling eyes is not part of the plan.

"April?" he asks, that damned gentle glint still seeing right through her. April realizes she's staring and possibly chewing with her mouth open. Paul continues, "I'm hoping we can talk."

April takes another sip of wonderful coffee and gestures to the two small chairs next to the table. "Of course, have a seat. We'll pretend we're in a cafe. One with really bad service though. They're not getting a tip from me!" Her heart pounds from his ominous suggestion that they "talk." Oh god, is he going to back out? He's going to say that he hadn't realized she still had feelings for him, but after her aggression last night he doesn't want to lead her on. He'll be flying home in the morning. He's going to be smug. Well, he can just go to hell.

Paul sits down, his back straight and his shoulders set. "This might sound strange," he begins while April glares at her coffee and waits to be rejected. "But this whole situation is strange. We met when we were so young, and we had a very memorable but short time together. I went through some stuff when I got back home, so maybe I built things up in my mind to be more than they were. I'll admit I thought about you a lot." His eyes lock with hers for the tiniest moment, enough for her to see a flash of sadness. April opens her mouth but Paul gestures for her to wait.

"You don't have to say anything. You said last night that you remembered me, even though on Facebook you said you didn't. Maybe we can just put it out there that you're having some conflicting feelings. We can talk about it if you want, or we can shove it under the rug and just go on with our business."

April doesn't know if she wants to hide under her bed or crawl into Paul's lap and ask his forgiveness. There he is again, accepting her baggage and not asking for more than she's ready to give. The way he looks at her makes her want to tell him, to admit those years of spring mornings when his touch came back to her. But it goes back farther than that, doesn't it—the reason why he scared her, and why she ran away. So far back that she'd have to start with being a little girl who sang too loud in the quiet house, and trying to find words for that made her so very tired. April wraps her hands around her warm coffee cup.

"Why did you come?" she asks softly. She looks at the table, not able to meet his eyes.

"A free trip to Paris?" he says wryly. He hesitates before adding, "And it looked like you needed the help. To be honest there's more than that. I think I just need some kind of closure."

"Closure," repeats April. A sensible word that tastes bitter in her mouth. Paul doesn't want to think about her anymore, not even at sunset on a beautiful June day.

"Now that I'm here, though," continues Paul, "Everything feels so complicated. We're not supposed to talk, and then we're supposed to kiss, and then we fly home. I'm right back where I was. So, what I'm hoping"— April holds her breath— "is that you and I could be...friends."

Friends. What a simple, complicated request.

"Friends," she repeats, echoing his words again like a freaking genius.

"Yeah, friends. It seems like a good place for a new start. Could we just...hang out today? Maybe walk around a little like we did before? Catch up on the last twenty years? Sneak around Gabriel?" Paul raises his eyebrows hopefully, but April notices his left foot nervously tapping.

She and Paul have been a lot of things to each other, but they have never been friends. April looks for as long as she dares at his dark eyes and hesitant smile. Here she is, a raw jumble of nerves and lust and confusion, and he wants to spend more time with her. It's more intimate than kissing, isn't it, to allow him to know her as she is now. She can give him just a little bit, though, enough to keep him here without tainting his nice, normal life with her brand of messiness.

"Paul, I would be honored to be your friend," she says. She gives his knee a quick squeeze but almost flinches at the heat and energy that spark on her fingertips from touching him.

April has what she wants: Paul ready to kiss her on camera. All he wants in return is a few crumbs of friendship from the real April. Maybe it isn't such a bargain after all.

Paul

Paul waits for April on the next street from the hotel, hopefully away from Gabriel's watchful eye. Why has he never noticed this terrible problem with his hands, and how they just hang there at the ends of his arms? Paul jams them in his jeans pockets, feeling like a pervert, then crosses his arms and leans against the building, feeling again like a pervert.

Thank God April is actually on time. He doesn't expect her to be, he realizes—she's the kind of person that guys like him wait for. She walks towards him, her hair damp and free, and her sundress scattered with scarlet polka dots.

After April slipped away, all of those years ago, Paul returned to the booksellers along the Seine, searching for another postcard of the smiling flapper with the light brown bob and yellow parasol. He couldn't think of anything else to do, and if he could find that postcard again, it would prove it had all been real. He never found it.

And here's April, twenty years later, smiling and beautiful and still the girl on the damn postcard. All she needs is a yellow parasol. He gave her that great speech about respecting her boundaries and being friends but seeing her smile like that is a stark reminder of how much she can still hurt him.

"Hello again!" April waves as she approaches. Paul overthinks what is the most friend-appropriate greeting: a hug, a handshake, or some kind of French cheek-kissing ceremony. He ends up patting her clumsily on the upper arm, possibly the worst of all options, especially as April glances at his hand in mild surprise.

"Well, I'm starving," she says brightly, adding after Paul stands there awkward and silent, "That croissant was amazing and probably saved my life, but I've always had an American appetite for hearty breakfasts. Plus, with the jet lag, my body is convinced it's missed a few meals."

This is a good start. April has a simple desire that her friend Paul can easily fulfill. He leads them to a crêperie he noticed yesterday, just a few blocks away. The morning is cool and misty, a little strange for June, but they choose an outdoor table. As April devotes her attention to the menu, agonizing over whether to go the sweet or savory route, Paul's mind again wanders to twenty years ago. With their shoestring student travel budgets, he and April never shared a meal at a restaurant. Not that he's wealthy now but imagine if on that first trip he'd had a credit card, a cell phone, and his own hotel room holding a queen bed with crisp white sheets. How unfair to have missed out on so much.

But April is here now, ordering a café latté and a spinach and brie crêpe from the waiter, who is clearly horrified by the combination. Paul isn't hungry—he's not much of a morning eater—but he orders a banana and Nutella crêpe and is rewarded by April's approving nod.

With food ordered, Paul doesn't know what to say next. He asked April if they could be friends, but the truth was, he doesn't have friends. He has siblings, and the employees at Stone Dry Cleaning. He seems to have Sid now, even if their friendship is a lot of Sid needling him about his hydrangeas. What do friends talk about, especially when they're a man and a woman, and even more especially when they've kissed, and when one of them had burst into the other's hotel room the night before and demanded that they kiss again, but just for practice?

He and April sip their coffees and fiddle with napkins and sugar packets.

Paul finally tries to break the silence. "How was your flight?"

Fortunately April doesn't give this stupid question the eye roll it deserves. "It was fine," she says. "A little long. I read a book Selma lent me and tried to sleep a little." She pauses, waiting for him to ask a follow-up question like friends probably do—inquire if the book was any good, or commiserate how hard it is to sleep on planes. Paul is stuck on April's mouth, though, and how mischievous it is, like she's always about to break into a witchy smile. And as his eyes linger on her lips, that's exactly what she does.

"This is weird, right? So, I guess we should catch up on the last twenty or so years? Very briefly, I'm divorced, and I live outside of Boston with my daughter Liza. She's twelve, except when she's thirty. I'm a home stager, which means I make houses look nice in a fake way, so people don't notice their flaws and pay more money. In my free time, when Liza is at her dad's, I like Zumba and thrift stores. I used to paint but haven't gotten back to it since Liza was born. And how about you?"

Paul wants to know more about what exactly home staging was, and what kinds of things she paints. But April looks at him expectantly, so he tries to match her businesslike tone.

"Single, no kids, never married," he begins, hoping it doesn't sound as stunted as he thinks it does. He's trying to come up with something not-depressing when April surprises him by leaning in and assessing him with interest. "Do you want kids?" she asks. "You still could. Men are lucky that way."

Paul is a little taken aback at her directness. Everyone tiptoes around these questions with him, knowing how loaded they are, except Teresa who just tells him to hurry up and have a few kids before he gets too old. But he likes the way she pauses tearing pieces off her napkin and waits for his answer with genuine interest.

"Well, it's a little complicated. In a way I already raised my kids. I have a brother and a sister—twins—about ten years younger than me. Our mother was sick for a long time, and after she died, I became their legal guardian."

April's face goes soft, and her busy hands still. "I never knew...I mean, we never talked about...How old were you?"

"Twenty-two. It was just a few months after, uh, I got back from Paris." *After you left me on top of the Eiffel Tower, wondering what just happened.* April's eyes widen in sympathy, and she places a hand over Paul's on the bistro table. He feels guilty for connecting her Paris memories with his sad time, but he hasn't told this story to anyone for a long time, and it feels good to talk. "My mother hadn't been well for a while when I left. We weren't sure what it was, but she knew something was wrong. When I got back, she told me it was ALS. She was going to slowly lose her ability to walk, and use her hands, and talk, and last of all to breathe. And I said don't worry about the kids. We'll be okay." Paul looks down at the table for a moment to steady his voice. "We thought she'd have a year. But she got pneumonia right after Christmas and that was it."

April blinks, her eyes glassy with tears. "Oh my God, I'm so sorry. How did you manage?"

"I don't deserve any praise or anything. It had to be done, and I screwed up a lot. Tommy's struggled with addiction and got into some trouble. And Teresa used to go for real losers. Her son's dad is the worst of them." Paul sees the pain in April's eyes, for a split second imagining it's pain over losing him, not automatic sympathy for his colossal fuck-ups. He quickly adds, "But everyone's good now. Tommy's sober and keeps coming up with what he calls 'disruptive innovations' for the dry cleaners—that's our family business, we own a pair of dry cleaners in Winnipeg. Teresa finally came home when Matty was six months old, and we kind of raised him together until she met Griff, her husband."

The waiter picks that moment to bring their food, setting the crêpes in front of them with just a little too much force.

"*Merci*," says Paul, glad for the distraction. He shouldn't have said all that, not if he wants April to believe she can count on him. But maybe she'll also understand that it's why she can trust him now, because he knows what it's like to feel everything you have slipping through your fingers.

April clears her throat and picks up her knife and fork. "I'm glad that things are okay now," she says. "They're lucky to have you. Not every family"— she gives a small, painful smile. "Well, not every family has someone that steps up for the kids like that."

April gazes down appreciatively and cuts a large bite right out of the center of her crepe, opening her mouth wide to take it all in. "Damn, that's good. So tell me more—do you live by yourself?"

"Just a high-strung dog that I inherited from an elderly neighbor. And even worse, I still live in the house I grew up in, with the curtains and sofa my mother picked out after they moved in."

The mention of the house sparks something in April. "Interesting," she says, cocking her head to one side. "That could go either way. Either charming or depressing." April eats quickly and happily now, and Paul slides half of his Nutella crêpe onto her plate.

"Is that your professional opinion?" asks Paul. "As a home stager, whatever that is?" Paul loves watching April eat, even if she's defying all laws of order by alternating between her savory crêpe and Paul's sweet one.

"Absolutely. Sometimes I get these properties that, no offense, reek of despair, but it's usually not the older houses with actual character. Do you have any pictures?"

Paul has a few photos on his phone, taken when he considered selling, and he wants to see April scroll through them with her serious nods and mischievous eyes. She hasn't changed, exactly, but her exuberance now comes with a streak of mature professionalism. He imagines this is the face she uses to convince her clients that she holds all the secrets to their happy ending. Paul gives up all pretense of eating and pushes his plate towards April as well as handing her his phone.

While she looks, Paul orders another crêpe with strawberries and vanilla ice cream. He wants to keep giving April things, and to see her keep eating like she's surprised that each bite was as delicious as the one before. Finally, she looks up at him with her new thoughtful expression, but somehow softer around the mouth.

"It's charming. Okay if I send it to myself?" She types her number into his phone and texts herself the pictures. "I have a soft spot for a vintage kitchen, though. Any realtor will say upgrade the appliances and install granite countertops, but sometimes I get tired of making everything look exactly the same. I'd rather take my time, really get to know the quirks of your kitchen before I just tear into it and really work it over…" April trails off as she realizes what she's saying, and as much as Paul would like to hear what comes next, they're saved by the waiter bringing the new crêpe.

"I thought about selling last year, but I never quite pulled the trigger," says Paul as April licks ice cream off the back of

153

her spoon. "I wanted a change, but in the end it wasn't the right change. I don't seem very good at change in general. I've been working at our dry cleaning stores since I was ten, doing pretty much the same thing as I am now." He couldn't make himself sound like a bigger loser if he tried, but maybe if he keeps feeding April she won't notice.

April picks up a whole strawberry by the stem and nibbles at the tip. "So, dry cleaning. Tell me about that. Or better yet, explain to me why you charge women so much more than men."

Not that again. Paul is saved from answering by a drop of rain on his nose. April feels one, too.

"Should we go inside?" he asks.

"Do you think we can make it back to the hotel before it gets going? My hair won't recover if we get caught in the rain, and I've got background interviews with Gabriel this afternoon."

Gabriel. Interviews. Right. Sitting with April feels so normal, maybe the first normal thing they've ever done. They'd talked about work, and their families, and the normal sort of things that people chat about. Maybe they're friends now, for all Paul knows about friends. But remembering that they're supposed to kiss in front of a small audience tomorrow is like a cold bucket of water. Last night, he'd felt close to wild with her in his arms, in a way he hasn't felt since that time he and April sheltered from the rain by the Seine. Only the shock of her throwing up last night brought him to his senses, such as they are. Tomorrow, he has to kiss her on camera and stay in total control, like the good guy he says he is.

The only way out is through, Paul's mother used to say. He just has to break down everything into steps, and the first step is getting April back to the hotel. "Sure, let's make a run for it," he says as he anchors some Euros under his plate.

He'll worry later about how to kiss her without imploding. If he isn't careful, he'll end up right back where he started, thinking about a kiss for years, but this time it will be worse because when she leaves, he'll know exactly what he's missing.

Paris, France 1999

April was watching the lovers when it started to rain.

She had noticed before how Paris was full of couples, touching, holding hands, embracing on park benches. Today, though, with Paul by her side, each couple she saw heightened the tingling electricity growing within her. A teenage boy slipping his hand in his girlfriend's back pocket, just at the lush curve of her ass, made April's mouth go dry. A young woman pressed a tall guy with a mohawk against a tree and languidly kissed him while his hands tangled in her hair, and a damp heaviness swelled between April's thighs.

When the raindrops started, Paul placed a hand in the small of her back and April wanted to grind against his light touch.

"Over there." He gestured with his chin to a small shelter, just three cement walls and a low roof. The open side was almost hidden by bushes, but they made their way through just as it began to pour.

The shelter was small and dim and smelled damp. They stood, facing each other. April was suddenly aware that for the first time they were, for all practical purposes, alone. The sound of the rain matched the rushing whoosh of excitement in her ears.

As April's eyes adjusted, she could see Paul's face. All day he had looked at her admiringly, often sweetly, but right now his gaze was a little dangerous. He had a few raindrops on his face that he didn't bother to wipe away, and his eyes...they were dark and intense and looking at April like he wanted to do something very bad—or maybe very good—to her right there.

She'd been thinking about kissing him for a while, but now that the chance was there, she didn't want to close her eyes. She wanted more of *this*, of his eyes raking over her body, of seeing herself through his eyes. She had never allowed desire to overtake her like this with any of her college boyfriends. She'd always put their pleasure first, and made sounds they would find sexy. Right now, though, with Paul's eyes growing darker and wilder, she felt her nipples hardening underneath her thin t-shirt.

"April," he gasped. He saw it, too.

"Shh," she ordered. "I want you to watch me. Don't touch. Can you do that?"

Paul's lips parted in silent surprise. He nodded. April cupped her breast and stroked a thumb over the hard nipple. Wetness surged between her legs, both from the electric connection with the nipple, and from the low moan that emerged from the back of Paul's throat.

April's other hand slid down her stomach, quickly undoing the button on her jean shorts and finding its way into her underpants. She loved the tension in Paul's shoulders as he watched, and the heat from his eyes in the dim space.

April moaned a little. She didn't mean to. She didn't even realize that people moaned unless they were doing it to perform for a guy. Her eyes never left Paul, so she saw him just barely lick his lips at her moan.

Her fingers kept moving, finding the familiar spot. But nothing was familiar about this. Her fingers worked feverishly, her breath growing ragged. Paul was close enough to feel the growing heat of his body, but his hands stayed by his sides. April's pleasure grew and grew as he watched, the taut control of his body together with the steady desire in his eyes.

"Can I talk?" he asked in a gravelly whisper. April nodded and gave her nipple another flick.

"April." His voice was shaky, but he still said her name carefully, reverently. "April, the way you look right now. Beautiful. So beautiful."

April felt sexy, debauched, maybe a little crazy, but after Paul said it, she realized she felt beautiful, too. She was touching herself, fully clothed, in front of a guy who couldn't take his eyes off of her, and she had never felt so beautiful. Her pleasure rose to a new level, and she moaned again.

"Yes," hissed Paul. "Yes, I want to see. Please show me. Please."

April felt like she was diving into a swimming pool, that terrifying split second in mid-air when there was no way to go back. You could only lose control and let gravity pull you down. She crashed through the water, holding her breath, and then moments later burst back through the surface, gasping for air.

"Fuuuuck," she panted, dazed with pleasure.

"Yeah," sighed Paul. "That was...thank you." He stood very still as April caught her breath and buttoned her shorts.

"Anytime," said April, and she laughed, free and joyful. The sound echoed in their little nook. Paul said she was magic, but surely he was the magic one, casting sex spells on her with his dark eyes and gravelly whisper.

None of it felt real: Paris, the Winged Victory statue, a shelter magically appearing in the rain, a man who could look at her like that. Then why did she feel like she was really herself, maybe for the first time?

Chapter 11

April

It's just a few raindrops at first. April follows Paul's relaxed pace back to the hotel, sneaking sideways glances. After hearing what he's been through with his mother and siblings, April sees how time and grief had shaped him—a depth of sadness never quite left the memorable eye smiles.

The deluge starts when they're still two blocks away. Plump drops of warm spring rain pour down, sticking April's dress to her body. If she was sneaking glances at Paul before, now she can't take her eyes off him. Paul with raindrops beading on his face inevitably brings back another time getting caught in the rain. The memory of Paul's hungry eyes flusters April so badly that she slips on a slick puddle and grabs Paul's hand for balance, or maybe he takes hers. At any rate, they burst into the Hotel Voltaire lobby wet, flushed, and hand-in-hand, only to be confronted by a wall of Gabriel, Selma, and an impossibly chic, unmistakably French man and woman.

Gabriel folds his arms and glares at April and Paul's clasped hands, shaking his head in resigned frustration like they're teenagers late for curfew. "Hello, young lovers," he announces drily.

Shit shit shit. Of course, Gabriel forbidding them from seeing each other is stupid, but it's his only rule besides not wearing green on camera. Besides, she needs Gabriel's support to make sure she comes across well in the commercial. She drops Paul's hand and casually runs her fingers through her wet hair.

Selma's eyes narrow knowingly at April's feigned innocence. Damn her ability to read April's thoughts. April glances over at Gabriel and braces herself, but he doesn't move.

After enjoying April's confusion for another moment, Selma gestures towards the new people. "This is Delphine and Aamir, the photographer and videographer for the shoot. Gabriel and Delphine met at the airport two years ago when their flights back from Art Basel Miami were delayed."

Delphine looks at April appraisingly, taking in the loud sundress and the wet hair that will clearly frizz as it dries. "*Enchanté*," she says politely. Delphine is about 35, Paris slim, wearing all black, with a pixie haircut and the cheekbones to pull it off.

Aamir nods agreeably and goes back to fiddling with his camera. He's wiry and attractive in the universal uniform of the artsy man: black jeans, expensive boots, and a leather jacket inappropriate for a June day, much less a rainy one.

April glances back to Gabriel to gauge his level of anger. He isn't looking at her, just glaring at his phone and pulling irritably at his tidy beard. This is even more unsettling than the tongue-lashing she expected.

April takes a deep breath. "Gabriel, I completely understand your anger here. You were very clear in your instructions, and since you orchestrated this whole reunion and got us a free trip to Paris, I certainly respect your wishes. But if you don't mind me saying, and even if you do, you are very young, Gabriel, and people are complicated." Gabriel raises his head and looks at her blankly. April gets the sense that Paul is doing the same at her side, but, as usual, once she gets talking it is very hard to stop. Also, in trying to convince Gabriel of the complexity of this situation and her own rightness in breaking his rule, she's doing an excellent job convincing herself. She continues defiantly, "I know you want some cute little story about two people seeing each other again and immediately starting where they left off twenty years ago, but so much happens over twenty years. Marriage, divorce, birth, death— it changes a person, Gabriel. I'm wiser than I was at twenty-one. I know now that I need to prioritize my own needs, and I will not apologize for putting myself first!"

April scans the group, waiting for someone to say something, but they all seem to be staring at her in confusion. Finally, Paul's warm hand slipped into hers.

"April and I needed to reconnect on our own terms. Unfortunately, that didn't fit with your vision for a dramatic reunion, Gabriel, but we will do our best to act surprised."

"Oh Jesus Christ," says Gabriel. He rubs his eyes and contemplates the ceiling before looking back at April and Paul like they're children announcing to a teenager that Santa isn't real. "I never thought you guys would stay away from each other. The idea was for you to get all excited about being forbidden to see each other, and bond against me, and have some steamy time in your hotel rooms. Then when you kiss later on camera, you're all hot and defiant with your big secret instead of two extremely awkward strangers. And lots of single and unhappily coupled middle aged singles see it and are filled with possibility *and sign up for a goddamn dating app!*"

"Oh," says April. Gabriel is smarter than she thought.

"Huh," says Paul.

"Nice," hisses Selma.

"*Très bien*," agrees Delphine, and Aamir nods and silently fiddles with his camera.

"Exactly." Gabriel folds his arms, just a little smugly to April. "And then maybe Heart2Heart gets another round of venture capital investors, and I don't lose my third job in two years. What I am pissed at is the French work ethic and the stupid handsome prime minister, and the goddamn mother fucking rain."

"He is not so good," says Delphine. Her accent is charming, her voice warm and musical. "They are saying that the *grève du travail* will begin tomorrow. The metro is already closed, and the other workers will join."

"The what?" asks April, looking from elegant nymph Delphine to fretful Gabriel to a surprisingly serious Selma.

"I think it's a labor strike," says Paul. "The unions have been in negotiations with the government for weeks." April tries to shut down the image of Paul reading *Le Monde* in his hotel room bed, swathed in warm, rumpled sheets.

"Yes, the strike," says Delphine. "Tomorrow everything will close to protest. The Louvre, the *Tour Eiffel*. Who knows when it will end." She shrugs elegantly, as if this is just another fact of French life, like perfect croissants on every corner.

"What are they protesting?" asks April. "Maybe it's no big deal and the government will just say yes."

Gabriel rolls his eyes. "No French labor strike has *ever* ended early because the French people will never give up having August off or retiring at sixty with a pension so they can spend their golden years playing *pétanque* while the rest of us poor fuckers bust our asses every minute of the day to keep from getting fired over email!" He starts pacing in tight circles.

"I always thought Americans should be more like the French that way," says April. "Did you know that drinking red wine…" Just as Paul shoots her a warning look, Gabriel checks his phone and bursts out with, "These fucking fuckers!" April wonders who the fuckers are in this case, the union members demanding fair treatment? The government moving the goalposts? Gabriel's apparently dick bosses at Heart2Heart? Capitalism in general?

"We have to do it right now. Go to the Eiffel Tower. I did not bring you here to wear *ponchos* and yell about your tender feelings over thunder, but it's now or never. And never is not an option." Gabriel looks at all of them expectantly. "Come one, move, people! Paul, go put on that blazer. April, do… something with your hair. This is happening."

"Is the rain supposed to continue like this?" asks Paul, somehow still calm. "I checked the weather last night and saw a chance of showers, but nothing like this."

"*Pluie torrentielle* with the thunder and lightning for the rest of the day," says Delphine, raising her perfectly arched brows in resignation.

April's brain, distracted by Paul's damp hair and Gabriel's tirades, finally processes what's going on. The commercial shoot is happening that evening. Recreate the kiss. Save her reputation. Make a clean getaway before Paul's thoughtfulness and perfect shoulders worm their way into her heart in a way she can't handle.

"Won't they close the tower if there's lightning?" Selma asks. "It's the highest point in Paris and it's made of wrought iron. It's basically a giant lightning rod."

"Yes, but it was designed to do so safely," replies Paul thoughtfully. "Insulated cables conduct any strikes to the top safely to ground. And if lighting hits the girders, electricity travels down the exoskeleton of the outside beams, which can't be accessed by visitors. It's absolutely safe."

April blinks hard. She wants Paul to say "girders" again, maybe while demonstrating how electricity travels by using his fingers on her own exoskeleton. But that's an inappropriate thought, especially in front of this audience. She and Paul are friends, and friends stay out of each other's girders. She's already barged into Paul's hotel room, but even worse they've gone out for a normal meal and chatted and reminisced like...like regular people. And French labor disputes and now pouring rain descended upon them like the wrath of a judgmental God.

So this is really happening. Maybe it won't be so bad. Going back out in the rain might at least drown out the flame of lust that those first raindrops ignited. She realizes that she and Paul are still holding hands and lets go, immediately shivering without his warmth. He eyes her with concern, and she smiles back reflexively—her polite, professional smile.

"Let's do this! Time to blow this popsicle stand!" she chirps. She's dangerously close to saying "Wonder Twin powers, activate!" when Selma's arm wraps around her waist and leads her to the elevator.

Once they're safely in April's room, with April wrapped in a dry robe, Selma hands her a towel and a glass of Champagne. "What the hell is going on here, Chickadee? I've barely seen you since last night, and then you text me that you're running off for a forbidden lunch date and you'll fill me in later? Well, guess what. It's later."

April sips the Champagne and squeezes her hair with the towel. "Oh Selma," she sighs. "There might be some things I still haven't told you about me and Paul. Besides that kiss on the Eiffel Tower there might have been an...erotic scene, on that first day we met."

Selma snatches the towel and throws it on the floor, grabbing April's shoulders as she rises to her tiptoes. "Start. Talking. Right. Now," demands Selma. "For twenty years I've listened to you go on about how you think cupcakes are overrated and how your big toe looks weird, but you forgot to mention this so-called 'erotic scene'? Wait, did you drag me along on a Transatlantic booty call?"

"No, that's not it at all!" says April, flopping face down on the bed. That is absolutely not why she was here. She is not thinking about Paul's booty. She sighs and turns her head to the side, purposefully facing away from Selma. "You know this is a business thing. But then I did something really stupid last night and went to Paul's room after we got back and asked if we could practice-kiss, but I threw up before we could try. And then today, he told me how he wants to be *friends*, and we had a nice lunch, and he's had a really hard life, and I guess I'm not sure if this is such a good idea anymore."

The bed trembles as Selma pounces next to her.

"You're suddenly realizing that all of this is a little... unorthodox? And I say this as a Jew who loves bacon." Selma pauses, and her voice changes to something softer and more tender. "When you asked me to come, you said it was strictly business so many times that I already sensed bullshit. Just don't bullshit yourself."

April rolls onto her side and peeks at Selma who mirrors her in the same position. Except Selma fits tidily on the bed, cheek propped in hand, while April's ankles hang off the end. Why didn't she tell Selma when she'd gotten back to the hostel that night, or any time in the last twenty years? Those few minutes in the rain feel like a fantasy–sometimes she wonders if she made it up. Telling Selma about it would have turned it into a funny story, a vacation sexcapade, instead of a moment when April felt completely free in a way that defied words.

"I just thought…" April starts, noticing a few grays in Selma's sleek dark hair. "I thought this would be easier. That seeing him again wouldn't get under my skin. I didn't think he'd still be exactly the same. But also different at the same time? I don't know how to explain."

Selma nods wisely, tucking a curl behind April's ear. "You are one messy bitch," she says fondly. She stands up, pulling April behind her and locating their Champagne glasses. "But messy bitches need amazing hair." Selma pulls over the desk chair and sits April down, running her fingers through the damp waves. "You are in danger of a rain-induced frizz out, so we'll go with some kind of braided crown. It's going to take a while, so you should probably start with that erotic scene."

April settles into the chair, closing her eyes as Selma's strong fingers work through her scalp. "Well, it was raining. Not steady rain like today, more like a downpour that starts and ends suddenly, and the sun comes out and it's like it never happened. Big fat drops of warm summer rain."

"Fast-forward to the sex stuff," says Selma, gently yanking a curl. So April does.

Paul

Paul is back in the lobby in half an hour. It didn't take long to comb his hair, brush his teeth, and change into his good jeans and new blazer. Delphine and Aamir have their heads together over in the corner, talking quietly, and Paul stands awkwardly as he waits for other members of the group, watching the rain through the front doors. Gabriel arrives next, wearing a black trench coat with black jeans and very shiny, very pointy boots. He buzzes with nervous energy, taking his phone in and out of his coat pocket and smoothing his perfect short beard until he almost bumps into Paul.

"Central casting couldn't have done a better job," says Gabriel, giving him a once-over. Paul isn't sure if it's a compliment, so he just nods and rolls back and forth on his heels.

"Gabriel," calls Delphine, "Let us shoot some interview with Paul. B-roll, like you Americans say." Before Paul knows what is happening, she steers him into an attractive corner while Aamir sets up an extra ring light.

"Pretend the camera isn't there," says Gabriel. "Act like you're talking to me. But don't say any brand names. And if I ask you a question, repeat the question in your answer, like if I say, 'What's your favorite color,' you say, 'My favorite color is blue.' And it's okay to curse, we can bleep it out in post. Everyone asks about that."

Everyone asks about cursing while being interviewed about their longtime crush? Paul really is out of step with the dating scene. He's still turning that one over when Gabriel begins talking in an unfamiliarly slow, patient voice: "Paul, how does it feel to be back in Paris after all these years?"

"Good," starts Paul before catching Gabriel's waving at him to continue. "Sorry, I mean, it feels good to be back in Paris."

Gabriel eyes him expectantly, and just as Paul realizes he's supposed to say more, Gabriel shakes his head and starts again with his sonorous radio voice. "What does it mean to see April again, twenty years after that kiss?"

Under the lights, in his new clothes, with Gabriel looking at him expectantly, Paul understands what it really means to be in a commercial. How is he supposed to put any of this into words? And does he even want to? He's here to help April but does that mean baring his soul to strangers in a hotel lobby?

"It means...seeing April means...well, it's like..." Paul feels Gabriel trying not to roll his eyes. "Can we start over? I'm sorry, I just don't know what you want me to say."

Gabriel practically vibrates with frustration under his stiff smile. "Just say something sweet for fuck's sake. Anything. Turn on that sad smile and charm them."

Paul tries to say something. Anything. April pretty. Paul sad man. But he opens his mouth, and nothing comes out.

"Gabriel, *tait-toi*, you make him nervous." Paul hears Delphine's musical voice, her pronouncing Gab-re-ELLE, and then she steps forward. "Paul, can you talk to me? I am just meeting you, and I want to know your story. Why does Paul Stone come to see a woman twenty years after one kiss?"

Her eyes are bright and curious, and she looks genuinely interested, not like Gabriel waiting for a sound byte. "Because...because it's April." Delphine nods, encouraging him. "And she finally needed me."

"That is very important, to be needed. And how do you feel to see her again, after such a long time?" Delphine quietly steps backwards behind the light and disappears in the glare. It's easier this way, being unable to see anything outside his

168

little bubble surrounded by darkness. This is the alternate world, the one where things aren't so complicated and messy and the truth inside his heart is easier to say.

"Seeing April again means...everything," he says, his voice surprisingly level. "Seeing her is like going back in time and remembering how young we were, and how excited about everything. But also, being old enough to know how special that is. You're lucky if it happens to you once, and it probably won't happen again."

"What do you mean, Paul? You're lucky if what happens to you?" says the light, musical voice.

Paul stares right into the ring light and sees stars. "Sometimes you get a flash that magic exists. You're lucky if you meet someone who feels right away like a missing piece of your puzzle."

"How does it feel to be separated for so long?" Delphine's disembodied voice is the voice inside his head, finally asking the questions he's never wanted to answer.

"Being separated felt inevitable. Even if I was too young to appreciate how special meeting her was, part of me still knew it was too good to be true. She was April in Paris, not April in Winnipeg. Maybe I didn't look for her hard enough because I never questioned it, that one minute she'd just be...gone. At least, before I met her, I always had this nagging feeling that something was missing, some part of me that would make the world and my place in it just make sense, you know? And I had that, just for a few hours. I found what I was missing. And missing it is better than wondering if it's even out there."

Gabriel steps into view, clearing his throat before asking in his sonorous producer voice, "So, are you saying that if there was some kind of website or app, say one for singles of your demographic, that you might have reconnected much sooner, or maybe never lost touch?"

The blatant reminder that he's shooting a commercial brings Paul back to his surroundings. Tasteful hotel lobby, rain beating against the full-length windows. And April, with Selma by her side, standing a few steps behind Gabriel, her lips slightly parted in tender surprise.

Paul likes April in all her forms—the twenty-one-year-old bohemian with a nose ring, the polished career woman, the April who barfed while wearing dirty yoga pants. This is something else, though. She's wearing a black, close fitting dress that shows the lushness of her body with a yellow scarf knotted chicly around her long neck. Her wild hair is contained in braids wrapping around her head, with a few loose tendrils softly escaping. She looks perfectly like herself and also like the most beautiful woman Paul has ever seen.

"April, talk about an Audrey Hepburn moment," says Gabriel approvingly.

April smiles, a little stiffly, looking away from Paul and finding something very interesting on the claret-colored carpet. He doesn't know how long she's been standing there, but clearly long enough to hear him spill his guts about stupid *puzzle pieces*, I mean, who even is he, talking in metaphors in a fancy Paris hotel. He wants so badly for this to be perfect for April, for both of them. He told himself that he'd come to finally end these daydreams of the mystery girl who got away—but there she is, right in front of him. She's real, and she needs him to do this photo shoot with her, and it's going to be perfect even if it fucking kills him. And from the sound of that lightning, it just might, girders be damned.

Gabriel follows Paul's gaze to April standing behind the camera and raises his eyebrows. Paul braces himself for another interview question, but Gabriel claps his hands together with lukewarm enthusiasm. "Thanks, Paul. That's good for now. We should go. Not like we're going to miss the sunset, but let's take advantage of any natural light that's still out there."

April steps out of her kitten heels and into a pair of rubber rain boots, bright yellow and decorated with black and yellow bumblebees. The heels disappear into her oversized shiny black purse. The sight of April in the elegant black dress paired with the bumblebee galoshes makes Paul's heart do something strange. It's so incongruous, so ridiculous, so... sexy. So April.

"Did you bring those from home?" he asks, trying to picture the magnificent brain of a person who packs rain boots for a five-day trip to Paris in one of the driest months.

"Yes," she says. "I hate wet feet. But don't think I'm always well-prepared. I forgot to pack socks."

"You can have mine," blurts Paul. She can have anything of his, anything at all.

April rewards him with another smile. "I might take you up on that. We can be sock buddies."

Sock buddies. That phrase, plus stepping outside into the rain that blows under their umbrellas and immediately soaks their legs, is a hard reality check. He told April he wants to be friends, and she's holding him to his word. It doesn't matter that the rain beating down on his umbrella sounds just like that little shelter years ago where he and April had been so very close.

"Sock buddies," he mutters to himself. To his family, he's the reliable guy. The one who drives you to the airport, who shows up at Stone Dry Cleaning on his day off. The one you give socks to on his birthday.

Well, then, he'll be reliable. He'll make sure this photo shoot goes off without a hitch for his friend April. He'll kiss her sweetly for the camera, without any of the ragged desire triggered by the raindrops. Afterwards, he will give her a pair of dry socks.

Paris, France 1999

"I should go."

"Don't go."

"I don't want to. But Selma will be worried."

"Can I see you tomorrow?"

"Yes. Of course. Later, though. We already bought tickets for the Catacombs tour in the morning."

"Meet me at 4 o'clock at the Eiffel Tower, April."

"That is the most romantic thing anyone has ever said to me."

"I hope so. If something comes up, leave a note for me on the bulletin board at my hostel. Auberge Internationale in the 15th arrondissement."

"Nothing will come up."

"Good."

"I have to go."

"I know."

"Paul? I really want you to kiss me right now. But don't. Because I don't want to say goodbye. Just, see you tomorrow."

"See you tomorrow, April."

April

April has pictured kissing Paul again in many different ways. In an airport, maybe, after bumping into each other during a layover. In Paul's hotel room, of course, when she got that brilliant idea that the two of them should have a practice kiss. But every time she tries to picture them kissing on the Eiffel Tower again, she draws a blank. The image of her and Paul, overdressed, with cameras around them...she can't see it. Maybe because that first time is still perfectly clear in her head.

It doesn't matter if she can't picture it because it's happening. They're in a taxi as she tries not to let her thigh rest against his, and Gabriel bickers with the driver in a mixture of English, French, and Spanish with what sounds like some Italian thrown in for good measure.

"He's either telling the driver to get us as close as possible, or to drive into the Seine." April is so lost in her own thoughts that she's startled by Paul right next to her, muttering into her ear. She gives a disconcerting wet snort of laughter and is immediately embarrassed, but Paul, as always, doesn't seem put off.

"And what is the driver saying back?" asks April.

Paul's eyes glint mischievously. "In French he's saying he will try but the roads are very bad. In what I think is Arabic, though, he's speaking a lot more quickly and less politely."

"So your Arabic is a little rusty. How embarrassing for you," says April with mock sympathy.

"I only know the swear words," says Paul, his lips in her hair as he speaks into her ear, giving them a private bubble within the taxi. "Or at least I think I know them. Mohammed—this guy that worked at our dry cleaners for a while—taught me a few words. For all I know he was teaching me nursery rhymes, but some of what this guy is saying sounds familiar."

"You're funny," blurts April. "I think I forgot that you were funny."

Paul looks surprised, then pleased. "Honestly, you might be the only person who thinks so. If you asked my family or my employees to describe me, I don't think 'funny' would be in the top ten."

"Maybe you're only funny in Paris," says April. She still feels very much like herself in Paris—impulsive, too talkative, taking up too much air and space in this cramped taxi—but when Paul studies her with his dark, patient eyes she believes he sees something different.

"Only funny in Paris," repeats Paul. "Like Jerry Lewis."

"Well," says April, "Parisians aren't really known for their taste. Except for food, fashion, and art."

April feels rather than hears the rumble of Paul's laugh. "I bet you're even funny in the States."

They've drifted together, his lips in her hair, their legs pressed together with her bare calf against his jeans. April is suddenly overwhelmed by intimacy, with the rain obscuring the outside world, and Gabriel and the driver still debating in various languages. She looks out the window, watching the drops stream down the glass. Back in the hotel lobby, when she came upon Paul's interview, she couldn't take her eyes off him under the bright light, talking earnestly to the camera. He looked like someone who could never lie. But then she'd heard him, talking about how he'd sensed even then that April would disappear.

"What did you do after?" April asks, still gazing out at the lights distorted by raindrops. *After I ran away. After I tried not to be like my mother.*

Paul knows what she means. "I looked for you. And then I sat on a bench until it got dark, in case you came back."

Paul on a bench, waiting for her, not quite willing to believe she would disappear after everything that happened. The image makes her heart crumple.

"I didn't come back," she says. A warm hand slides over hers for a moment.

"It sure did take you a while," says Paul.

They linger in the silent moment, until the taxi brakes suddenly to pass through a large puddle.

"We've been driving for a long time," says Paul. "The hotel isn't more than a kilometer from the Tower." April realizes he's right—she's been too wrapped up in their conversation to fully pay attention to the route. Surely, they passed that horse statue before.

"Gabriel, why is it taking so long?" she says, bursting their private cocoon.

"Road closures," grumbles Gabriel. "Street flooding, or an accident, or maybe just a blockade of drowned Parisian rats. Who knows. Who cares. I told him to find a different way." His phone pings. "God damn it, Delphine says that Rue de Charles is closed, too." Delphine, Aamir, and Selma are in a second taxi with the camera equipment.

The taxi passes by what April recognizes as the Carousel near the Tower. She glimpses up for the familiar, graceful shape, but if it is there it's concealed by the mist and clouds. While she cranes her neck awkwardly, the driver slams on his brakes and the car hydroplanes, barely missing the car in front. April falls backwards and finds herself lying over Paul's lap. She blinks up at him, and he looks down in surprise and then concern.

"Are you okay?" he asks.

April is fine, but her mouth doesn't seem able to form words, and anyway it's very comfortable lying like this, with Paul's strong thigh against the back of her neck and his warm brown eyes on her body. Paul opens his mouth to ask her again, but his voice catches on the "are", and he just gazes down at her with dazed surprise, like she fell out of the sky onto his lap instead of sliding over from the adjacent seat. April stares back.

"Hi," she finally says.

"Jesus Christ," spits Gabriel. "Keep it in your pants, you two. This is as close as he can get. We have to walk the rest of the way."

The taxi is warm and dry, and Paul's thigh is a firm yet comfy pillow. April wants to stay right here, not search through the rain and fog for the Eiffel Tower, like a ghost from her past. But she's come too far to mess up her perfect plan now. Besides, if she doesn't kiss Paul in front of the cameras very soon, she might accidentally kiss him for real.

Paul

They're too late.

Paul holds the umbrella over he and April (mostly April, not that it matters since the rain blows at them sideways) and tries to keep up with Gabriel as they stumble across the Esplanade. Just as the Eiffel Tower's base comes into view, they see the electronic bulletin board flashing: TOUR EIFFEL FERMEE/ EIFFEL TOWER CLOSED. A group of protesters with umbrellas and raincoats hold drooping signs and banners, hand-lettered with *"En Greve"* and *"Non Macron!"*

"Nooooo!" Gabriel groans and runs ahead while Paul wonders if he should follow until he feels April's arm settle around the crook of his elbow, impossibly warm through layers of clothes and jackets and driving rain.

"This is bad," says April. "The strike has already started. It wasn't supposed to start yet. That woman—that Delphine—said it would start tomorrow. Paul, this is bad." Her voice is strained with rising panic, and Paul waits for her to continue her April-esque stream of consciousness, but she just stares at the protesters. If April is too stressed to talk, Paul really has to do something.

"Let's get a closer look," says Paul. Better to keep moving and get rained on than stand still and get rained on. "Maybe Gabriel will figure out a plan." As they get closer, though, a knot of worry grows in his stomach. The top of the tower is hidden in fog, the base disappearing into the clouds. Even a flash of lightning doesn't illuminate anything. The Eiffel Tower has disappeared.

A clap of thunder, and April flinches, squeezing his arm. From the other corner, Selma, Delphine, and Aamir come into view, Delphine looking aggravatingly unperturbed in a red belted raincoat and clear umbrella. Selma waves with both arms, and they all walk briskly towards each other and the stump of the tower, catching up to Gabriel who stopped to check his phone. He looks up unsurprised to see the core group assembled around him.

"Delphine, you said we'd have more time!" says Gabriel. "Why is the only efficient thing that has happened in France in the last fifty years this particular protest on the one day I need some of that French bureaucracy and red tape?"

Delphine shrugs. "These things move very slow until they are fast," she says. "We will come back."

"But we can't come back," protests Gabriel, and if Paul didn't know better, he would think his confident young friend is scared. "This is it. This strike could last a week, or a month, or who knows how long? And if I don't get all the footage by the day after tomorrow when we fly out then I am screwed."

"Gabriel, I'm sure if you talk to your bosses, they'll understand that these are circumstances out of your control," says Paul soothingly. If he keeps Gabriel moving forward, then he can prevent April from panicking and hold this whole circus together. "Tell them you need an extra day or two and have them change the tickets."

Gabriel closes his eyes for a moment and opens them with a new look of grim determination. "That is not an option," he announces, more to himself than to Paul. "I'll make this happen or go down in flames."

"Too wet for flames," mutters Selma, but Gabriel is already striding towards the line of strikers and police officers. Paul is torn between following him, staying and holding the umbrella over frozen April, or maybe helping Aamir rearrange the tarp blowing off the equipment.

Paul takes April's cold hand and leads her to catch up with Gabriel. He can manage this. Surely there's a solution where April starts chattering again, and Gabriel goes back to being overconfident and sarcastic. Paul takes care of people, that's what he's good for. He failed his mother, he failed the twins when they were younger, but he's not going to fail April. They are friends, damn it, and he's going to make things right for her. Even if it means wrapping one arm around her waist under this too-small umbrella and kissing her softly until her lips warm and her cheeks turn pink, then kissing her purposefully while the rain pours down everywhere except in the little world under their umbrella.

Paul is gripping April's hand very tightly. *Focus, buddy,* he orders himself as they catch up with Gabriel near the protesters. *You're here to make April's life easier. Kissing is for cameras.*

April

Rain pattering on the umbrella, protesters chanting in French, thunder. Flashing lights from a police car, bright yellow rain slickers, the Eiffel Tower swallowed by clouds.

It's too much for April to process, and her brain whirrs in circles.

They can't recreate the kiss tonight. Gabriel says this is the only chance. No kiss, no commercial, no public redemption. Back to the identical houses, erasing their history for identical buyers full of the same determination to lead a picture-perfect life. Back to waking up alone every morning and putting on the navy pantsuit and nude lipstick, trying not to talk too much. It's like April is standing on a cliff as the swirl of sound and wind around her pushes her closer and closer to the edge. Only Paul's warm hand holding hers anchors her in place.

Why did Gabriel say this was their only chance? Why would Heart2Heart bring them all this way and not give them an extra day or two? It doesn't make sense, but nothing makes sense right now in the churn of noise and lights. April watches as Gabriel approaches the protesters and tries to cut through their line to an empty-looking tourist information booth. The protesters hold up their signs as barriers and April sees their mouths open and close angrily while Gabriel dodges from side to side looking to break through their ranks.

Two police officers, all in black with neon yellow safety vests, near Gabriel. They walk slowly but steadily, ignoring the rain as it falls on their black hats, and April's disorientation sharpens into fear. "Paul," comes out as a hoarse croak, but he's already seen it. "Wait right here," he tells her, but April can't let go of his hand. She doesn't want to be alone in the rain watching everything fall apart. Shouldn't everyone go home, where it's safe? Except April is tired of being safe.

Gabriel gestures wildly at the police officers—pointing to the missing top of the tower, back to her and Paul, waving his phone around—but she can't hear anything over the strikers' chants and a fresh clap of thunder. One of the officers grabs at Gabriel's phone, and Gabriel jerks back, knocking the second officer with his elbow. Then lightning. The first officer steps towards Gabriel and lays a hand on his shoulder. Gabriel pushes the hand off and springs forward, slender and quick against the imposing black form. Then his partner grabs Gabriel from behind, pinning his arms behind his back and blocking his body from April's view. She opens her mouth to scream but nothing comes out.

Paul pulls them forward, April following because she's forgotten how to let go. He calls to Gabriel, then in French to the police officers. April doesn't understand, but the policeman loosens his grip on Gabriel's arms. Paul keeps talking, with Gabriel interrupting and trying to shrug his arms free. The protesters chant, the rain falls, April holds Paul's hand. In the lights and the rain and the noise, Paul is the only thing that makes sense.

Delphine is there now in her red raincoat, followed by Aamir. She looks possibly more elegant wet, and the police stand still listening to her authoritative French. And Selma, dear Selma, also appears, resting her cheek on April's other arm. April leans into her, seeking more support to stay upright.

But April only looks at Paul, like he's the answer to all the questions on the tip of her tongue. He still holds her hand.

Paul

"They weren't going to arrest me," says Gabriel as Paul pulls him back to the street, following Delphine and Aamir away from the Eiffel Tower. "My brown ass deals with New York cops every day. These French ones are just glorified hall monitors."

Paul glances back at April, sharing an umbrella with Selma right behind him. He thinks he can hear her yellow boots splash through the puddles, though it's hard to hear anything over Gabriel and the rain.

"I tell you, I had everything under control. I know what I'm doing. I just need to come up with Plan B."

Delphine halts and spins around. "Gabriel, *tais-toi*. You are very lucky right now." She inspects the rest of the group. "Everyone will come to my home. We will drink something, become dry. We can do nothing more tonight."

Before Paul can question if this is a good idea (it probably isn't), silent Aamir magically flags down two cabs. He leads April and Selma into one, leaving Paul to squish between Gabriel and Delphine. This is definitely not his first choice of groupings, especially with Gabriel fidgeting and talking.

"I can still make it work. It's barely lunchtime in New York, I have a few hours."

Delphine vaguely hums in agreement or appeasement.

"It could have been so perfect," Gabriel continues, hunched in the backseat with his arms crossed and his sharp elbow poking Paul's ribs. "The golden hour, the same angle as the original shot, with the telescope in the background. See how the perspective makes him look taller?" Gabriel reaches his phone across Paul to show Delphine the original photo. Paul is forced to look at it along with them, since they've apparently forgotten he's there.

"We have a couple of sweet kids here," Gabriel sighs. "I wanted to capture that feeling of hopefulness. Just had to keep Paul from looking too sad or April from seeming too...flighty."

Delphine studies the photo thoughtfully. "She is very, how you say, flighty. And Gabriel, I am very concerned about her hair. You did not hire the *coiffeur* like I said, and her hair is very disobedient."

Paul tenses as they talk about April. She'd hinted sometimes that other people saw her as, well, a lot, and hearing Gabriel and Delphine dissect her in the cab like this makes him protective. He's seen April in her joyful and flustered and talkative moments, but he's witnessed that softer side, too, that Gabriel and Delphine know nothing about.

All three of them stare at Gabriel's phone for another moment.

"So what happened next?" asks Delphine. It takes Paul a moment to realize she's talking to him. "After the kiss?" prods Delphine.

The crowds, the noise, the cool hand in his one moment and gone the next.

"She...vanished," Paul says.

"Vanish? You mean, like, she is gone?" says Delphine. "Gabriel, you did not tell me this."

Gabriel slides his phone back in his jacket pocket. "I guess I didn't know exactly. You literally mean right after this picture was taken, she ghosted you?"

"There were so many people," says Paul. "Everyone was pushing, trying to get on the elevators."

"Damn, that's cold," says Gabriel. "Sorry, Paul, I can tell you still like her, but that was not a nice thing to do."

"So what?" snaps Paul. "So what if she's not nice? So what if her hair is crazy and you think she talks too much, or whatever. She's interesting and funny and lights up every goddamn room that is lucky enough to have her walk into it. Who cares if she's nice? I'm nice, and let me tell you, it hasn't done much for me."

Paul glares straight ahead, watching the windshield wipers try to keep up with the deluge, but he senses Gabriel and Delphine's glances at each other, like they can't wait to get away from him and dissect what he said. Everyone is silent for the rest of the ride.

Soon they're in a quiet neighborhood of small buildings. It's still early in the long summer evening, but the skies are dark, and sheets of rain continue to pour down. The other taxi arrives a moment later, and Delphine leads them all up several flights of stairs and opens the door to a small, high-ceilinged apartment with parquet floors.

A small boy, about two years old, stacks wooden blocks on the floor while a white-haired woman mends a small shirt.

"*Merci*, Alice," says Delphine, picking up the little boy and balancing him on her slim hip. "Everybody, this is Nico. Say *bonjour*, Nico." The boy buries his face in her shoulder, and Aamir rubs his head affectionately.

They're a family. Paul hasn't been sure if Delphine and Aamir are more than colleagues, but now he sees that while they'd been bumbling around Paris's biggest tourist trap trying to stage a great love story, all that time their photographers have the real thing: a partnership, a welcoming home, a beautiful child waiting for them. He's trying so hard to keep things going for April's sake that he lost track of the big picture. The whole thing is cringeworthy, and now he's in a stranger's perfect apartment with wet socks and no romantic photograph.

Aamir walks the babysitter to the door, chatting in French, while Delphine bounces Nico on her hip.

"Please, will you sit?" she says, gesturing to a small couch, a few chairs, and an oversized bean bag. The furniture is a mix of elegant pieces and stuff Paul recognizes from IKEA, but it's modern and whimsical here, not sad and lopsided as it is in his house. As he sits, though, Delphine hands the child to Aamir and gestures for Paul to follow her into the next room. "You will help me carry the glasses," she says firmly, like someone who isn't used to being disregarded.

Paul follows obediently. The kitchen is what he thinks of in his limited experience as typically French—narrow, with miniature appliances to his Canadian eye. It's spotless, but there's a carton of intensely red strawberries on the counter and a colorful sippy cup drying by the sink. He looks around for whatever glasses he's supposed to carry, but instead finds himself crowded into the far corner by Delphine. For a terrible moment he thinks she might kiss him—maybe she and Gabriel had signaled to each other he needs actual kissing lessons, and for the second time in twenty-four hours he's getting roped into a practice make-out session. Up close she's very attractive, but Paul can't imagine kissing anyone with such a serious mouth and angular cheekbones.

Delphine takes him by the shoulders and whispers loudly, "Paul, you must tell me, do you want this? Gabriel thinks you carry a torch for April all these years. If you kiss her again, maybe it never goes away."

"Why..." stammers Paul. "Why do you say that?"

"They say French women know about love. Maybe this is true? I hear that in America they don't even give the new mothers *la rééducation périnéale*. How can this be?" She peers at Paul expectantly while he translates in his head—perineal re-education? Huh. He would have remembered Teresa mentioning that.

"*Alors,* the nurse to help you recover the vagina after the baby?" Delphine shakes her head in frustration. "To put the electrodes in the vagina to tell if you do the exercises correct? So you do not *fait pipi* when you sneeze and can have an orgasm again with your husband?" Paul's growing alarm must be obvious because she looks at him with true pity. "I see that French women are the experts on love after all. With our happy vaginas." Paul did childbirth classes with Teresa but even their instructor hadn't said "vagina" as many times in one minute as Delphine.

Delphine opens a cupboard over Paul's head and takes out stemless wine glasses, lining them up on the counter.

"I see the way you look at April," she says matter-of-factly, opening a drawer and fishing out a wine key. "Like she is beautiful and special. Your eyes, they stop looking so sad."

"What about her? How does she look?" asks Paul, surprising both of them with the edge of urgency in his voice.

Delphine takes a bottle of wine from the compact refrigerator. "I do not know," she says thoughtfully as she twists the corkscrew. "She is someone who talks a lot, so you do not notice what she really thinks. She does not have her heart on her shirt sleeve like you. So I am worried for you."

Paul swallows hard. The idea that Delphine sees his feelings so clearly, not just his longing for April, but his loneliness and his vulnerability, is mortifying. But she's speaking plainly to him, and she deserves the same in return.

"Thank you," he says. "You are very perceptive. *Perspicace,*" he clarifies in French. "And you're probably right. I'm good at hiding things. Sometimes from myself. So, I think you are right about my feelings for April. But I have everything under control. Whatever happens I can handle it."

Delphine raises her eyebrows doubtfully but nods her pointy chin while expertly sliding the cork out of the bottle. "I hope you are right, Mr. Paul Stone," she says. "But be careful. Love is not the same as a happy vagina. Sometimes even French women make a little *pipi*."

Paul hums in agreement like this is very profound advice. And maybe it is? He watches her pour the wine, an elegant twist of her wrist preventing drips between glasses. He told Delphine he has everything under control because that's how it felt when April held onto his hand at the Eiffel Tower. It's the moments when she isn't looking at him, and he has a chance to think, that everything goes sideways.

Paris, France 1999

Paul walked alone over the Pont des Arts on his way back to the hostel, pausing to watch the river flow under the bridge. In Paris, the Seine was part of the city. With graceful arcs, it cleanly divided Paris into the Rive Gauche and Rive Droite. Stone embankments turned it into something urban and dignified. Back in Winnipeg, where the Assiniboine and the Red River met at the Forks, there was a recreational park with boating and splash pads and a Riverwalk. Families picnicked, teenagers sunbathed, and children screamed as they ran through the fountains. The Seine would never.

In Paris, Paul was part of the city. Back home, he was the steady and reliable son of Deirdre and Eddie Stone, helping out at Stone Dry Cleaning since before he could see over the counter. But like Paris, he had two parts. And Paul had never let anyone cross the bridge to his romantic and dreamy Bank. Funny how it came so naturally with April.

What happened when Paris Paul went back to Winnipeg? Would he return to being the guy with no bridge between his Right and Left Banks? How could he keep his family going and still be the man who swept a girl off her feet in Paris? All he knew was something had shifted inside him, and he wanted more than what he'd left behind.

April

April tries not to gulp her glass of Sancerre as she hunches awkwardly on Delphine's elegantly low sofa. She didn't plan on drinking tonight, not after last night's fiasco in Paul's hotel room, but there's a whole new fiasco now that requires a glass of wine. One minute she'd been standing in the rain clutching Paul's hand like a life raft, the next she was hustled into a taxi with Selma and Aamir, and now she's attempting not to drip on a chic velvet couch while figuring out what the hell just happened.

Selma perches next to her, perfectly sized for the sofa but eyes darting around suspiciously while she taps her fingers on her wine glass. Selma had been uncharacteristically silent in the taxi with April and Aamir, and she'd grabbed April's wrist as they walked up the many stairs to the apartment.

"Something's off here, Chickadee," she'd muttered as they approached the second floor. "As much as I like Gabriel, he clearly doesn't know what he's doing. What the hell was he thinking with the police? And then Delphine dragged us all back here before anyone could say anything? Who is she, anyway? She's too gorgeous to be trustworthy."

April didn't disagree, but her head felt so heavy, and she was tired of planning the next move. "Maybe you're right," she hissed, pulling her wrist back from Selma's grip and trudging forward. "But what am I supposed to do?"

"For starters, we could get the hell out of here," said Selma. "Find a new hotel, spend the next few days actually enjoying Paris."

"But what about…"

"What about it?" interrupted Selma. "What about your little plan to make you Miss Congeniality of the internet?

190

Fuck that, April. Not everyone is going to like you, and that's okay. If no one hates you, you're not doing it right."

Easy for Selma to say, she'd always been the tough one. She would have no problem telling Melissa Valentine to get lost. April, though, had too much at stake. She thought of all those unread messages piling up, all those anonymous people seeing the messy, chaotic bitch underneath the pantsuit. She doesn't want to lose her business, but she also doesn't want to prove them right.

"I don't want anyone to hate me," said April, shaking her head. "This can still work. Paul will figure out something."

Selma's eyes flashed dangerously. "Maybe Paul is not the solution to every single one of your problems," she snapped and stormed up the stairs, following Aamir into the apartment.

When they walked inside, April was surprised to see the toddler. Selma also was visibly taken aback and excused herself to use the bathroom. April hadn't imagined sophisticated Delphine as a mother, and she looked like some kind of "woman who has it all" stock photo with adorable Nico on her hip. The apartment effortlessly combined the French proportions of high ceilings and tall windows with sleek, comfortable furniture. It was elegant and homey, striking that perfect note of longing in anyone who entered. It was that note that April was always seeking when staging homes, and she had forgotten how powerful it was to be on the other end.

Now here they all are, wet and dazed and perched around the living room. April wears a towel over her shoulders like a shawl, and Gabriel has one turbanned over his damp hair. Selma's expression is stormy even while she's swathed in a gaily striped bathrobe. It can't be later than seven, but after everything that's happened it feels like 2:00 AM. It reminds

April of those after-parties in college, when no one wanted to stop drinking and go home alone, so they clung together until everyone either passed out or made a bad decision to carry them through the rest of the night.

At the Eiffel Tower less than an hour ago, Paul was her rock, but now he's on the floor making block towers with Nico. She's pretty sure that Delphine keeps appraising her with sharp eyes, or maybe someone with such perfectly arched eyebrows is incapable of looking another way.

While they drink wine and make stilted conversation about the rain, Delphine brings out a chic and simple spread of baguette topped with butter and radish slices, skinny twisted breadsticks upright in a glass, and a terra cotta bowl of big, green olives. April takes a piece of baguette and bites in, marveling at how the thick spread of butter mellows the spicy radishes, a sprinkle of coarse salt crunching between her teeth.

"This is amazing," April exclaims, feeling like an ignorant American.

Delphine looks around for a seat, finally perching on Aamir's knee. "*Merci*," she says so politely it's like a slap in the face.

Selma takes a breadstick but only snaps it in half without taking a bite.

Gabriel clears his throat dramatically and lifts his glass. "Everyone. So, that happened. Thanks to everyone for keeping me out of Paris jail. Even though I could have handled it, and I'm almost a little curious. But we have other things to figure out, which we will do. In the meantime, thank you to Delphine, our beautiful hostess, and to Aamir..." Gabriel's voice is a little husky and choked. "To Delphine and Aamir... damn, you two beautiful people make this all look very easy."

What is a young, worldly, single person like Gabriel seeing that moves him so much? Delphine, her angular body nestled into Aamir's lap, his hand comfortably on her hip. A Paris apartment with high ceilings and an eclectic mix of vintage furniture with IKEA basics. A beautiful toddler giggling as Paul playfully stacks blocks higher and higher. A fantasy of a happy home, except it's real. She lifts her glass and joins the toast.

Gabriel continues. "Thank you for the change of scenery. Thank you for the food and drink. *Santé*, my friends."

"*Santé*," April echoes. She's filled with longing, but what for? Does she want to be the chic woman with an adoring partner? Or maybe she wants to be the little child on the floor, surrounded by laughter, not constantly aware of the tension between mother and father that can snap at any moment.

They all drink to Gabriel's toast, and Aamir raises his glass. "To love," he says in a shy, heavily accented voice.

"To love," they all chorus.

Paul looks at her, his face soft and concerned, and April blinks away some stubborn tears. Before she lets her guard down under his caring regard, before she starts crying for the little girl who tried to make everyone happy, April turns brightly to Delphine and Aamir. "So, how did you two meet?"

Delphine smiles like April is a small child or a well-trained dog. April's read how French people consider it extremely rude to ask what someone does for work—maybe asking how they met their partner falls into the same mysterious category of tacky American conversation starters.

"We were very young, at a concert. I had a cigarette and needed a match. He had a match and needed a cigarette." Delphine shrugs, like this is the most obvious, boring story imaginable. April nods enthusiastically, feeling foolish, feeling the tears threaten to return.

Gabriel shakes his head wistfully. "So, you just...saw each other, and talked to each other? How do people *do* that? I mean, how did he know you were single, and straight, and not totally insane?"

Delphine carelessly waves her hand. "Then he would just have a cigarette and try again with the next pretty girl."

Aamir tightens his arm around Delphine's waist. "I know. I know she is for me."

"That's it, that's what I don't get!" says Gabriel. "How do people know these things? Whenever I see a guy that, you know, does it for me, I imagine going up to him and just saying hi, how's it going? And then, this guy, even in my dreams he looks at me like I'm a creep for bothering him while he's just trying to listen to a podcast on the damn L train, or his boyfriend who's sitting right next to him and I didn't even notice gives me this death stare and they start making out right in front of me." He cringes visibly just thinking about it, his white towel turban trembling.

As someone who talks first and often ends up cringing later, April is sympathetic. She tries to give Selma a wry smile before she remembers that Selma is mad at her, or maybe she's mad at Selma. Anyway, her friend is distracted by little Nico crashing a toy car into his blocks.

Gabriel leans back on the couch and sighs. "So then I go home and swipe through Tinder or Grindr, but then if I match with someone, all I can think about is how even if we do meet each other and hook up, then some little part of me for the rest of my life is going to be thinking about him, you know? Wondering if I'll walk into a party and he's there, and if he is, does he remember me, and is he there with another guy? And then I have to spiral into why he likes the other guy better than me, the neurotic weirdo he hooked up with one time." Gabriel polishes off his wine. "Why doesn't he love me?" he jokes, but with a catch in his voice.

Selma pats his hand. "That sounds exhausting."

Gabriel nods sorrowfully. Selma finishes her wine in one gulp, and her eyes narrow into that sharp, challenging look that April both loves and dreads. It's someone else's turn to get one of Selma's signature tough love lectures, though there's something worryingly dangerous about her mouth right now.

Selma's pats change to a firm grip on Gabriel's hand. "Honey, how old are you? 23?"

"24?" Gabriel answers hesitantly.

"Okay, that makes a lot of sense. Look, you and I are the only single adults in this room." April protests but Selma cuts her off. "And I would say the only queer ones, but I don't like to make presumptions. I am 42, I've been at this a lot longer than you, and I'm going to give you some advice." Gabriel nods, looking both scared and curious. "I'm not going to tell you that people aren't thinking about you as much as you think they are, or some bullshit like that. People are curious about other people, and we watch each other. I know when I'm at yoga, for damn sure I'm judging everyone else there. Because it would be unbearable if I didn't! Who wants to stay in their own head and think about their same stupid problems all the time? I'll still be worried about my saggy butt and lack of retirement savings tomorrow, so at least for now I can watch you trying not to fart during downward dog."

"Hear hear," yells April. This is the familiar Selma.

"So just accept that everyone is watching you and put on a good show. When you're meeting your Grindr guy for a drink, just assume that the married couple at the next table on a 'date night' ordered by their marriage counselor is eavesdropping, because they don't have anything to say to each other. Go with it. We're all playing a part, so just have some fun. If he's a dick, fuck him—literally or figuratively, your choice."

Gabriel listens very intently, squinting in concentration. "But what if…" he starts hesitantly. "What if he's nice? What if I like him?"

"Then he knows the game, too," says Selma. She slumps back on the couch, suddenly exhausted. "And you both keep playing your parts of nice boyfriends until one of you cracks. First person to let it slip that they're actually a bottomless pit of needs and wants loses. Then you press the reset button and start over with someone new."

An awkward silence. April swallows a lump in her throat at Selma, usually so larger-than-life, looking so tiny and tired. She isn't wrong, though. Wasn't that exactly what happened with April and Danny? When April wanted Danny to see her ugly parts and love her anyway, she realized he couldn't. Maybe no one can.

"I'm sorry, but that's terrible advice." Paul's voice startles April out of her thoughts. He slides up from his spot on the floor onto the couch, realizing only afterwards that he's now thigh to thigh and shoulder to shoulder with April. He studies her knees intently while April debates scooting over. Her body is already settled against Paul's, though, nestling into the familiar way that the two of them just *fit*. Paul gives a choked cough as April realizes she's burrowed in even closer, caught in Paul's gravitational pull.

Everyone waits expectantly for Paul to continue. Even little Nico must be wondering what is more important than block towers. Paul clears his throat, his jaw set with determination to get his words out.

"Gabriel, what Selma is telling you won't get you what you want. A good friend of mine told me that what women want is a man who knows how to take care of his plants." He scans the group, noticing their rapt attention. "At first, I thought he just wanted me to mulch my hydrangeas, but he's right. If you want love, you have to do the work. Maybe sometimes it's hard, or sometimes it's boring, but you don't give up, and then, if you're very lucky, your plant blooms for you. If it doesn't work out, and you water and prune and mulch and the plant still dies, well, life's terrible secret is that you'll survive. Maybe you'll be sad for a long time. But then someday you'll be ready to try again, even if it doesn't work out a second time." He pauses, gathering his thoughts, while the heat of his body travels through his jeans, though April's dress, into her chilly skin. "Because we're humans. And love is all there is."

The room erupts: Selma's protests, Gabriel's questions, Delphine's offer of more wine, Nico's bored whimpers, Aamir's French words of comfort. Only Paul and April are silent, though April's sure her thumping heart can be heard over the hubbub.

And love is all there is.

April has been pretty sure she wants to have sex with Paul for a few hours now (or maybe for twenty years) and his willingness to show his big romantic heart to a roomful of cynics clinches it.

And he wants to be friends. She'll show him friends.

April discreetly brushes her fingers over the back of Paul's hand. "Let's get out of here," she murmurs and watches those careful dark eyes spark in agreement.

Chapter 12

Paul

Paul's nerves are tightly wound all evening, his senses on high alert. The mineral smell of olives. The ticklishly soft rug when he sat on the floor. The edge of raspy tiredness in April's voice.

Cynicism is exhausting. Paul bristles remembering Gabriel and Delphine picking apart April in the taxi. Selma's lecture on the impossibility of true love, especially against the backdrop of Delphine and Aamir's happy home, is the last straw. She didn't say anything he hasn't thought before, but right now it feels like a crossroad, where he can either stay on the same meandering lonely path he's been on for years or veer off into an unknown route.

And now April wants them to leave together.

Paul thinks about that kiss all the time. What he doesn't think about, because it might wreck him, is April in that dark nook, raindrops spattered on her t-shirt, her eyes wild and her lips parted. Right now, with April so close to him that one of her amber waves tickles his neck, he'd give anything to teleport together to his hotel room with its big bed and locking door. And apparently, astonishingly, April wants the same thing. If the intensity of waking up in his room scared her this morning, she's over it. And Paul's sick of pretending he doesn't want every single thing she'll give him.

The rest of the group chats quietly, somehow oblivious to April's invitation hanging in the air. Aamir scoops Nico and carries him to bed, Gabriel is on his phone, and, well, now Selma is perched on Delphine's lap. He wants to turn that pairing over in his mind, but right now his sole objective is to leave this small gathering with April as discreetly as possible.

While Paul debates faking a phone call or maybe a medical emergency that can only be helped by someone with gray eyes and a wide grin escorting him to his hotel room, April rises. "Thanks for a lovely evening, Delphine. Paul and I are going to head out now." She offers a hand to pull him off the couch, and just like that, they're at the door.

"Bye," calls Gabriel, not looking up.

"À *demain*," murmurs Delphine, her gaze locked on Selma.

"Uber," says Selma, giving them an offhanded wave.

And that's it. Down the stairs, back to the rain, into a car. So much for Selma's theory that everyone is always observing you.

Paul is human, damn it. And love is all there is. And April smells like wine and rain and some herbaceous scent dabbed behind her ears.

They're quiet on the ride back to the hotel, but it isn't uncomfortable. It's peaceful, knowing what they each and what the other person wants, and it's all happening soon, so what is there to say? They squeeze into the tiny elevator, and April presses the button for Paul's floor. That feels right, too. They can redo that first awkward night, with April's messy attempt at seduction. They can redo everything. Maybe they'll even see the top of the Eiffel Tower from his window as it lights up against the night through the rain and fog.

Paul closes the door. Locks the lock. The room is dark, and he pauses for a moment, reading April's body for signs of hesitation.

April nods as she steps towards him. Paul reaches out, brushing a loose tendril off her cheek. The rain has changed April's hair into the curlier, wilder shape he remembers, and feeling it spring against his finger wakes some bottomless yearning inside him. He closes the distance between them, keeping one hand by her cheek and the other drifting down to the small of her back. For the second time in his life, he doesn't think and just kisses.

Once he starts, everything is easy. April's mouth smiles under his at first, but soon she relaxes in his arms, her lips parting against his like she has a secret, and the secret is that she wants more kisses.

They just kiss for a long time, holding each other in the middle of the room. Every time part of Paul's brain thinks to invite April over to the bed, or offer her a glass of water, he quickly loses his train of thought because kissing April is just completely perfect. He'll probably never stop. Their first kiss was like this, the feeling that time and space and reality were suspended, and all that mattered was being close to April, hearing her sighs, feeling her mouth on his mouth and her soft skin against his fingers. Except this time, they're all alone, and no one is going to stop them.

Paul wants more skin, more perfume, more April. His fingers brush the back of her neck, and she shivers. Is it desire, or hesitation? He draws back and looks at her with her swollen lips.

"Whatever you want, that's what I want, too," Paul says. "If you want to keep kissing, or move over to the bed, or order room service and watch a movie."

April grins wickedly. "I want to do all of those things. Starting with the second, and then the first. Definitely the third one later." She steps backwards, pulling him with her, and they fall onto the bed. Paul freezes a moment with how incredibly good it feels. Pressing up against April while standing was nice, but pressure and gravity and not having to focus on staying upright does wonderful things for him. He's suddenly aware that April's naked body is just underneath her thin dress and his own naked body, especially the growing hardness in his pants, is asserting itself. He adjusts himself to make it a little less obvious, but April's hands slide down his back, right onto his ass, and presses him into her.

"Hockey ass…" he thinks she mutters, but that doesn't make sense. Then he's lost in a helpless grind as her long legs wrap around him.

It's a lot, and it's happening fast. Paul thinks of himself as a considerate lover, doing his best to make sure his partner is comfortable and enjoying herself. If that constant wariness came at the expense of ever losing himself in the moment, well, that's just how it is. But when he props himself up on his elbows, brushing back April's hair and trying to read her expression, she sighs happily and arches up to kiss him again. He pulls back, enthralled by her neediness, and watches her reach for him.

"What are you…?" she protests. "Get back here. I waited twenty years for this, and you're going to make it worthwhile."

Paul brushes his fingers over her breast, tracing the hard nipple.

"April," he says hesitantly. "This doesn't feel real. I've thought about it for so long, and now that's happening, my twenty-two-year-old self is yelling at me to hurry up, and my forty-two-year-old self is telling me not to mess this up."

"Why not both?" says April.

Paul laughs. He can't remember the last time he laughed in bed with a woman, if ever. April's joy at being there with him, and her trust that he can make her feel good, makes him determined to be the man she sees. He's kissing her hungrily now, gripping her hair, her shoulders, her thighs.

His body is coming to life, like pins and needles in a sleeping limb, and it would hurt if it didn't feel so fucking good.

April

April knows about sex. She's a little out of practice, but you don't forget the basics—how to slow things down; how to moan helpfully when your partner stumbles on the right spot; how to bite your bottom lip and tousle your hair like a sexy underwear model.

But here, in this dark room with the rain still falling outside, she's in danger of forgetting everything she ever knew, from the *Cosmo* thing with the scrunchie to Selma's illuminating reasons why she should keep her fingernails very short. Because calm, competent Paul Stone is absolutely taking her apart with his kisses and his fingers and his wild, ragged breathing.

A hand gropes her back, searching for a zipper or buttons. She reaches to help but just tangles their fingers which is nice but doesn't move things forward. "Wait, wait," she finally gasps, and Paul immediately stills. "Buttons. Can you?" With Herculean effort she flops onto her stomach. Paul lifts her hair to kiss the back of her neck, then slowly, so terribly and wonderfully slowly, unfastens the ten buttons of her dress, delicately kissing each new bared inch.

They work together to pull it over her head, and April only gets stuck once, giggling helplessly with her arms pinned to her sides while Paul yanks this way and that, muttering curses. Freedom—and nakedness—are all the more glorious once she's released.

Paul spoons her from behind, kissing her neck, hands grazing over her breasts, her stomach, lightly tracing over the front of her underpants. "I want to watch you again," he says, his voice gravelly and a little dangerous. "I need to see your face again when you come. Please."

Please show me. Please. Those desperate, ragged words came to her over the years when she least expected them. They snuck up on her when she was listening to Danny pontificate about his new watch, or hopelessly scrolling through dating profiles. Hearing 'please' again from Paul, so rough and needy, breaks any last remaining defense she might have had. She's going to make this so good for him. For them.

April reclines luxuriously against the pillows, like one of the lush odalisques from the Louvre. Her fingers tease their way down. Paul is on his side next to her, his head propped up on one hand while the other circles her nipple.

When April finds the spot, already slick, she gasps. Paul's eyes never leave hers while he pinches and rolls her nipples, working them in a relentless rhythm that pushes her own strokes. Her blood pounds in her ears, but she can still hear his murmurs of *please* and *yes* and *so beautiful.* When she reaches that terrifying, wonderful point of no return, Paul holds her through her shudders and kisses her temple as her body goes limp. "That was perfect. You were perfect," he whispers into her hair.

"Pants off. Now," commands April once she can talk. Now it's her turn to peel away Paul's reserve and see him absolutely lose his mind.

"Absolutely. Um, I have condoms in the bathroom. I'm not presuming anything, but should I get one? And I didn't bring them thinking...this would happen. My sister always puts a few in my shaving kit when she comes over. Even when the ones from last time are still there."

April smiles. Discombobulated Paul is a blabbermouth, just like her. "Get the condom. Stop talking about your sister," she says sternly. Paul is obedient, tossing a condom on the nightstand. She shucks his pants and then, after a moment's hesitation, his underwear.

April likes what she sees.

Naked Paul is more confident than clothed Paul. He dives onto the bed while April unwraps the condom and rolls it on him with more wrist action than necessary. She needs him to catch up with her and cross that line to debauched.

"I want you to come again, with me inside you. I know how you look, now I want to know how you feel. I want to feel you all around me."

"Jesus," April groans. She's just as ready and desperate for him than if she hadn't been coming all over her hand a few minutes ago. "Better get to it, then." She pulls him on top of her and into her, and they both freeze for a moment with the cosmic revelation of how fucking good this is going to be. "Go," she hisses, and Paul starts thrusting, smooth and slow. He's everywhere, inside her, around her. His body covering hers, his breath in her ear.

He moves faster and she pushes against him, building towards something monumental that neither of them can take back. April gets there first, grinding against Paul with abandon as wave after wave of pleasure crashes over her. Paul isn't long after, and now it's April's turn to watch. He's on his elbows, flushed, eyes wild and black in the darkness. "Oh God," he pants as he comes. "April. My April."

April laughs. Or sobs. Or something in between. "My Paul."

Paul lays his head on her shoulder, catching his breath. "Don't go. Just stay with me, okay? Spend the night? Just don't go."

Those words are a splash of cold water on her loose, sated body. Paul isn't looking at her, his cheek still on her breasts.

"I won't go," she says. Not this time.

Part 3

Chapter 13

April

April stays.

She stays while Paul brings her a glass of water, somehow courtly while stark naked. She stays for his unhurried kisses over her neck and shoulders and drifts off to sleep as he makes his leisurely way across her collarbone. She stays to wake to the beginnings of gray morning light and feels Paul pressing against her back, an arm protectively over her waist, and she thinks *finally* before she falls back to sleep.

When she wakes again, the room bright and sun-dappled, she knows Paul is awake even though he is perfectly still behind her.

"Hi," she says, covering his hand with hers.

"April," he says, and it's groggy but still achingly happy.

"You're a good sleeping partner," she says. "No snoring."

"You're an excellent sleeping partner. You only hog the covers a little bit."

"Who, me?" April gives him a playful hip check, only to grind up against....oooh, yes.

"Anyone ever told you that your hypnic jerks are out of control?" says Paul, lightly dragging his fingers across her butt.

"My *what*?" April turns over to face him.

"Your hypnic jerks. It's when you're falling asleep, and your body does this involuntary muscle spasm. I had to hold on for dear life with all the twitching."

"I think you're a hypnic jerk." April experiments with a finger to his ribs. "Ah, ticklish," she says triumphantly.

Paul barks a laugh and tries to kiss her but kissing with morning breath is not on the table. She wriggles and giggles until he finally gives up aiming for her mouth and moves his morning kisses down between her legs until she isn't giggling any more.

April lies back on the crisp white sheets, her body as molten as the sunlight speckling the ceiling. So this is what it's like to be April in Paris. Graceful, happy, sexy...and then Paul does some combo finger-and-tongue move that short-circuits her brain.

"Okay, but..." she starts weakly when she remembers words again. "I really do have to brush my teeth. I think there's moss growing on my tongue. You can even come with me and kiss me as soon as I'm done."

Paul pulls on jeans and a soft-looking t-shirt and fishes April's dress off the floor. He buttons her up much more efficiently than he unbuttoned last night but distractingly smooths out the wrinkles with his big warm hands until they fall back on the bed.

"Is this how you iron clothes at your dry cleaners?" purrs April, pulling them both up to standing. "Come on. Toothbrush. Coffee." She tucks her underwear in her purse, picks up her loud yellow galoshes, and leads the way barefoot downstairs to her room, feeling Paul right behind her with a hand on her waist and lips grazing her hair. She tries not to smirk as they pad silently down the carpeted hallway like teenagers sneaking home after curfew.

And like a disapproving aunt, there is Selma cross-legged in front of April's door, also wearing yesterday's rumpled clothes. April freezes and then sways as Paul knocks her off balance.

"Oh, hello there," says April with elaborate casualness.

Selma shows a split-second flicker of surprise at Paul's hand on April's hip before standing and composing her face to neutral.

"Hi, Chickadee. Hi, Paul. I don't suppose you two are coming back from a morning jog."

"Nope," says April. "And I don't suppose you've been to morning mass at Sacré Coeur."

"Not a chance."

"Well then," says April.

"Well indeed."

April tries to have a stare-down but smiles first. The whole idea of her and Selma slutting it up in Paris in ways they only dreamed of twenty years ago is too delightful.

"Were you waiting for me?" she asks.

"My room key is in your purse. No one is at the front desk, and I thought maybe you'd popped out for *petit dejeuner*."

"Oh, shit. Sorry, Selm. You shouldn't give me these things to hold on to. Or you should wear clothes with pockets."

"And spoil the clean lines on this tunic? No, thanks. As soon as you excavate my key I'm off for a shower. So what's the plan for today? The Metro is closed from the strike. Which is something I would know if I'd tried to take it back to the hotel this morning."

Right. The morning light peeking through Paul's curtains. No rain. April automatically recites the familiar checklist to herself: recreate the kiss, save her reputation, and go back home to Liza. Two days ago, she'd have said there was no room in the plan for a night of hot sex, but everything is a little fuzzier now. She'd had sex with Paul because she wanted to, and because not having sex with him was a stupid waste. There's no reason they can't still find a way to get the promo done and figure out what the rest means later.

April opens her door, and Selma follows her inside. Paul lingers awkwardly at the door, like he's not sure if he's invited.

"Come in," she tells him, dumping the contents of her purse on the bed to find Selma's key.

"Nice panties," says Selma, scanning the detritus of the purse.

"Always good to carry around a spare. Here's your key."

"Thanks." Selma looks back and forth between Paul and April with a glint in her eye. "So, do you two need a practice-kissing coach? Wouldn't want it to look inauthentic for the lonely hearts out there."

"Maybe you should share why you went off on the concept of love last night, and then started canoodling with the lovely and terrifying Delphine."

"Yeah, sorry about all that," she says brusquely. "Exposure to domestic bliss has a weird effect on me. I feel the need to corrupt it." She shrugs. "The tot goes to bed early. I love an accent."

"Sweetie, I'm afraid their domestic bliss is off the charts now," says April. "And this is coming from someone who lived in superficial domestic bliss for years before realizing how miserable I really was."

April is surprised to feel Selma's small, warm hand slip into hers. "There's a lot of ways to be happy," she says. "You just need to pick one and give it a chance. And try not to listen to bad dating advice from your best friend."

Paul clears his throat hesitantly. "And, uh, did Gabriel…"

Selma steps back in horror. "Oh God, no. It was just a civilized little *ménage à trois*, not some depraved orgy. What do you think I am, Paul?"

Paul is adorably flustered, clearly pondering the fine line between *ménage* and orgy.

"No, my dears, Gabriel stayed a while after you left. Aamir tried to give him dating advice, but Aamir was speaking French, and Gabriel was speaking Spanish, so I'm not sure how much stuck. And then he got a bunch of texts and rushed out of there like his hair was on fire. Maybe the guy from the plane found him on Grindr."

April hopes that's the case. If everyone in their little group got laid last night, they will hopefully be in a good mood and ready to regroup and move forward. But for now, she really just wants to brush her damn teeth.

"Okay, well, bye, Selma. Congratulations on the sex."

"I'll draw some conclusions based on your purse panties and say you, too. Keep me posted. Bye, Chickadee." She pauses for a moment, looking at Paul, her face growing serious. "It's good to see you again, Paul. You turned out okay." And she slips out the door.

April turns to Paul, ready to laugh over Selma's escapade or her strange little benediction on the way out, but Paul is standing by the dresser with a soft, dreamy smile.

"April," he says. "You had it all along." His fingers trace something on the dresser, half-hidden under her sunglasses. "You kept the postcard."

He picks it up carefully, a little worn around the edges but still bright and cheerful, the girl and the yellow parasol and the Eiffel Tower. April flushes, like she's been caught in a lie. It's just a postcard, for God's sake.

"I did," she says. "I was going to show you. I always kept it, to remind myself it was real. The girl with the parasol, and the boy with the book."

Paul looks at the card again. "I never noticed him. The boy with the book." His thumb brushes the figure in the background, a dark-haired young man sitting on a picnic blanket with a book in his lap but looking up at the girl.

"I did," says April. "I noticed him, and I never forgot him." Something in her chest cracks as delicately as an eggshell and warmth flows to the tips of her fingers.

"You're still the girl with the yellow parasol to me," says Paul, and then April is in his arms being kissed like the dream girl in the picture, not a single mom with morning breath. April has never been kissed like she's the heroine in a book, and Paul's kisses are gentle and worshipful. It's wonderful, of course, but something about it felt almost ticklish. She pushes against him, looking for more pressure, something to ground her against his reverence. Clearly the postcard has a big impact on him, in fact...

"What if," says April, her words garbled against Paul's kisses until he dazedly pulls away. "What if we did the postcard? In a way, it's as much our story as that photograph. I'm the girl with the parasol, you're the boy with the book, the Eiffel Tower is right there in the background."

Paul blinks, his lips still twitching like they haven't gotten the message that kissing is on pause. April's excitement builds, though, and she rocks back and forth on her toes, her hands on Paul's chest.

"Do you get it?" she says. "We recreate the picture on the postcard for the ad campaign. In my interview, I'll talk about how you bought me the postcard, and I kept it all this time. People will like that, right? I have to tell Gabriel. And Selma.

What should I wear? Do you think we can find a yellow parasol or umbrella somewhere?"

Paul covers her hands with his, and she feels the thud of his heartbeat slowing under his soft t-shirt. "I know where to get a yellow umbrella," he says slowly.

"Really?" says April. She feels her smile growing so big her cheeks hurt. "Oh, Paul. I knew I kept the postcard for a reason. I'm so happy right now."

"I'm so happy for you," says Paul, but there's a slight worry crease between his dark eyes. "I'll make sure this works, April." He brushes his thumb along her jawline. "But just one thing. Could you give me an hour, just you and me, before we talk to Gabriel?"

"An hour or two for what?" April's eyes drift over to the bed, but Paul shakes his head.

"Later, I hope. Right now, I really have to show you something." He swallows. "I know the priority has to be the ad campaign, but last night was, to sum it all up in a huge understatement, amazing. And before we get caught up in all the Heart2Heart stuff again, I just want a little more time together."

April's surprised to realize she wants that, too. Maybe everything is going to work out after all—she can get a new photo, change the narrative online, and make up for so much lost time with Paul.

"Okay," says April, raking her fingers down his chest and watching with satisfaction as his eyelashes flutter. "But can I shower first?"

"I'll allow it," says Paul, his hands drifting down to her hips. "Meet me in the lobby in twenty."

"Whatever you say, sir," says April breathily. She nips Paul's ear, and he gives her a quick, hard kiss before heading out the door. Before he turns the knob, he looks back with those intense dark eyes.

"Don't be late," he says in a husky voice that sends a thrill down April's spine and walks out.

April hurries to the tiny bathroom and turns on the shower, catching sight of herself in the mirror. She's flushed, hair frizzing in all directions, a smudge of last night's lipstick on the corner of her mouth—in other words, a hot mess. And she feels incredible. Now that they had a workable Plan B, her mind is free to wander back to last night and how completely right it felt to wake up with Paul wrapped around her. They're going to have to talk at some point, because April wants more of Paul's quiet looks and hockey ass. She has no idea what that future could look like, though. For now, she can only think about one more stolen hour with Paul before they face reality.

Paul

Paul heads back to his room, catching a quick glimpse in the bureau mirror of a barely recognizable guy with a goofy smile and tragic bedhead. He's in the shower lathering up his chest and singing—singing!—so loudly that he almost misses his phone ringing. Katy Perry warbling "Last Friday Night" edges into his rendition of "Benny and the Jets" though, and he dives for a towel, barely getting it around his waist and dripping all over the floor as rushes into the room, his heart racing.

"Last Friday Night" is Tommy's ringtone. He'd ironically programmed it into Paul's phone himself after he got sober. Paul hates it but changing it would admit how he doesn't think the song is ironic at all. The clock reads just after 9AM, which means 2AM back home. In the past a 2AM call from Tommy could mean a ride to the ER after punching a wall, or another angry, drunken tirade about how Paul needed to get off his case. It's been years since that kind of call, but Paul instinctively braces for the worst.

It's a Facetime call. Paul tries to angle the phone away from his worried face and naked chest, and his voice comes out more brusquely than he intends. "What is it, Tommy?"

"Just checking in on you, bro. Making sure you've actually left your hotel room since you got there." A smile tugs at Tommy's mouth. Paul instinctively scans him as best he can on the tiny screen: no beer bottles in the background, pupils not dilated, not slurring. Something about his eyes, though, is especially bright and glittering.

"Isn't it, like, the middle of the night?" asks Paul. "Is everything okay?" Please let everything be okay. Paul just wants to dry off and meet April in the lobby without dealing with any drama back home.

"Yeah, yeah. I just couldn't sleep, and I felt like talking. I figured you'd be up with the time difference. I want to tell you something. Remember when we were kids, and Mom would watch *Roman Holiday* or one of those other old movies on TV? She would let us stay up for the whole thing because she said it was bad for our growth to go to bed before the happy ending. Anyway, I've been thinking about that a lot lately. Mom believed in happy endings."

Paul remembers that. She'd been strict about bedtimes except for those occasional nights when one of her favorite movies came on. He pictures her in her blue housecoat on their brown sofa, a twin snuggled at either side.

"She didn't get one," Paul says flatly. Why is Tommy calling him at 2AM to reminisce? Paul's optimism for the day ahead slowly leaks out of him, like he's a balloon and Tommy is a thumbtack.

"Maybe not," says Tommy. "But she still had faith they were possible. Maybe we can earn them. I mean, look at you in Paris, really going for it." On the screen, he nervously rubs his light brown hair and looks directly into the phone. "Have you ever been in love, Paulie?"

Something isn't right. He and Tommy don't talk to each other like that. Even over Facetime, Tommy is flushed and fidgeting.

"Are you drunk?" blurts Paul. Tommy flinches, but Paul keeps going, as if by talking he can keep the familiar panic at losing his baby brother under control. "Did you take something? Tell me you didn't drive."

"Jesus, Paul, what the hell are you talking about? It's been three years, and your mind goes straight there."

"What am I supposed to think? It's the middle of the night, and you want to talk about mom, and if love is real?

Come on. I know what it means when you're like this." So easy to fall back into old habits, hiding fear behind anger. In a strange way it feels good, after all the new emotions he's been hit by in the last forty-eight hours.

"That's what you really want, isn't it," says Tommy. "You want me to be drunk right now so you can come to the rescue. Dude, you're in *Paris*. Put that big old spotlight on yourself and ask why you're so focused on what you think I'm doing. You think about yourself."

"What's that supposed to mean?"

"It means...*fuck you!*" Tommy ends the call.

Damn it. Damn Tommy for dragging his mind back to real life. But also, damn Paul for being a total jerk. For a minute on the phone it was like Tommy needed him again.

Paul wants to tell Teresa to check on Tommy, but that would mean waking up Griff and Matty as well and having to explain exactly why he's accused Tommy of being on something. The evidence is flimsier and flimsier as he plays it back in his mind. Anyway, if Tommy's drunk, it's so late back home, he'll just sleep it off. Paul will call in the afternoon, just to make sure everything is okay.

Right now, though, he has more important things to do.

Last night—and this morning, too—was incredible. April was as joyful and warm in bed as she is out of it, along with something else Paul hadn't seen before until he had smoothed her sweaty hair back and peered into her eyes in the dark. She'd been so still, taking in every bit of him, that he'd thought for a moment maybe everything would just work out.

Knowing that he and April have one more hour together before moving onto her new plan, Paul grins stupidly, sprawling mostly naked on his bed. He'll take her to that special place, the one where he keeps picturing her. Then they will take a picture, not one up on the tower but something closer to earth signifying how they've been connected all these years, with April keeping the postcard. Not the kiss photo, which was also the photo of just before April left. For this picture, he will sit next to her and smile, and then afterwards they'll talk and figure out some way to keep being the girl and boy on the postcard.

Paris, France 1999

"Selma, please come with me. What if he's secretly an ax murderer?" pleaded April. She was already late.

"Then meeting him at the Eiffel Tower is about as safe as you can get. Just don't go with him to a second location, like Oprah says." Selma was lying on the bottom bunk in their hostel where she fit perfectly, unlike April whose feet hung off the top bunk. "I already told you, I don't want to be a third wheel, I'm tired from the Catacombs, and I don't like heights. Just let me stay here with the guidebook and figure out the best hostel in Prague."

April slid off the top bunk with a thud. "Please?" Her voice quavered, and Selma opened her eyes.

"Hand me my shoes," she said. "I don't know why you're so nervous, though."

April wasn't nervous about seeing Paul again. She was downright scared, and not because she thought he was bringing an ax. Already she couldn't stop thinking about him, and they hadn't even kissed. Yet. Yesterday felt like a dream, from crashing into Paul on the street to locking eyes in the dim sanctuary. Meeting him again today would make it all real, for better or for worse.

As Selma put her shoes on, April imagined what advice her mother would give her right now. Not that her advice was objectively any good, but it was the only way that April could still hear her mother's voice. The two of them at the kitchen table while her father worked late, her mother chain smoking and talking too fast. Sharon telling her everything she was going to do, was going to be, if only she hadn't been trapped into marriage by Hank Andersen. She was going to travel, and feed starving orphans in Africa, and start a band in Berlin.

She would have had plenty of boyfriends to buy her things and take her dancing. If only she hadn't gotten pregnant when she was twenty-one and married the guy. April should never let a man tie her down like that.

Even at thirteen, April saw the flaws in Sharon's argument. That advice, though, recited to her so often, stuck in her head like an incantation.

April didn't want to meet a nice guy right now. She'd overheard years of screaming and pleading, and saw Hank slowly withdraw from his wife and daughter until he was a silent shell. When April was fourteen and her mother left for good, it was one of those days where Hank had decided to try again with a big bouquet of red roses. When he realized she was gone, he threw the roses on the floor, stamped on them until their potent sweetness filled the room, stormed into his room and shut the door. He didn't come out until the next day while the cloying smell went from fresh and floral to tinged with decay. April didn't clean them up because it was the only sign of her mother left in the house.

When Hank came out, he didn't say Sharon's name until two years later when they got that call that she had been hit by a truck while biking, just a few hundred miles away in Provincetown. And then he went back to never saying it, and to minimizing his contact with the daughter who looked and sounded like her.

"Are you coming or what?" April snapped back to the present moment, where Selma was standing impatiently by the door.

April was going to hurt a man someday. She already knew this, and even after just one day with Paul, she didn't want it to be him. But not to show up at all was unspeakably cruel in its own way. She would meet him, with Selma in tow, go up and look at the view, and tomorrow get on that train to Prague.

Chapter 14

April

Before she heads downstairs to meet Paul, April thinks about checking Instagram. She's too happy to deal with all that crap right now, she decides as she pulls on a blue batik skirt and a t-shirt she stole from Liza with a big Huy Fong Sriracha label. Soon Gabriel and his PR machine will redirect the conversation, and she can go back to her old life, turning homes that reek of despair into something aspirational.

But what about a whole life that reeks of despair? whispers a tiny voice from deep inside. April pauses, one sandal on, and sits heavily on the bed. The joy from last night with Paul is like a flashlight, exposing the dead space and cluttered corners of her life back home. And she isn't sure there are enough throw pillows in the world to fix it.

April wants to hear Liza's voice, but it's 2AM in Massachusetts. She wants to talk to her father, but besides the time difference, she knows speaking to him always starts off hopeful and leaves her feeling worse. She wants to talk to her mother, but that's impossible.

Thinking of her mother brings that familiar flutter in April's chest. She knows from experience how quickly it can grow into panic if she isn't careful. Deep breaths, apply lipstick with a steady hand. Count backwards from ten, then start again. Throw her hair into a ponytail, put on sunglasses, and head downstairs to meet Paul. Avoid the claustrophobic elevator. Avoid any mirrors to remind her how much she looks like her mother right now, burning with nervous energy.

And downstairs, see Paul, feel her heart lift at his reliably strong shoulders and serious mouth. Slip her arm into his and say, "So where are you taking me, my mysterious Winnipegatonian?"

"I regret to say we call ourselves Peggers," he says, and April giggles. She's always giggling around Paul.

Paul and April leave the hotel and walk slowly, arm in arm, making small observations about the smells from the bakery, the rattan chairs lined in front of the cafés, the carefully dressed old women walking their little dogs. It's late morning on a Friday, but the streets are full of people attending to the small duties and pleasures of the day.

As they stroll, the neighborhood grows more elegant, with residential buildings giving way to high-end shops. There are less women with shopping bags and more tourists in sneakers. A flash of color catches April's eye, and she stops in her tracks, drawn in by the sight.

"This is what you wanted to show me," she says—not a question—and squeezes Paul's arm. He squeezes back and flashes her a crinkly eye smile, making something in her chest spark.

In a row of elegant sandstone storefronts, one has tall, graceful arches revealing a passageway between buildings. The tops of the arches are lined with colorful umbrellas, their open tops facing the street in pops of fuchsia, orange, yellow, and robin's egg blue. April sees more bursts of color inside the entrance.

"Shall we?" says Paul, adorably a little nervous.

"Yes, please," says April, whispering like they're entering a church.

April and Paul walk through the arch and into another world. It's a stylish, open-air mall of fancy boutiques and smart cafes, but April only has eyes for the rainbow canopy of umbrellas suspended in midair, completely enclosing the passageway. Individually, they are utilitarian, fabric on a steel frame with a sturdy handle. All together, though, they are art, and she feels her goofy wide grin spreading on her face.

"It's called Umbrella Sky," says Paul. "It's by a Portuguese artist named Patricia Cunha. She goes all around the world arranging umbrella installations–over eight hundred just in this one."

"Like Christo meets Mary Poppins," sighs April.

She's still taking it all in. The sun shines through the umbrella canopy like a stained-glass window, throwing a colorful riot of shadows on the pavement. April sees with delight that her arm is splashed with orange, then yellow, and she twirls for Paul to see the changing vividness reflecting off her skin. The colors and shadows create a wonderland, and the hidden passageway is a magic spot in the middle of Paris where ordinary rules don't apply.

"I knew you'd like it," says Paul and gives her a quick, shy kiss on the cheek. "The day I got to Paris, I was so anxious, and I just walked all over the city. I was trying not to think about you and all of a sudden, I wandered into this, and it was like all my memories of you had manifested right in front of me."

God, her mother would have loved this. She would have said, "April, I want to live in an umbrella house, just like this. It's like being inside a bouquet of lollipops." And April's father would have to say something about how wet you would still get in the rain, with the imperfect coverage of the umbrella canopy.

April doesn't usually remember her mother being happy. The primary memory is Sharon hunched over the kitchen table, voice scratchy with cigarettes as she recites all her grievances. There was so much more, though. She and April would also sing along to her Heart records, pouring every ounce of emotion into "Crazy on You" and "Barracuda." April would make them tuna sandwiches for dinner, and Sharon would set out cloth napkins and light candles. More than once, she woke April up to see a particularly beautiful sunrise, silently wrapping her in an afghan and leading her outside, never letting go of her hand as they watched the tender violets and yellows fade into day.

April doesn't want to be frightened of disappointing people anymore. Her mother had so many beautiful qualities, but her father was too conventional to see them. If Hank looks at April and only sees something that he can't understand, well, then maybe April should stop trying so hard. Maybe she's okay just as she is.

And here is Paul, beaming at the sight of her bathed in blue and yellow and purple. His own face is splashed with green and indigo. If Paul looks at her and sees someone special, well, maybe he's right? She'd been too young the first time they met, too caught up in her own vision of what a fling in Paris should look like. If the last twenty years have taught her anything, it's that perfect moments like she and Paul keep having are a rare and sacred thing. She has no idea what a future with Paul could look like, and how their lives in different countries could ever be combined. But for the first time, she's not scared to dream about it. She steps into his arms and kisses him hard, their colors coming together in a beautiful mosaic.

Paul

Paul could look at April looking at the Umbrella Sky all day. Now, the whole world can see how she looks to him, radiating joy and flashes of color that change as she moves and talks and smiles.

After she kisses him, he's so happy he can hardly breathe. "You look like you belong here," he says, words inadequate for how he wants to remember this moment forever. "April in Paris."

"But it's June, silly," she laughs and strides ahead through a side passageway, the prism of umbrellas stretching in every direction. Paul follows, pulled forward by April's momentum. He watches her silhouette against the Umbrella Sky. Even from behind, her crackling liveliness is still obvious in her quick steps and wild curls.

Paul is so captivated that he almost crashes into her when she stops short (like the first time they met on the sidewalk, like the second time in the pharmacy. Maybe colliding with April is just part of being around her.)

"Steady there, cowboy. Wait a sec," April says, fishing around in her bag, which was the color of a lime and woven from straw. She manages to dig out her phone. "I need to get a picture for Liza." She snaps multiple photos, moving around to catch different angles and dropping to a knee at one point.

If April is thinking of her daughter, no doubt she's remembering her life back in Massachusetts. April has a career and a house and a family. Even if they didn't live in different countries, would she want someone like Paul in her life, whose only friends are his siblings and his equally lonely neighbor, and whose job revolves around convincing athleisure-wearing Millennials that dry cleaning is worth their time? Though Tommy is going to change all that, isn't he, with his apps and Prosecco and probably karaoke nights and a disco ball unless Paul steps in.

Tommy. Paul cringes thinking of their fight earlier. He'll text Tommy once he gets back to the hotel and make sure he's okay. Paul tries to take care of people, even when they act like they don't want him to. At least April still needs him for another day, and if he's lucky she'll need him the day after that, and then maybe one more?

April, practically lying on the ground to get some new angle on the umbrella canopy, smiles and holds out her hand. He pulls her up with a little too much force, and they stagger and laugh against each other until they regain their balance.

"Say umbrella!" says April, stretching out her arm with the phone for a selfie. Paul hasn't stopped laughing or looking at April, can't stop looking at her as her eyes reflect the entire rainbow. She looks back at him and leans over to whisper against his skin, "I don't ever want to forget this."

She snaps a photo.

"I couldn't if I tried," says Paul, gently taking April's phone and slipping it into her purse. "I never could."

They stand there, not quite kissing but feeling each other's closeness, until Paul realizes they're blocking half the passageway. A fearsomely elegant *jolie laide* in what even Paul can tell is a Chanel suit harrumphs as she squeezes by.

"How about some coffee for the walk back?" he says, reluctantly disentangling himself from her long arms.

"Always," says April, sneaking in a last pat on the butt that makes Paul swallow hard.

"Be right back." And he is, just a few minutes later, with two lattes and a mysterious paper bag under his arm that's a secret, maybe he'll show April later if she's a good girl, which means no slipping her hand into the back pocket of his jeans, or maybe just for a minute, but they really should get going and tell Gabriel about the new plan.

"So, tell me about Liza," he says while they sip their coffees and stroll. "I mean, if it's okay for me to ask about her."

"It's okay," says April. "Liza is…well, she's both my twin and my polar opposite. She's always quoting Coco Chanel, you know, 'Before you leave the house, look in the mirror and take one thing off.' I've always been more of a 'Add three more things' person."

April trails off, and Paul tries to read her face. Liza's name must be a sharp reminder of April's real life, thousands of miles away. Paul has never knowingly dated someone with children.

"How did she feel about you coming on this trip?" asks Paul.

"She was pretty excited about it. I haven't dated much since my divorce, partially because I didn't want to traumatize her, but she was ready to act as my matchmaker and my agent to get me here."

Paul nods, but he's not sure. Aren't twelve-year-old girls unreliable narrators? Teresa was twelve when Paul returned from that first trip to Paris, and those months of watching their mother slowly lose control of her body turned his little sister from a shy homebody to a sullen teenager who communicated mostly in eye rolls.

"I miss her like crazy," says April, giving a sad, adorable little sniffle. "She's why I'm here. Not just because she wanted me to, but because I need to keep my business going and not be some crazy lady on the internet." She glances at Paul. "Does that sound terrible, to say that she's why I'm here? Because I'm so glad I came."

"Not terrible at all," says Paul. "You sound like a good mom." After he says it, he realizes how true it is. April is a mother before anything else. She might not have space for him in her life. But that thought slips out of his mind as they walk, heads bowed together, April smelling of sunshine and coffee. Paul leads them back to Hotel Voltaire easily, his steps sure and his sense of direction keen. He carries April's present under one arm and guides her with the other. He can't wait for her to open it and smile her sexy jack o'lantern smile just for him.

As they round the corner, Paul sees Gabriel pacing the sidewalk in front of the hotel. He squeezes April's arm and gestures with his chin until she sees him too and nods, eager to share their idea. Paul should be used to Gabriel pacing dramatically by now, but something about the scene looks off, and uneasiness gnaws in his stomach. As they get closer, Paul can tell Gabriel has been up all night, and not in a sexy way. He wears his same black clothes from Delphine's, the coat rumpled and the shoes muddy, and the swoop of his hair is flat on one side. He's holding a cigarette with a long cone of ash on the end and striding in tight circles, continually looking at his phone, starting to rub his eyes, and startling himself with the lit cigarette.

Gabriel doesn't notice them until they are almost at the perimeter of his pacing circle. A quick moment of relief is quickly replaced by his usual sharp tongue. "Jesus, don't you two ever read your texts?" he snaps, but there's an unfamiliar wobble in his voice. "I've been trying to find you all morning. The concierge said you both went out ages ago. Oh my God, I'm so fucked."

Paul pulls his phone out guiltily and sees the string of texts from Gabriel. He looks at April who shrugs.

"Sorry Gabriel, I saw you texted a few times, but I figured we'd be back soon, and it would be easier to talk in person," she says. "Paul and I figured out a great new plan. While it doesn't literally recreate the original photo on the Eiffel Tower, it truly captures the essence in a way that might be even more authentic than…"

Gabriel cuts her off with something between a sarcastic laugh and a choked sob.

"What's wrong?" she asks. "Is it going to rain again?"

"Rain. If only," says Gabriel. He runs his fingers through his hair, which is in a wild pouf where it isn't flat. "It's over."

Paul doesn't like any of this. "What are you talking about? What's over?"

Gabriel leans back against the hotel facade and slides down the wall until he's sitting on the dirty sidewalk. "Everything," he says with a painful, incredulous laugh. "The app. The photo shoot. Paris. My career. Janice said the Feds showed up at Sergei's apartment in the middle of the night with a search warrant, but he was already on a flight home to Kazakhstan with what's left of the investors' money. Heart2Heart is done, and I'm lucky if I don't go to jail."

Paris, France 1999

The Eiffel Tower was crowded that day. In his well-thought-out itinerary, made in his bedroom back in Winnipeg, Paul planned to visit the Eiffel Tower early on his last day, as the pinnacle of his trip. He thought carefully about avoiding crowds in order to get the best view. But after meeting April, none of those fussy things were important. The crowds were festive, like a carnival.

It was the golden hour when they bought their tickets to go up. The late afternoon sun brushed the whole city with warm light. Even Selma looked soft and luminous in the glow as she refused to let Paul get her a ticket. "I'll stay down here and find a falafel vendor," she said. "I don't do heights."

The elevator was packed, and even Paul was feeling unpleasantly crammed and jostled as they rode up. He stayed close to April so he wouldn't lose her in the crush. Fortunately, April stood out. At least he couldn't take his eyes off of her. She was taller than most of the other tourists, and while she'd changed out of her cut-offs into a plain black slip dress over a white t-shirt, the late afternoon sun had transformed her hair from dark bronze to burnished gold.

When they stepped out on the top deck, Paul felt April's hand grip his tightly. They let the crowd sweep them towards the barrier and caught their breath at the same time as the famous view revealed itself. The streets, alternately winding and geometric. The Seine sinuously dividing the city. The golden light everywhere, dripping off white buildings and lighting up the river.

Paul turned to April, who was so close to him that their bodies pressed together. The light picked up her faint freckles, and he brought his hands to her face, lightly sweeping his thumbs over her cheekbones. It was a perfect moment in itself, seeing and being seen high over the City of Lights. But April's lips parted slightly and without even thinking about his hands or his breath, Paul closed the last few inches between them and kissed her.

Surrounded by hundreds of people, he kissed her like they were all alone. The crowd moved around them, seeming to not see them or not care, and April's lips were so warm and soft and tasted like honey. Paul never wanted this to end, but his damn mind kept straying to the future, when he would be home, responsible for a sick mother, pre-teen twins, and two dry cleaning locations. He tried to stay in the moment–warm, soft, honey–but the panic was rising, and he pulled back.

"April," started Paul. She opened her eyes, the evening light sparking flecks of gold in the gray. He shouldn't talk. He should just keep kissing her, but the idea of never feeling this again was too much to bear. "I had this premonition I'd meet someone in Paris. But it was a selfish feeling, like, it's my turn, time for something good to happen for me. Meeting you was the opposite. I want to give you everything, wrap up this view so no one else can have it and put it in your pocket to keep forever."

April was still so close, he could see her dark brown eyelashes. She started to say something and swallowed, digging her fingers into his shoulders. "You aren't selfish," she finally said.

"I don't want this to end," said Paul. "I know we just met, but you're the best thing that's ever happened to me. I can't imagine you being out there and not knowing what you're doing. I want to write to you and call you and come visit you in the States if you'll let me." April tensed in his arms, her fingers gripping his shoulders so hard now it should have hurt, but the idea of her stepping away hurt more. "Say you'll let me." He barely recognized his own voice, deep and gravelly with need.

April pressed into him, burying her face in his shoulder while he wrapped his arms around her waist. Paul felt her sigh, her hot breath against him, and he tried not to squeeze her while he waited for her answer. Finally, he felt rather than heard a murmur of "okay" into his neck as she slumped against him. He let himself hold her as tight as he wanted, barely registering that if he let go, she would have slipped to the ground.

Chapter 15

April

April doesn't understand.

"What do you mean, Heart2Heart is done?" she demands as Gabriel just stares at the pavement in front of him. "You didn't even hear our plan for the new photo. You'll love it–it's fun and whimsical and references that first meeting from a fresh angle."

She waits for Paul to chime in, but he's nodding studiously at Gabriel like he's working out a tricky math problem. Does Paul think if he just stands there looking handsome and befuddled, everything will somehow work out?

"I was going to tell you earlier, but Paul asked me to wait," she adds. Why doesn't Paul say something?

"April," says Gabriel from the sidewalk, leaning back against the brick building to look up at her. "You don't get it. This is over. There is no more Heart2Heart, and thousands, well maybe dozens of active singles will no longer find love. The Feds are going through the company records as we speak, and I've got a sinking feeling they're going to find this was Sergei's plan all along."

"The plan was to sink the company and run off with the investors' money?" asks Paul. "But you had an office in New York. And a website."

Gabriel stands up, accepting a hand from Paul, and brushes off his dusty pants. "Yeah, well," he says, resuming his pacing. "Any ten-year-old can have a website, Paul. But you have to believe me, I really thought I could fix things. Ronnie and Sergei said it was just a rough patch, but I should have known they were desperate when they hired an equally desperate brown guy who would work for cheap. I was supposed to get them good PR which they could channel into a pitch for the series B financing."

"And that's where we came in," says Paul.

April starts to understand, or at least she feels her stomach lurch.

"Every company demands to go viral," continues Gabriel, still a blur of movement making April seasick. "Like you can just snap your fingers and get 500,000 retweets. They have no fucking idea. I tried everything. I knew time was running out. I was about to catfish Anderson Cooper as his high school crush when I saw a sweet little photo from the previous century of some kids kissing on the Eiffel Tower."

"But we have a new idea," repeats April. "I wanted to tell you right away, but Paul said to wait." Gabriel just has to understand that they can still do this. They don't need a camera crew or make-up. They can go to the Eiffel Tower esplanade right now, far from the strikers, and Gabriel can take the fucking picture on his phone.

"So what happens next?" asks Paul. He's still maddeningly calm. "We just…go home?"

"That is precisely correct," says Gabriel. His gaze darts back and forth between them, something unhinged and a little scary in his elegant face. "I still don't think you guys quite get it. They froze all company assets and canceled my corporate card. I don't know how we're going to pay for the hotel rooms. At least I booked round trip tickets home."

The cavalcade of words break through April's stupor. *Closed up shop. No Eiffel Tower. No ad campaign.* Less than an hour ago she stood under the enchanted umbrella canopy, where everything felt possible, but now...

"No!" she manages to say. "No. This is unacceptable. You have to fix this, Gabriel. You told us to come to Paris, you said you could help me, so do it."

"April," says Paul, "I know you were counting on this, but we'll have to find something else."

How is Paul so fundamentally decent, with his soft t-shirts and his patience with Gabriel's stupid story? Not like April, whose confusion is giving way to white-hot rage. Something is slipping out of her grasp, and the harder she tries to hold on, the quicker it slithers away.

"Nope," she says. "We already have a new plan. We should have told Gabriel right away, Paul. If you hadn't made me go see the umbrellas, we'd have already taken the picture."

"April..." starts Paul, reaching for her hand, but she flinches away. She can't stand for anyone to touch her right now. A vein in her head throbs, and her skin feels hot all over.

"April, believe it or not you are not my main concern right now," snaps Gabriel. "I have nothing to go back to in New York, and I cut some corners to make this trip happen, which won't look good in a serious audit. I'm not your savior to get back in white lady America's good graces." He looks April up and down, and she feels him seeing beyond her lipstick and cute outfit into the dark, hungry part that feeds on praise and attention and is never satisfied.

Gabriel laughs bitterly. "Maybe we both got what we deserve. I tried to convince people that they could be less lonely if they tried our dating app, and it was total bullshit. But you're worse than me because you'll do anything just to look good to people you don't even know. Your so-called scandal would have blown over in a week or two, but you'd rather drag people that care about you into some kind of fake fairy tale."

April is furious. Her jaw clenches and her eyes narrow as she stares Gabriel down. How dare he go back on his word! How dare he say those things about her! She feels that ugliness deep within her coming out, the red-faced, incoherent, rage-filled woman who looks and sounds so much like her mother.

"You don't know me," says April menacingly. "You have no idea what my life is like. I have a business, and a daughter to support. I'm not some kid playing at being a big shot in the big city. I came here to get that picture. That's all I care about. So you can help me, or you can go fuck yourself."

Gabriel shakes his head. He's calm now, unsettlingly so. "I choose B," he says. "Sorry, Paul. You're a good guy. I shouldn't have gotten you mixed up in this." Gabriel storms into the hotel, almost knocking over the bellhop.

April spins around back to Paul. A dark flush creeps up the back of his neck, and his hands are jammed hard in his pockets. April's head hurts, and she has a twisting feeling in her belly seeing herself as a passer-by would: an angry, messy woman driving people away.

Paul takes his hands out of his pockets and raises them in surrender before April can flinch away again. "I'm sorry," he says.

April would rather he yell, or storm off, or even throw something at her. Instead, he's giving her the same calm blankness her father always gave her mother when Sharon just needed him to feel something, to take on some of her overwhelming emotions so she wouldn't have to bear them all.

"I shouldn't have gone with you this morning," says April. Paul winces, and she hates herself.

"A couple of hours wouldn't have made a difference," says Paul. The flush on his neck spreads to his ears but not to his face. Maybe that means he's angry underneath it all. April hopes so.

"Maybe it would have," she snaps. "You don't know. I thought you were here to help me."

"April…" starts Paul.

"No, I mean it. I shouldn't have come here. This was all such a mistake."

"Maybe," says Paul.

April startles. She expects him to keep trying to calm her down, to bury her feelings and stop yelling on the sidewalk. Paul notices she's at a temporary loss for words, and he keeps going.

"Maybe it was a mistake," he says, "But I don't regret anything. My brother says I should take a hard look at myself instead of worrying about other people, but I don't want to do that. I like thinking about you, and what I can do to make you happy. I don't know how to fix this, though. I'm sorry."

The anger leaks out of her like her Instant Pot on slow release, and April feels sick with shame. She can only look at Paul's feet, his clean sneakers and neatly tied laces.

"Please go away," she whispers. She hears his intake of breath like he's going to protest and then her own voice, brittle and thin, "Please."

The sneakers step closer. "I'm leaving," says Paul's voice. "Take this. Don't worry, I'm not going to touch you. I just… well, I really wanted this to work."

April takes the paper bag without looking up. The sturdy sneakers walk out of sight. She stands there for a moment, too drained to move, feeling the shape of the bag. She knows what it is, and the realization kicks her in the gut.

She forces herself to open the bag and look inside, like pressing on a wound. It is a yellow umbrella, like the beautiful, useless ones of Umbrella Sky. Like the girl on the postcard she'd kept all these years. Paul remembers her as that girl–pretty, bewitching, nothing dark or messy behind her wide smile. She'd almost believed it, too.

Paris, France 1999

April kept her face on Paul's solid shoulder, listening to the hum of the crowd and Paul sighing in her hair. Right here, on the top of the Eiffel Tower, kissing and talking about the future, should be the happy ending, she thought. The culmination of the movie montage. Maybe the credits could start rolling while they clung to each other and the sun set over the city. Before real life went on, and she screwed it all up.

April opened her eyes. From this high up the city flattened into a map of itself, the streets and buildings just lines and curves. Only yesterday, she and Paul had wandered Paris, but she couldn't relate those charming nooks and alleyways to anything from up there. There must be hundreds of couples too small to see thinking they were discovering the real Paris. Paris was full of young lovers. April wasn't special.

"What do you see?" asked Paul, moving so they stood hip to hip looking out over the railing. He looked a little sad, and April realized Paul always looked a little sad.

"Everything," said April. And nothing. They agreed when they met not to talk about life back home, but Paul had broken the pact. He wanted to keep in touch, to visit, to learn everything about her. And she, in turn, would learn why he was a little sad, and she didn't think she could bear it.

"Everything," repeated Paul, like April had said something wise instead of fumbling. "I think you're everything." He leaned in to kiss her again, and it already felt so terribly familiar, so dismayingly right. If their last kiss felt like the end of a movie, this one felt like real life. Paul's hand was sweaty, April's nose itched, but they were kissing like a conversation. It was wonderful and unbearable at the same time. It was like touching a hot stove, where you know it will hurt so much worse once you take your hand off.

April broke away "We should head down," she said. "Selma's been waiting for a while."

"Sure," said Paul. "Let's crash back down to earth."

The sun had set, and much of the crowd swarmed towards the elevators at the same time. An elevator came and was quickly filled to capacity while people around them shoved and pushed. April felt herself moved by the surge of bodies, like all she had to do was go limp and let the crowd carry her. Her hand slipped out of Paul's, and she didn't turn around. She caught another wave of bodies flowing into the next elevator. The doors closed. "Paul?" she asked, but she knew he wasn't there, and no one could hear her anyway.

When they finally hit the ground level, April sidestepped the elevator crowd, watching them stream by. Now that she was free from the crush, she was gasping for air. She stumbled back to the Esplanade to find Selma reclined on the grass.

"Honey, are you okay?" asked Selma, hopping up. "You look like you're having a panic attack."

"I'm fine," said April. "No, that's not true. I'm not fine. Selma, let's go to Prague tonight. If we go now, we can grab our bags at the hostel and make that night train."

Selma looked concerned for a moment, but the pull of a new adventure was too much. "Brilliant," she said. "Let's do it."

Paris was full of lovers. April wasn't special. But she couldn't bear for Paul to realize it.

Chapter 16

Paul

Paul doesn't go back to his room. He can't handle seeing the bed where he'd curled around April just this morning. He has nothing to offer her now, not if they can't pose for a happy picture. He sounded calm and measured when he said he would make a plan, but inside he was unsteady and just trying to buy some time.

Gabriel is back on his phone, grimacing and waving his free hand. Paul slips down the street to a café and parks himself at one of the more shielded outdoor tables. He considers ordering a glass of wine, or even better a shot of tequila, but sticks with his usual cafe crème. The coffee arrives quickly, and he makes a big ceremony of stirring and crumpling sugar packets before realizing he has no desire to drink it.

He's tapping the cup with his spoon, annoying even himself, when he sees a tall man striding by with a toddler on his shoulders. It's Aamir the photographer and his little son Nico, and Nico is happily licking an ice cream cone that's already dripping down his arm. Paul sits perfectly still, blending into the background, and the pair pass by him as they chat and laugh and drip a trail of melted ice cream.

Paul is relieved to avoid a conversation right then but also a little deflated. Seeing the happy father and son pair just reminds him how alone he is. Not just alone, but lonely.

Paul's phone buzzes. He wonders for a second if it might be April, calling him to say...what? That she still wants to see him, ad campaign or not?

It's Teresa. As much as Paul doesn't want to talk, he always picks up for family.

"Hey, everything okay?" he asks.

There's silence on the other end and finally an intake of breath, like she's trying to calm down enough to get some words out.

"Oh, Paulie, I'm so glad I got you," says Teresa in a quavering voice. It's been a long time since she called him Paulie, and he pictures her ten-year-old self cajoling him to buy her candy.

"What's wrong? Is Matty okay?"

"Matty's fine," she says, and Paul has a quick moment of relief before she continues, "It's Tommy. There's been an accident."

Paul's brain sputters, trying to make sense of her words. An accident. That word means everything from peeing your pants to dying a violent death.

"What do you mean an accident? What happened, Tree?"

"I'm still not sure. He was driving somewhere—it was 3AM and the roads were empty—and they think he swerved to avoid an animal or something. They took him to St. Joe's. He's still unconscious, Paulie."

Paul's gut twists. He knew Tommy was angry after they talked, and it turns out he'd been angry enough to get in his car. "He was drunk, wasn't he," says Paul before he can stop himself.

Teresa pauses. "I don't know," she says, and Paul hears her shock that he's already focused on blaming someone. "I hope not."

"At least he didn't hurt anyone else. They'll send him back to jail, Tree. I need to call his lawyer from last time." Paul's been so wrapped up in his own drama that he hadn't done the simplest thing after Tommy's suspicious call. He should have told Teresa to check on Tommy, or called the Winnipeg police, or something.

"Paul, let's just focus on Tommy waking up again, okay?" says Teresa with a shrill edge to her voice.

"You focus on that," says Paul. "I'll see what I can do to save his ass. I'll get a flight home tonight."

"I hate to make you leave your big reunion. But I really need you." Teresa is crying softly now.

"It's all over," says Paul, and it sounds dark and ominous. The staged reunion is over, but everything else is over, too— the spark, the hope, the feeling that he can return home different than he left. "I'll call the airline now. Don't talk to the police. See you tomorrow."

Paris, France 1999

The bulletin board in April's hostel was in the same place as in Paul's—a noisy, shabby lounge that smelled like unwashed clothes and hashish. It was covered with scraps of paper—lined and unlined, even some backs of envelopes, with handwriting ranging from artistic to barely legible. Most of the notes were in English, and Paul read through them again.

Joelle H.- Meet Allie and Nicole at le Pantheon at 10 and bring A's earrings. Dress sexxxxy.

Seeking travel buddy- anyone heading to Barcelona want to team up with a chill guy?

Ronan- We moved to the Tres Amis hostel in the 9th. Come find us tomorrow morning. This place sucks. M & S.

Angie please let me explain. I'll come back tomorrow.

Nothing for him. Nothing that said, *Paul, I had to rush Selma to the hospital, meet me here tonight* or even just *P.- I'm sorry. -A.* Nothing to make sense of how April was there one minute, kissing him and letting him say those things about visiting each other, and then the next minute she disappeared into the crowd.

He asked the irritable woman at the front desk if April and Selma had checked out, describing the tall and short Americans. The woman looked at him suspiciously for a moment but told him that the loud girls had left suddenly last night. No, she didn't know where they were going, but they asked if the train station was within walking distance. The tall one had no manners. *Américaines*, she sniffed.

Paul went back to the bulletin board and read each note again. A layer of older notes peeked out from underneath. Had these other people found each other? Was this all that connected people in the world, a designated spot where you pinned up a scrap of paper and hoped that it met the right eyes?

What was he supposed to do with these feelings that had blossomed inside him over the last two days? What could he do besides add his own note to the board and get ready to fly home.

Chapter 17

April

April is staring at her reflection in the mirror, holding the yellow umbrella open over her head, when Selma quietly slips into her hotel room.

"Cloudy with a chance of shitstorms?" asks Selma with unusual softness.

"I'm such a stupid bitch," says April, looking at her pale face and red eyes. "Everything is a mess."

Selma gently takes the umbrella out of her hands, closes it, and tosses it on the bed. "I know, sweetie. I just saw Gabriel."

"So you know it's all over? No reunion kiss, no commercial, no chance to get my business back in the good graces of the Melissa Valentines of the world. Plus we're stuck with the hotel bill."

"He told me all that." Selma sits down on the bed, her feet barely touching the floor and her hands folded in her lap.

"Then how are you so calm?" demands April. "Why aren't you yelling at me and telling me to get it together?"

Selma pats the spot next to her on the bed. April obeys, sitting with a reluctant sigh.

"So what happened with you and Paul?" asks Selma. "Gabriel said he left you at a standoff, and no one's seen Paul since."

April doesn't want to talk about that part. The creeping shame returns, how she'd flung Paul's considerate words back in his face. Women like her shouldn't be around kind men.

"It's better this way," says April flatly. "The whole plan would never have worked."

"April." Selma takes April's hand in both of hers. "We've known each other for a long time. I'm going to yell at you a little because I care. But first I need to say that I'm sorry."

April doesn't expect that. "For what?"

"For letting you run away twenty years ago without asking any questions." says Selma, squeezing April's hand tighter. "And for not realizing that we were running away until it was too late."

April tries to protest, but Selma cuts her off with a warning glance.

"I didn't say anything when you left Danny because he was never good enough for you, and now he's just about the best ex-husband ever. But running away from people before they can run away from you is not a good look."

April nodes as the wave of shame returns.

"And Chickadee, anyone who's had half a dozen therapy appointments can see that we need to exorcize your mom's ghost from your life. It's very sad what happened to her. And your dad is kind of an asshole and always will be no matter what you do. But she was just a sad, troubled woman who didn't get the help she needed. She doesn't have any power over you anymore."

It sounds so simple when Selma says it that way, just a few words to describe the twisted knot inside her. "I'm four years older than she was when she died," whispers April. "How is that even possible? Why do I still feel like she's always watching me? I can still hear her voice when I'm upset. She's saying that no one will ever understand us, or love us, so we have to count on each other."

"Okay, this is the part where I yell. Tell her to shut the fuck up!" Selma glares while holding April's hand so gently. "You have me. And you have Liza, and you're an amazing mother to her. You and Danny have the most functional co-parenting relationship I've ever seen. Seriously, sometimes I want to marry him myself so I can divorce him and have the most amazing ex-husband ever, too."

April laughs, or maybe sobs, or does an embarrassing cross between the two that involves snorting and tears.

"What do I do, Selm?"

"Do less, baby girl. This whole April in Paris scheme is some of your finest work in terms of overthinking and adorable drama. You and Paul could have taken a selfie on the first day and posted it to show you'd reconnected. Even if you'd done nothing, the whole scandal, as you call it, would have blown over by now. So what's the real issue here?"

April takes a deep breath and tries to clear her mind of the swirling tornado of shame. What's left is Paul, his dark eyes, his gravelly voice, the shoulders that covered her in bed last night. She thinks about Paul at 22, and the way he already knew how to ask the right questions. She thinks of Paul today, and that patient, fond expression he gets when she can't stop blabbing.

"I want Paul," she says, and her voice is clear and calm. "I don't even want the cameras and the interview. I don't care what strangers think of me. I just want Paul to keep looking at me the way he does. I don't know how it can work, but there has to be a way."

"Then what are you doing here with me weeping and holding hands? Go find him. Or should we hatch another madcap scheme, maybe something with monkeys?"

"I'm thinking I stand under his window with the Moulin Rouge cancan dancers," says April, feeling a small, growing warmth in her chest.

"Let me go talk to Gabriel and deal with the other shit," says Selma. "Just be prepared that we may have to spend tonight in a cheap youth hostel. Hope you don't mind the top bunk."

"God, can you even imagine that we slept in a room full of strangers like that?"

"If we'd had the internet back then, we'd still probably be friends with all those weirdos. We'd know that the guy from Missouri who used to cry at night is now a state senator or something."

April shudders. "Gross. Though maybe Paul and I would have never lost touch."

"No regrets," says Selma. "Let's just say that the time wasn't right. And now it is. So go get'em, tiger."

April stands up but pauses for a moment before leaving, looking at her determined friend. "Selma, are you sad that you're not pregnant?"

Selma gives her a tired smile. "Not sad, no. I never thought I'd be a good mom. I just liked thinking, even for a few weeks, that there was a plan for the rest of my life. But it looks like I'm back to making it up as I go along. Anyway, I'm more of the cool aunt type. I'm looking forward to taking Liza to get her belly button pierced when she's 16."

April tries to give a stern glare but smiles instead. She is so happy right now. "How about we stick to a nose ring?" she says, kissing Selma on top of her head before she runs out the door.

April heads for the stairs, fluffing her hair and wiping her eyes as she walks. She can't wait to tell Paul that she didn't mean what she said, and that she wants them to be together however they can. She imagines the way his eyes will light up first, and then a big smile spreads across his face as he takes her in his arms…

Paul's door is open. April raps on it a few times and peeks inside. Instead of Paul, a hotel maid strips the bed.

"Excuse me!" says April, startled. "I mean, *pardon*. Where is…*monsieur?*"

"The man is gone," says the maid in English, barely looking up from her duties.

"Gone where?" asks April, perplexed. Did she mean he had stepped out for a few minutes? But there are no signs of Paul left in the room. His suitcase is gone, along with the jacket hanging on the back of the chair, the book beside the bed.

"Gone away," shrugs the maid. She gathers the sheets and walks around April to leave the room. She reaches for the doorknob, giving April a meaningful look that clearly says time to go.

For the first time, Paul isn't waiting for her somewhere. He's finally had enough, and now he's gone.

Chapter 18

Paul

By the time he lands in Winnipeg, Paul is so tired he can't think straight. Teresa sends him updates which come through sporadically on the airplane Wi-Fi. Tommy is still unconscious. They gave him a CT scan. The doctor is worried about brain swelling. Paul's been in this place with Tommy before, angry and guilty and scared.

Paul's been here before with April, as well—returning from a magical few days with her in Paris, knowing they'll never see each other again.

He takes a taxi directly to the hospital and almost runs down the hallway, still pulling his suitcase while he looks for the room number Teresa texted.

And there it is. Tommy, still and pale as a corpse in the hospital bed. Only the pinging monitors and IV bags keep Paul from immediately screaming that his little brother is dead.

Teresa paces by the window, texting and muttering to herself, and a vaguely familiar woman in dark-framed glasses knits in a chair by Tommy's bed.

Teresa sees him standing in the doorway and rushes to hug him. "Paulie, you're here!" she says. "I'm so glad to see you." Her face cracks for a moment and she looks like a little girl. "I've been so scared."

"How is he?" says Paul gruffly. If he lets go of his poker face, he'll turn into a blubbering mess.

"He hit his head pretty badly on the windshield. The doctors say they need to do some evaluations once he wakes up, and the sooner he wakes up, the better."

"What about the police?"

Teresa looks at him reproachfully but answers. "They said they want to interview him when he's conscious. And they took some blood. Haven't heard any results yet."

"He wasn't drunk," says the woman in the chair. "I told you, Teresa, and I'll tell you, too, Paul. He texted me around 3AM that he couldn't sleep. He seemed really upset so I told him to come over. He was on his way to my apartment when he crashed. I talked to him right before he got in his car."

Paul looks at her again. Now he remembers. The dry cleaners. Mad about higher prices for women's clothes. Sarah? Simone! "Simone!" he says proudly, forgetting the rest of the situation for a moment. Simone looks back at him, unimpressed, and continues knitting a yellow stripe on her blanket.

"It's almost 9," says Simone. "They're going to kick us out soon." She stuffs her knitting in a tapestry shoulder bag, stands up, and hugs Teresa hard. "Good night, Reesie. Call you in the morning." She nods curtly at Paul.

As they watch her leave, Teresa slides an arm around Paul's waist. "So you've met Simone? I think it's brand new, but she's hardly left his side." She rests her head on his shoulder and sighs. "I'm so glad you're here," she says. "Seeing him like this...I hate it so much. I didn't think we'd ever be here again."

Paul gives her a squeeze. "Me neither." But that isn't true. He is terrified every day that if he takes his eyes off Tommy, this very thing will happen. And there he went off to Paris, no less, to try to recapture the last moment his life had been more or less carefree. He won't make that mistake again.

Paul's job is to take care of other people. That's what he's always done, and that's what he will continue to do. Paris is over. He'll never go back.

April

"I'm sure all three of us can fit in the bed," says Selma.

"Well, you would know," snaps April, sharper than she intends.

"Could you two please refrain from working through your personal issues right now?" pleads Gabriel. He's in some loose drop-crotch black pants and a very soft-looking, perfectly distressed t-shirt, either ready to lead a yoga retreat in Tulum or bunk down with two grouchy middle-aged women in a single hotel room to save some money before they can fly home the next day. "I am still feeling the aftershocks of losing my job and possibly being under investigation. And I, for one, am appreciative of Selma's offer to share her room tonight. Not to mention her behind-the-scenes manipulation to get the hotel to reduce our bill in exchange for Delphine taking those new photos for their website." He looks at himself in the mirror and carefully dabs lotion around his eyes. "Obviously, it is not our business to connect how soon after a threesome Selma got Delphine to come to our rescue. So I am going to brush my teeth and try to get some sleep on a small corner of this bed before I go back to New York and ruin my last remaining dignity by breaking into the former Heart2Heart offices to clear out my desk."

After Gabriel marches into the bathroom and shuts the door, April can't help herself. "Thanks for being so good in bed that we don't have to pay the hotel bill."

"What can I say, it's a gift," says Selma. "But don't sell yourself short, not all of us can do sex stuff in a park that haunts a man for twenty years." She rifles through her cosmetics bag on the bureau, but April catches her concerned sideways glance in the mirror.

"You don't have to worry about that any more," mutters April.

"Chickadee, of course I worry. When I saw you heading off to find him this morning, you looked like you'd swallowed sunshine. And now, it's like no one showed up to your birthday party."

"I don't look that bad. That's the saddest thing I've ever heard."

Gabriel comes out of the bathroom. "What's the saddest thing you've ever heard?"

"That Pedro Pascal is probably straight," says Selma, and they both watch a silly grin bloom on Gabriel's face. "Okay, stop mooning, everybody. Gabriel, tell April again what Paul said."

Gabriel sighs and recites, "Paul texted me to say he had a family emergency and was leaving tonight. No, he didn't say what kind of emergency. No, he did not include any emojis that might reveal his state of mind."

"See?" says Selma. "People have emergencies."

"80% of family emergencies are just excuses to get out of awkward situations," grumbles April. "Remember how many times during college exams that your," she holds up her fingers in air quotes, "Grandmother died."

"Paul is better than us."

"That's true!" says Gabriel. "He said to please let him know if I ever come to Winnipeg, and he'll take me to his favorite Thai restaurant. I mean, obviously I'll never go, and if I did, I would not be sampling the so-called ethnic cuisine, but it's still very thoughtful."

April can imagine Paul saying that. Hell, he would no doubt also pick Gabriel up from the airport and give him a guided tour.

But who does those things for Paul? Was anyone picking him up from the airport? April pictures being the person that Paul counts on to be waiting at the baggage claim, but she lost that chance screaming at him in the street.

"I was so horrible to him," she says. "And then he gave a polite excuse and left. It's pretty clear what happened. Anyway, I don't want to talk about Paul."

Selma sits on the bed, back against the headboard. "Paul who? Lucky for us that all of our lives are messes, and we have many other topics to discuss."

"Absolutely," says Gabriel. "Me next. Please tell me how I'm going to break the news that I'm coming back to Cranston to share a bedroom with my grandmother." He flops on the bed on the other side of Selma. "And then tell me how to get my old job back at the Body Shop. But first...fuck it, April, I know you don't want to talk about it, and I probably shouldn't tell you this..."

"But you're going to," interrupts Selma.

"Yes, of course I am. I just thought you might want to know that I think Paul really cares about you. I think he loves you."

April cringes, the words as painful as if Gabriel slapped her. The thing is, though, she knows that already. The way Paul looks at her, and kisses her, and bought her a goddamned yellow umbrella— well, it's obvious. But it's not enough. She'd been cruel, and thoughtless, and he realized that a future with her was impossible. Paul loves her, she knows it, and it only makes things so much worse.

But she still wants to hear Gabriel say it. "How…?" she sputters. *How do you know? How could it possibly be true?*

"He came to find me," says Gabriel, "After you, I maybe stormed off a little, too."

"And he tried to fix things," says April softly. "He always tries to fix things."

"He didn't try to fix anything. He just thanked me. For bringing you two back together. For making him realize there was still magic out there, especially in Paris. And he asked me to help you, if I could."

April's eyes stung with all the salty tears she was holding back.

"Help me with what? Become less of a bitch?" She tries to laugh.

"He asked if I could do anything to help your business. Still get you some good PR or something. He said he didn't want you to regret any of this."

"I regret nothing," says April.

Selma's eyes light up, and she sings in her best Edith Piaf, "*Non! Rien de rien…*"

Surprisingly, Gabriel grins and joins in: "*Non! Je ne regrette rien…*"

They look at each other, realizing no one knows any more words, so they sing the same two lines over again, each channeling the ennui of the great chanteuse until April claps her hands over her ears.

Gabriel flops back on the bed. "I will try to help you, if I can," he says. "I should have said this before, instead of all that ridiculous shit about how we're in some liar's club together, but I think you were brave to come here. Heart2Heart sucks, God rest her soul, but I'm starting to think that anyone who puts themself out there deserves a fucking medal. And a boyfriend."

"A medal and a boyfriend," says Selma, raising an imaginary glass. "Hear hear!"

Gabriel clinks his imaginary glass to hers. "If I can't get you a medal and a boyfriend, April, I'll start with leaving you a bunch of good Google reviews."

"That would actually be great," says April. "And it's okay what you said. Or maybe not okay, but I get it. I was trying so hard to convince myself that this was all strictly business, so I should be glad I at least convinced you." She lays back on the pillows between Gabriel and Selma. Being squeezed between two friends helps her heart hurt just a little bit less.

At least she has Liza to go back to, and work. Though retreating back to the world of home staging, wiping away the personal touches and lived-in feel of a house, sounds barely tolerable. She agreed to this whole trip so she could save a business she doesn't even want, and she lost the thing she truly cares about along the way.

Boston, Massachusetts 2007

"No," said April. "I am not wearing that stupid thing tonight." She flung the cheap tiara with the attached veil on the bed.

"Come on, Chickadee," said Selma. "It's your bachelorette party. If you're going to make me wear that taffeta bridesmaids' monstrosity, then you can wear this out dancing."

April chewed her lower lip. She'd been doing that a lot lately. "I'm sorry about the dress, Selm. Danny's sister freaked out when I said I wanted the bridesmaids to pick out a black cocktail dress that they liked, and somehow she put herself in charge of all things bridesmaid. And then Danny's mother added fifty of her closest friends to the guest list. And even Danny, when I told him I didn't want any flowers, said we had to have them because his godmother is a florist and is doing all these red rose centerpieces as a wedding present."

"You're having roses?" asked Selma quietly. She was the only person who really knew what that meant.

"Just the centerpieces. And my bouquet. Danny says I need it for the pictures and for the whole throwing thing."

April felt Selma's hand grab hers. "I'm only going to say this once, Chickadee, and if I'm wrong then please forget it. I like Danny. But I've got my car out there with a full tank of gas. We could be in New York before anyone notices you're gone. I'll do everything. You won't have to talk to anyone. Just blink twice, and I'll haul your ass out of here right now."

April felt a lump rising in her throat. This would be the time, wouldn't it? This would be the time to tell Selma that she wasn't sure if she should do this. Could do this. That Danny was fun and got along with her father and the sex was good, but April knew something wasn't right.

She didn't say anything. Calling off her own wedding two days beforehand was the kind of messy, dramatic thing her mother would do. Hurting a nice guy because he wasn't able to give you that thing you wanted, even if you weren't even sure what it was, was exactly what her mother had done. If April made different choices—marrying the laid back guy, finding a respectable job, keeping a peaceful home where kids weren't responsible for parents' moods—then she would be a different person.

April cleared her throat and did her best to smile. "Everything's fine. Just nerves."

"Of course. Very normal blushing bride kind of thing. Speaking of which, I need to finish my toast for the reception. Does Danny's grandmother know that you got busted skinny dipping in your neighbor's pool when you thought they were on vacation?"

"Yes, Selma, that's exactly the kind of story you should share. I knew I was very smart saying you could give a toast."

"Oh, Chickadee, come one. We had fun, didn't we? Remember college? Remember that summer on the Vineyard? Remember Paris?"

April felt her heart beating faster.

"Oh, and that guy who showed us how to get the Louvre, and then we met him the next day at the Eiffel Tower. He liked you."

April tried to make some kind of joke but her mouth was dry.

"What was his name? I wonder if he's on Facebook. Maybe I could track him down and invite him to the wedding. See if he wants to speak now or forever hold his peace."

"Jesus Christ, Selm, leave it alone. I'm marrying Danny in two days, and you don't need to save me."

Selma gave her a quick look. "Of course not, April. I'm sure you know exactly what you're doing."

April did know what she was doing. She was marrying Danny, she was going to be just enough in love with him to make her happy and not so much in love that she lost control. She wasn't going to remember what it was like on the Eiffel Tower, in the golden light, with Paul, before she ruined everything.

Chapter 19

Paul

Paul's house is dark and musty, like he's been gone five weeks instead of five days. He drags his suitcase inside and opens the refrigerator, suddenly realizing he's starving. Just the same condiments and orange juice he left behind. Nothing has changed.

As he debates eating dry cereal or just going to bed, his phone pings. It's Sid.

I see your lights on. I have leftover spaghetti.

Paul's first instinct is to immediately turn off all the lights and sit in the dark, but the doorbell rings. So that's what it means to have a friend— someone who feels entitled to barge in whether you want them or not. Though he's surprised to realize he actually does want to see Sid, and it isn't just the spaghetti.

Sid has a packed Tupperware and carries Muffin under one arm. "How is your brother?" he asks, handing Muffin to Paul and striding into the kitchen.

Paul fills Sid in on the factual parts of Tommy's condition and scratches Muffin behind the ears. She looks a bit tidier and more symmetrical in her fluff than when he left, like one of Sid's neatly trimmed azaleas. He lets Sid heat up the spaghetti and even serve it to him on a real plate with a fork and a napkin. He's too tired to move after he finishes eating, and Sid takes his empty plate, washes it, and puts it away. And instead of grabbing the dish rag out of his hand, Paul just feels relief.

**

The ringing phone startles Paul out of sleep, and he's not sure where he is. Back in Winnipeg. 5:27AM. Teresa on the phone. There must be news.

"What is it?" he asks, his heart pounding.

"The hospital just called," says Teresa, and Paul can't speak, can only feel his stomach clenching.

"No, no, Paulie, it's good! He's awake! He's a little confused but he's talking and everything."

"Thank God," Paul croaks. Somehow the possibility of an early morning phone call with good news hadn't occurred to him.

"I'm leaving for the hospital after I get Mattie up. Should I stop by for you?"

"No, I'll meet you there." Paul needs to get things in order so he can be in control when he sees Tommy.

By the time Paul arrives at the hospital, he's showered, drunk a big mug of coffee (black, since he didn't have any milk), and looked through his file folder labeled "Tommy-legal" to get the lawyer's phone number. He's googled "impaired driving third offense" and "alcohol rehab Manitoba." He also texted Caridad from Stone Cleaners to confirm that she's opening. Somehow, he even found a few minutes to visit Melissa Valentine's Facebook page. He has to scroll down quite a bit to find the old picture of him and April, and no one's left a comment for a few days. Melissa is busy experimenting with smoothie recipes and promoting a new skin care line.

April must be on her way home now, no doubt excited to see her daughter. It seems like the internet outrage has died down. What was the point of that whole trip, anyway? She could have just waited patiently for the trolls to work out their feelings and get distracted by the next thing. Of course, waiting out his feelings hasn't worked for Paul, but surely April could have held on for a few more weeks.

When Paul walks into the hospital room, he's surprised to see Simone already there. She sits in the chair next to Tommy's bed in her overalls and hipster glasses, leaning in close to Tommy and touching his arm with a startling tenderness. And Tommy. Tommy is pale, with the beginnings of a scraggly beard, but he smiles and looks at Simone like she brought him back to life herself.

Paul pauses there in the doorway, unable to move. He'd rushed home, thousands of miles and three connections, to take charge of this situation, and here was his brother, awake and healthy and clearly in love.

Teresa sees him and pulls him into the room.

"Hey bro," says Tommy. He's trying to sound casual, but his voice is hoarse and weak. "Sorry to make you cut your big trip short. When'd you get back?"

"Last night," says Paul. Is Tommy going to ask next how his flight was? Why is everyone acting…normal?

"I begged him to come back," says Teresa, brushing her fingers to Tommy's cheek. "I hope I didn't mess up anything hot and heavy in Paris."

"Yeah, well, I'm used to you guys screwing up my social life," says Paul. "Same old, same old."

Everyone looks surprised at his sharp tone.

"Simone said you were asking about the toxicology report," says Tommy. He's already remembering to be guarded around Paul. "The doctor came by earlier and said they had the results. No measurable alcohol. I wasn't drinking. I don't do that anymore."

Paul waits for relief to flood over him. He waits for his body to rush over to Tommy and break into the group hug. But he's frozen, like a stranger watching from the doorway. They didn't need him to come home. Paul never felt so lonely in his life.

"Maybe you don't do that anymore," he says, looking at the happy group holding hands on the bed. "But you did. You drank, and you hurt yourself, and you went to fucking jail, and every time I cleaned up after you."

"Paul," gasps Teresa, but Tommy says. "It's okay, Tree. Let him say what he needs to say."

"You just take it for granted that I'll be there no matter what. Maybe next time you crash a car, drunk or not, you can do it when I'm not on vacation."

"Stop it," says Teresa. "Go home and get some rest, Paul."

"I'll leave," snaps Paul. "But I don't have time to *rest*. I need to go to the cleaners and make sure he didn't fall asleep at the wheel there, too. You take all the time you need, both of you. I'll take care of everything, like usual." He wants to storm out of the room, to give them a taste of life without him, but then he makes the mistake of looking at Tommy, his little brother, his little brother who nearly *died*, and Paul starts to cry, hard and loud.

He hears his choking, ugly sobs but it's like it's happening to someone else. Teresa guides him into a chair, and Tommy reaches for his hand, and Paul just bawls so hard the chair shakes. There's no relief in tears, though. Inside his heart is cold and heavy like a dead thing.

April

For someone who claimed they were going to Paris to save their small business, April's been strikingly negligent in keeping an eye on AA Home Staging over the past five days. So, on her first morning home she gets to work, starting with her email. Beyond the usual spam there are about a dozen emails with subjects like "Jezebel" and "You never deserved him" and "I am praying for you." After a moment's hesitation, she deletes the whole inbox. None of the messages could say anything crueler than what she says to herself.

With increased energy April opens Instagram and scrolls through notifications. She's never devoted much energy to her business account, just dutifully posting the occasional photo of a staged room with its bare tabletops and seasonally appropriate accent pillows. Most of the new comments are along the lines of "DO NOT HIRE THIS WOMAN. SHE IS A SLUT AND WILL STEAL YOUR HUSBAND," which April thinks gives her too much credit. Delete.

One recent picture in her timeline, the foyer in a cute split-level, catches her eye. A half-moon table with a vase of white roses, partially reflected by a large gilt mirror. April remembers clearing away the kids' hockey gear and hanging the mirror to hide some smudges on the wall. The owner, a recent widow moving closer to her parents in North Carolina, was a little shocked. "Isn't that bad feng shui," she said, "To have a mirror facing the entrance? Not that I believe in all that, but I can imagine being startled by my reflection every time I open the front door."

She was right. April isn't a strict adherent of feng shui or any other design principles, but she always felt a sense of unease entering that house, with the choking scent of roses and the unexpected glimpse of her own reflection. But the pictures looked good and gave the cramped 1970s home a feeling of elegance that matched the statelier homes in the neighborhood. Still, the photo makes April remember everything that bothers her about her work. Prioritizing aesthetics over comfort, erasing all the little imperfections that make a house into a home. April likes a little clutter, damn it. That forgotten mug of coffee on the desk, the nick in the molding from an errant basketball—that's what makes a home special.

Impulsively, April runs upstairs to her bedroom. This room is actually *her*, with the colors and textures of her special things. Honestly there's some ugly crap, too, but isn't that just life. She'd claimed that the wall striped with nine different shades of yellow was waiting for her to pick a color, but really she just *likes* it that way. She wants them all.

Before she can overthink it, April takes a photo of her bed with the slightly tattered crazy quilt and pile of mismatched pillows. She captures the morning light pouring through the sheer curtains and the half piece of toast with almond butter on a cobalt pottery plate that she'd been too tired to finish last night. She posts it to Instagram before she can change her mind, captioned with her favorite Virginia Woolf quote: *"No need to hurry. No need to sparkle. No need to be anyone but oneself."*

"Mom?" Liza slips into the room, another jolt of energy in the bedroom. "What are you doing? You're not going to paint again, are you?"

"Hi, baby. You're up early. Nope, I'm keeping it just like it is."

"Good. I like it."

"Me too. You know, it makes me think of my mother." April puts her arm around Liza and leads her down to the kitchen, pouring orange juice and popping slices of bread in the toaster. "I've never told you much about her."

"I know," says Liza. "Grandpa never mentions her either. I always thought it was because you were both mad at her."

April refills her coffee and takes a sip while she thinks about this. "Not mad," she says. "At least not me. But I've always felt a lot of complicated things about her. She had a lot of problems, and we didn't know how to help her. She hurt us a lot, but I can see now that she hurt herself more."

"Is that why you and Grandpa are so weird with each other?"

So much for keeping that complication of that relationship under wraps. "I think I remind him too much of her," says April, "And I'm always trying to act like the daughter I think he wishes he had. It's kind of a mess."

"Mom, no offense, but that's really stupid."

"You're right, baby. It's totally stupid." The toast pops up from the toaster, and April butters it and sets it in front of Liza. "Sometimes I think it's too late to fix it."

"I don't think so," says Liza. "Last time we went up there, he told me this story about how when you were my age, you said all his ties were too boring, and then you made him a tie that was all yellow and purple and stuff, and it was so beautiful, and he still has it somewhere."

April remembers this very differently—she had worked for hours to sew the necktie, using the prettiest fabrics from her scrap bag. Her father said something about how colorful it was, and she never saw it again. The idea that he'd held onto it all these years makes her equal parts thrilled and angry. Maybe there's something there still worth working on.

"But Mom, you haven't even told me about Paris," says Liza, taking a gulp of juice. "You said you were too tired to talk last night. What was that guy like? Did you kiss him in the Eiffel Tower again? I bet Dad five dollars that you would."

"He said I wouldn't?" asks April, more curious than annoyed for once at Danny pretending to have insights into her mind.

"He said you seemed, um, conflicted. And that he'd never heard of the guy so it couldn't be a big deal." Liza folds her toast and eats it in three bites.

"Well, you both lost. Or you both won," says April.

"I have no idea what that means," says Liza, "And I'm going to be late for school if I don't get dressed. Just tell Dad to give me five bucks." She shoves the second piece of toast in her mouth and leaps up the stairs.

In her quiet kitchen, April lets herself spend a few minutes thinking about what Paul was doing right now. Maybe his family emergency was actually real. Maybe he was in that crazy mustard-colored kitchen drinking coffee and feeling sad. Maybe she should text him to see if he's okay. Or maybe she should give him some space while she figures out how to apologize for the terrible things she said.

Chapter 20

Paul

The morning is already warm, and it's hot as hell working the shirt finishing machine in the back of the shop. Paul's put himself on shirt duty for the last week, sweating and grunting while the industrial fan blows hot air back on him and drowns out any friendly chit chat from the counter. He doesn't work the machines much anymore, not unless one of the regular employees is sick, but he needs to lose himself in the discomfort and routine of lining up the cuffs and collar to be pressed between sheets of hot metal.

Tommy has been conscious for eight days, home for five, and he and Paul are still very careful around each other. Everyone is careful around Paul since his meltdown at the hospital, and he doesn't want to talk about it. So he works as many hours as possible, takes solitary runs along the river, and in the long June evenings sits with Sid on his front porch while Sid teaches Muffin new tricks like "sit pretty" and "shake."

He doesn't think about Paris, except for when he does, which is all the time.

Lift the top of the press, put the shirt on the buck and do up the buttons, wipe the sweat off his forehead with a red bandana...

"You were always so slow with the buttons."

Paul startles and spins around, almost burning his hand. Tommy is right behind him. He looks okay, just a few fading bruises on his cheek.

"It's a good thing business is bad, if that's how long it takes you to do a shirt."

Paul steps aside, and Tommy deftly closes the buttons and slides the blue check shirt into the finisher to be pressed on the form. Paul reaches in the wet box of laundered shirts and grabs one, fitting the cuffs and collars over the curve of the press. When the blue check shirt is done, Paul transfers it to a hanger while Tommy buttons the white one on the shirt buck.

Finally, Tommy speaks. "So, it turns out when you have a concussion, you can't read or watch TV or do anything but lie around and think."

"Sounds like hell," says Paul lightly. He's sure where this is going, but at least they're talking.

Tommy smooths the shirt collar. "Remember when I was on the hockey team in high school, and you came to all my games? You'd give me all this advice after, about how I should work on my speed, and not give the goalie any clues where my shot was going."

"And you told me to mind my own business."

"I told you to shut the fuck up. That I didn't need any pointers from some guy who never made the team."

"Yeah," says Paul. He remembers it all well—Tommy's bursts of anger, his own feeling of helplessness.

"It took me a while, but I figured out why you never played in high school," Tommy says, looking intently at the shirt he's buttoning.

"I wasn't good enough," says Paul, pulling out a pink one from the wet box.

"That's a load of crap, you were fine." Tommy encases the hung shirts in plastic sheath with a flourish and finally looks at Paul. "Simone pointed it out to me when I was bitching about you always being on my case. You didn't play so I could play. You were working here, and driving Mom to doctors' appointments, and doing your geometry homework while making tuna noodle casseroles, and I was an ungrateful little shit. I should have listened to you. I should have listened to you about a lot of things."

Paul opens his mouth to protest—he's the one who should be sorry, he's the older one who should have made everything okay. But Tommy looks like he has more to say, and this time Paul is going to listen. Paul silently picks up the next half-pressed shirt and holds it out for Tommy but doesn't let go.

"What I'm trying to say here is thank you," says Tommy. "For everything you did for me and Teresa. You missed out on a lot." They each hold a sleeve, looking more at the stripes than each other. "And you weren't wrong to assume I was drunk when I called you. I don't have a great track record, and I need to keep proving myself. But believe me when I say I haven't had a drink in three years, and every morning I wake up and tell myself, one more day, buddy. Don't let today be the day you fuck all this up."

For all his worrying about Tommy staying sober, Paul has barely considered what it means to actually be him, to wake up every morning and make the decision to fight his addiction one more day.

"I always thought," says Paul, "that if you couldn't stay sober, it was because I wasn't trying hard enough."

Tommy scoffs and grabs the rest of the shirt. "Sorry to disappoint, but it has nothing to do with you."

Those words echo through Paul, like a mallet striking a gong. *Nothing to do with you.* In fact, the harder he'd tried, the more he'd pushed Tommy away.

"Why did you call me in Paris, anyway?" asks Paul. He wants to rewind back to that moment and really listen. "You said you wanted to tell me something."

Tommy grins goofily as he reaches overhead for a hanger. "I wanted to tell you that I'm in love!" he says. "This whole thing with Simone is happening really fast, though, and I was feeling a little freaked out. I guess I just wanted to hear your voice."

The press beeps, but Paul doesn't move. He's messed up so much, but he's still the one Tommy calls.

"You could have died," says Paul, his voice cracking. "I was so scared." The machine beeps again shrilly, but he fumbles reaching for the handle. Tommy's strong, wiry arm reaches around him and lifts the top before sweeping Paul into a bear hug.

"I'm sorry, man. I've put you through a lot." Tommy squeezes so hard that Paul can't breathe, and that's just fine.

As the brothers let go of each other with many shoulder pats and subtle eye wiping, they hear an elaborate, attention-getting cough: "AHEM." Simone has her knitting bag on one shoulder and a folder under her arm, and she's a little misty behind those hipster glasses.

"Caridad said you guys were back here. Can I assume that some awkward things were said leading up to this bro hug?" She looks back and forth between them. "Thank fucking god. Men," she sighs dramatically, but she gives Tommy a look that even Paul can read: *Are you okay?*

"Let's clear the embarrassment at having feelings and talk business," Simone says, handing Tommy one last hanger while Paul turns off the press. "I brought those mock-ups for the new promotion."

Tommy looks sheepish. "Babe, we didn't get to that part yet. Paul, Simone was helping me with some posters to advertise some of that stuff we talked about. Home delivery, partnerships with local companies, all that stuff, but we weren't going to do anything without you."

"No time like the present," says Simone, opening her folder and laying out some papers on an empty ironing board. Paul picks up the first one that catches his eye, a colorful cartoon of a woman with red lips and a dramatic cat eye in a masculine business suit, and a broad-shouldered man with glasses in a purple sundress. "No more pink tax!" it says. "Everyone is equal at Stone Dry Cleaning."

He feels Tommy and Simone waiting for his reaction. He's ashamed by their nervousness. Why did he care so much about doing things the way his parents had always done? Why shouldn't Tommy try something new, even if it didn't work out in the end?

"I love it," says Paul. "Let's do it."

"Are you sure?" says Tommy. "It's a work in progress. I mean, I've been playing with various price points to see where the sweet spot is, but there are still a few kinks left to work out."

"I'm sure," says Paul. "You've worked harder than anyone these last few years, and I should have listened more to your ideas. I trust you. Let's give it a try."

Tommy and Simone exchange thrilled smiles, and Tommy grabs her and twirls her around. Paul loves seeing them so happy, even if it reminds him how lonely he is.

Tommy notices Paul's expression fade, and he keeps one arm around Simone and reaches out the other to squeeze Paul's shoulder.

"Teresa says you came back from Paris early because of the accident. I'm really sorry you had to do that. But you don't have to give up things for me anymore. I don't know what happened over there, but your guy Sid keeps texting me to say he thinks you got your heart broken, and that we need to stage some kind of reunion of the reunion."

"You and Sid text?" How long had that been going on?

"I guess I was on your emergency contacts list for the dog. And Sid thinks if we make you happy then Muffin will be happy. Plus, he's a decent guy, I think he doesn't want you to be sad, either."

"I'm not sad," protests Paul.

Simone peers at him over her glasses. "I know I'm new around here, but for a guy that has such a full, enriching life, you have some major sad puppy eyes. I don't know who did what to who, but you've got it very, very bad."

"She's right," says Tommy, grabbing Paul's shoulders and bringing his face so close that Paul squints. "Your eyes are like these fucking deep wells of sadness, and they're giving me the creeps. Can you text her and say you're sorry for whatever the hell you did, so I don't have to look at this any more? You're like that velvet painting of the crying clown that Grandma had. Ahh, make it stop!" He crushes Paul's face to his shoulder in a half hug.

"It's more complicated than that," says Paul, his voice muffled in Tommy's shirt.

"Like hell it is," said Simone. "What women want is a man who can say he's sorry."

And she and Tommy pretend to look through the poster drafts while Paul digs out his phone, finds where April texted herself the picture of his kitchen, and types the first word that comes to mind.

April

April's Instagram post of her bedroom gets more likes and comments than anything she's ever shared. An artist she admires shares the picture, adding, *This is life: colorful, joyful, and a little messy.*

A longtime realtor contact stops returning her calls, but a new agent invites her for coffee. Twice someone comments "Bitch" under an old photo, and April clicks the delete key with satisfied vigor. She takes more photos of eclectic corners and objects around her home: the comfy chair she's always meant to reupholster, its faded fabric contrasting harmoniously with a faux fur throw; her mother's old Nancy Drew mystery books with their matching yellow spines on her kelly green bookshelf; an endearingly lopsided terra cotta bowl, made by Liza, and filled with smooth stones gathered on beach trips.

A yellow umbrella makes a few appearances—hung upside down like a chandelier, or held by a woman in front of a pear tree, the budding fruits visible but her face obscured.

Then, after she's almost given up hoping for it, her phone pings. It's a text from Paul. Just one word...*sorry.*

You spend your twenties carelessly optimistic, not caring how your hopes and dreams inevitably crash into everyone else's. You spend your thirties too busy for reflection, following the rules because without that roadmap for work, children, and marriage, life is chaos. And what about your forties? April has spent hers mentally apologizing—to Danny, to her father, to the memory of her mother, to her clients as she depersonalized their homes. When's the last time she said that word out loud?

April remembers Paul talking to the camera back in the Hotel Voltaire lobby, and how his face went from surprised to embarrassed to a little bit awed when he saw her. In bed together, Paul touched her like he wanted to learn everything about her. She'd always told herself that her marriage to Danny failed because he didn't really know her, but that was a two-way street. April never really gave him the chance. She preferred to be a simpler version of herself around him, and to smile and say thank you when he brought her roses on their anniversary, rather than be her true, messy, imperfect self.

April doesn't want to be that simple version of herself anymore. And she wants to make a real apology.

Me too, she texts back and presses her phone to her chest like it's an actual love letter, hoping to feel the ping of a response against her heart. There is nothing.

**

So April keeps working. Saturday marks nearly two weeks since she returned, and with Liza at Danny's, April heads to her favorite flea market. She needs a few picture frames and vases for her work inventory, plus it's a beautiful late June day in New England, probably one of the last before summer's humidity creeps in.

April rambles happily through the flea market, doing a first loop to check out the merchandise before circling back to focus on a few things that catch her eye— just the way she and Selma used to scope hotties at college parties, she smiles to herself. She's wearing her April at the Flea Market in June uniform: canvas pants with lots of pockets, a worn linen shirt tied at the waist, and red Chuck Taylors. She tries to confine her hair to two braids, but curls sneak out from under her red sun hat.

April pauses by a table of old dishes and kitchen supplies, habitually scanning the plates and casseroles for vintage Fiestaware. She smiles at a set of mustard-colored bowls, an exact match for Paul's kitchen counters. She takes out her phone to look at that photo again with its yellow-on-yellow theme. No reek of despair there. Maybe a touch of melancholy from the kitchen's obvious lack of use. With some care and attention, and a few of those turquoise place settings over there to pop against the yellow, she can show Paul how special that kitchen really is. April likes those mustard kitchen counters, damn it.

And she loves Paul.

The thought hits her like a bolt of lightning, more thrilling than finding a full set of cobalt 1950s Fiestaware. At twenty-one, she'd been too scared to know how precious and rare it was to connect with another person like that. Two weeks ago, in Paris, she'd been too scared— not to mention too damn stupid—to see that she'd been given a second chance. Now she knows for certain that she wants, and wants to deserve, Paul, with his shoulders and deep brown eyes and infinite patience.

So what now? April buys the turquoise dishes, of course, even though she hasn't completed her loop around the flea market. She doesn't even bargain, surprising the seller who has already sized April up as a canny shopper. Some things are too precious to risk losing by playing games.

She heads back to her car, her purchase already heavy and awkward. Her phone starts ringing as she gets close, so she hustles to the car and plops the box on the roof. She rushes to answer without even checking who's calling.

"April?" says a man's voice, familiar even after a few weeks apart.

"Gabriel!" she says. "I'm so happy to hear your voice! Like, even I am surprised how happy."

"Likewise," says Gabriel, "I never call people, but some weird little part of me got excited to actually talk to you. I tried to suppress it, but here we are."

April remembers how much she likes sparring with Gabriel, who can take it and serve it right back to her. "So, last time I saw you, you were broke, unemployed and chronically celibate."

"And last time I saw you, you were catastrophically in denial. But enough about that. I got a job offer–I can't really go into detail yet, but we have synergy with Maypole.com. You know that site, right? Furniture, home goods, Buddha statues for suburban yoga moms."

"Of course I do, that's huge! Congratulations! I steal ideas from their website all the time."

"Yes, again I seem to be catering to your demographic. But look, in all sincerity, I'm sorry about what a shitshow things turned into in Paris." He pauses meaningfully. "Have you talked to Paul?"

"No. Have you?"

"A couple texts. He just said things are okay. Which I take to mean he's desperately sad. Listen, I've got a proposition for you. I might have pitched a certain idea at my new job."

April listens with great interest. "I'll do it," she says before Gabriel can even finish.

Chapter 21

Paul

So Paul fell back into his routine, though it wasn't quite the same routine that he left. Sid stopped by most evenings for a beer and a chat about the latest Blue Jays game. Paul went to Matty's softball games and thought about coaching hockey again next season. He even offered to have Matty for a sleepover so Teresa and Griff could have a date night, which they accepted enthusiastically. Simone stopped by the store for lunchtime meetings, and she, Tommy, and Paul ate the exotic sandwiches she brought, full of things like tempeh and alfalfa sprouts, while discussing new business ideas.

So Paul was very busy. So busy that sometimes he went for an hour or two without thinking of April's long arms around him, and his hands raking through her wild bronze hair.

Sid invites Paul to the Flower and Garden show at the convention center downtown, and he makes it clear that he isn't taking no for an answer, even when Paul explains how very busy he is.

"You're not busy," says Sid. "You're effectively filling up the hours in your day. There's a difference."

The convention center is a wonderland of display gazebos, gardens, shrubs, fountains, flagstone patios, and flower beds. Disoriented by the collapse of the division between inside and outside, Paul follows Sid around while Sid says cryptic things like, "Japanese salmon rhododendron. Someone's got a sense of humor."

Paul examines the pink blossoms. "Those would look nice by your steps," he says, hoping he's being helpful.

Sid barks out a laugh before turning to see Paul's blank face. "Oh my God, you're serious," he says. "Sorry to laugh. It's just that...this is Zone 3, Paul. Only the hardiest plants for us. If you want to live among Japanese salmon rhododendrons, you need to head south, my friend." Sid pauses to pick up a pack of seeds and hand them to Paul. "Zone 6, maybe. Like Boston."

After April's text, that *Me too* that felt like a window cracked open between them, Paul waited for more. What was she sorry for, exactly? For agreeing to come to Paris in the first place? For leading him on, when she was just there to save her business? Or was it a belated apology for twenty years ago, slipping away in the crowd at the Eiffel Tower without a word? He started too many responses, and then it was too late. Again.

"I mean it, Paul," says Sid. "You clearly haven't wanted to talk about what happened in Paris, so I tried to be patient, but the Blue Jays are terrible this season, and I want to know why you haven't called April. Your brother thinks..."

Paul wants to bristle at Sid and Tommy discussing him behind his back, but instead he feels the beginning of a warm glow. Still, he interrupts out of habit. "I know what Tommy thinks. He thinks I should call April, and say, hey, Winnipeg is lovely this time of year—which it is, but only this time of year—and invite her for a visit. And she'll leave her kid and her job and show up the next day, and say, wow, I love it when middle-aged men keep their home as a shrine to their late mother! And tell me more about the dry cleaning business… what's your favorite solvent, perc or 1-bromopraopane? And please introduce me to your nosy younger siblings, your spoiled dog, and your one friend who can't stop talking about salmon at a flower show."

Sid looks at him calmly before going back to perusing the rack of seeds. "It sounds like you are very secure in exactly what your brother thinks. But what do you think?"

"I think…" starts Paul, but no words form. He tries again, "Well, of course I…" He turns away from the seed rack and strides toward a miniature cottage with an attached water wheel spinning in a babbling brook. What even is this place?

Sid sits down on the decorative stone bench surrounded by tulips and pats the place next to him. Paul sits heavily and again tries to speak while Sid pretends to read the back of a seed packet. The flowers are strangely odorless, and Paul thinks of how April hates roses. Paul almost envies her this definite conviction, even if it is painful for her. What does he hate? What does he love?

Paul leans back on the bench. "Tommy and Simone and I have these lunch meetings sometimes where we brainstorm ideas. Or they do, and I try not to shoot all their ideas down right away. They get really excited about stuff like making us a logo and an Instagram page, and how we can convince Gen Z to properly care for their clothes instead of wearing disposable stuff from H&M or whatever." He glances at Sid, who nods.

"Dry cleaning your woolens—good. Sweatpants—bad. But what does this have to do with you?"

"That's just it," says Paul. "I don't know. I inherited the business, and I more or less inherited Tommy and Teresa. It's like someone else chose my life for me. But now I see Tommy and Teresa making their own choices and getting excited about their lives, and I think, what gets me excited like that? Because it's not dry cleaning. And no offense, but it's not gardening. It might not even be Winnipeg."

"Forgive me for stating the obvious, but could it be April? Or is it just a coincidence that you have returned from Paris and suddenly these feelings appear?" asks Sid with raised eyebrows.

Paul is very still for a moment, taking in the wonderland of flowers. It's beautiful, but it isn't real. Kind of like Paris. If he and April see each other again, it has to be real, not hiding behind the spell of the City of Lights.

"April doesn't like flowers." He says, and Sid flinches slightly and then composes his face into purposeful neutrality.

"Some people do prefer succulents," said Sid.

"I don't even know why," says Paul. "There's so much I don't know about her. Like if she ever wants to talk to me again."

Sid nods. "And the best way to ascertain that is to attend the Winnipeg Flower and Garden show with your neighbor. I understand completely."

Paul snorts and then remembers he's feeling sorry for himself. "Before I went to Paris, you told me that women like a man who can take care of plants. What if I can't? What if all my plants shrivel up and die, or decide that they can take care of themselves better than I can do it? Maybe everyone would be better off if I didn't get any new plants."

Sid stands up and holds out a hand to Paul. "Come with me," he says, pulling Paul up and steering them through the crowd towards the periphery of the displays. Near the exit, in a dark corner, he stops at a shelf of plants. These are different from the proud, flourishing dahlias and roses that make the convention center into a movie set. Even Paul can see that they are too small, or lopsided, or yellow where they should be green, or brown where they should be yellow. A crooked, handwritten sign says "50% off. All sales final."

Sid decisively selects one of the plants, a spindly, cactus-like thing that droops on one side and has no leaves on the other, like a bad haircut. He hands a two dollar coin to a bored teenager sitting nearby and thrusts the plant at Paul. "Christmas cactus. Give it some sun. Don't water it too much. It will produce pink flowers in December. Or maybe not this year. That's fine, sometimes it takes a while."

Paul takes the plant in both hands like it's a delicate baby animal. "You make it sound easy," he says skeptically.

"It's not difficult. You don't have to be perfect. But you need to show up."

Paul looks at his friend, who had shown up for him so many times over the last two weeks. Sid hasn't done anything but reliably knock on his door at 7:30PM and rant about the Blue Jays' pitchers, but it's a reminder that Paul has a friend. Maybe even a friend and a half counting Gabriel and all his texts. Paul hasn't been the perfect father-figure, or business owner, but he shows up every day. He'd shown up for April when she needed him, too. Maybe if he shows up again, he can find out what she wants, if she ever wants to talk to him again.

Paul clutches the cactus to his chest and nods. "OK," he says.

***

A wave of thunderstorms moves through overnight, and on Monday the air is clear and fresh and smells like wet earth. Paul opens a window as he sets up his computer in the unused dining room to prepare.the quarterly business taxes. He spends more time at home lately instead of holed up in the windowless back office at Stone Cleaner's. Somehow home doesn't have that same claustrophobic feeling that it did just a few weeks ago.

Paul's phone pings. Gabriel. "You are still in Win opening right," which Paul assumes was an autocorrect for Winnipeg, surely unfamiliar to Gabriel's phone. He's going to text Gabriel back after he finishes the taxes, and after he figures out exactly what he might want to say to April. He needs to have his thoughts collected before he talks to Gabriel—the last thing he wants is to get swept up in another crazy scheme.

When the doorbell rings, he considers ignoring it, but Muffin rushes to the front door, happily yapping, so Paul follows. He opens the door while still trying to decipher a handwritten note Tommy left in the till about taking some petty cash and doesn't even look up while he waits for Sid's usual "Hello, my beauty. Hi, Paul."

"Hello, Paul," says a woman's voice. It can't be. Paul looks up from his paper. It's April.

April

Glasses.

After picturing this moment so many times, April's brain now fizzes and sputters like that ginger ale she'd sipped on the plane to calm her stomach. *Glasses. He's wearing glasses.* There is Paul, standing in front of her at last, but April's plan for a coherent and thoughtful speech is no match for the unfamiliar silver framed glasses that make Paul look like a stern geometry teacher who brings candy for the class on test days.

Paul regains the power of speech first. "April?" he croaks, taking her all in: cropped jeans and peasant blouse, clutching that small box she'd packed so carefully back in her kitchen. She hopes he likes what he sees, that April-not-in-Paris after a long day of traveling is still someone who can make Paul-with-glasses smile. April knows she's missed a few steps that a normal, sane person might take in getting from Point A to Point B. Even Gabriel cautioned her that she should wait a few days, until he was able to confirm that Paul was in town and up for this whole scenario, but April had already arranged to swap custody days with Danny. Plus after waiting twenty years the first time, she simply could not wait another day to see Paul again.

"What are you...? I mean, how did you...?" starts Paul. He takes off his magical glasses and rubs his eyes like he can't trust his vision before putting them back on. That glimpse of Paul's naked eyes breaks the spell, and April manages to talk.

"I drove. From the airport, I mean. Not from my house," blurts April. She has so many things she plans to say, but maybe starting with logistics will settle her nerves. "Did you know that it's a twenty-eight hour drive from Boston to

Winnipeg? How is that even possible? I mean we're on the same continent, even though you live north of North Dakota. I bet it's not even a twenty-eight hour drive to Paris, if there was a bridge of course."

"Maybe a bit more than that, I'm sure it's over 5000 kilometers," says Paul, again with that sexy teacher vibe. She can't help a delighted snort while Paul says, "Never mind, never mind. I just can't believe you're here. I've thought about you. A lot."

"Me, too," says April, holding the box tighter. She can't help noticing that Paul looks maybe more stunned than happy, and the little dog is giving her the stink eye like it knows just what she did. Now that she's here, she can really see how impulsive her plan is. April looks around at the quiet street and tidy houses in contrast to her badly parked rental van with a mysteriously sticky steering wheel.

Get your shit together, April, she tells herself. She's come too far to stop now. She just needs to explain to Paul her perfectly rational reason for being there before she gets to her stupidly romantic one.

"Anyway, thank God you're home," she says brightly. "Gabriel said you guys haven't talked in a while, and you weren't answering his texts or calls, so I was nervous. It was his idea for me to come, you know."

At the mention of Gabriel's name, Paul's shoulders tense.

"Is that yours?" he asks, noticing the van for the first time. "Is Gabriel inside?"

"No, just me," says April. April didn't like the guardedness creeping into Paul's eyes, the muscle twitching in his jaw. Does Paul wish Gabriel was there to be a buffer between them? She needs to cut to the chase and explain the deal. "He's got some kind of mysterious new job connected to Maypole.com. You know them?"

"I guess," says Paul. "I think my sister orders stuff from there."

"Gabriel thought I could redecorate your house as a promo for Maypole. You said you were thinking of selling but didn't know where to start, and they do stuff like that all the time, before and after type stuff." April looks for some reaction from Paul, but he stands in his doorway, his warm eyes growing guarded. His expression makes her nervous, and the words bubble out of her mouth. "He feels bad about Paris, and how he screwed up. Or like he would say it, 'overestimated Heart2Heart's capacity for investment in its future.' Did he tell you how he and Selma and I spent the last night in Paris in one bed to save money? They both snore. Anyway, he was thinking about you a lot, and he was worried about you and your whole family emergency, and he misses you and wants to make sure you're okay."

April stops for a breath. Putting all her emotions onto Gabriel is a safer bet while Paul's face looks...blank. April almost reaches out and brushes his cheek until he sets his jaw with resignation, and she flinches.

"You want to redecorate my house for an internet story," he says quietly, looking somewhere over her shoulder. "Okay. Fine. Do you need me to sign something?"

April shakes her head.

"I guess you should come inside, then," he says and finally opens the door wide.

April follows Paul into the house, noticing how he shifts his body to give her plenty of room as she passes him. This really isn't the reception she expected. She certainly didn't think he would wrap her in his strong arms and kiss her senseless as soon as he saw her, but...okay, to be honest, that is what she thought. As much as she told herself that it was reasonable for him to be surprised and a little cautious when she turned up on his doorstep, she assumed he'd share her uncomplicated joy to reunite in his own house, with not only glasses and bare feet but bare calves and a threadbare Winnipeg Jets t-shirt that looked soft enough to sleep in.

"Well, this is it," says Paul, gesturing to the cozy but worn living room. April notes the built-in bookshelves and an unused-looking fireplace, as well as some faded green carpeting that surely hides original hardwood floors. She can work with this. But then she sees Paul crossing his arms protectively and not quite meeting her eyes. She has to work on that, first.

"I hoped you'd be glad to see me," says April.. "And it seemed like you were for a minute."

"Why are you here?" asks Paul, and April can't stand the hurt confusion in his voice. "Why did you show up on my doorstep with no warning with your enormous van, looking more beautiful than ever? Because if this is another business proposition, I'm not sure if I can take it." Paul rakes a hand through his dark hair and finally looks into April's eyes with his familiar intensity. "I'll do it. You know I'll do it. If it means that you get one less mean email, or if you fall asleep a little sooner at night, of course I will. But just know what you're asking of me, to act like one of your clients instead of the guy who thought of you every day for twenty years and seems destined to do it for twenty more."

April catches her breath. Of course Paul thinks she's there to use him again. Showing up out of the blue is the move of a desperate businesswoman, not just a stupidly naive person in love. She hid behind the work excuse in Paris. She's hiding behind it now, using Gabriel and Maypole as a protective shield.

"I was so happy when you texted me," says April slowly. She wants to smooth the anxious creases in Paul's forehead as quickly as possible. "It helped to know that you were out there and thought of me sometimes. Maybe part of me just always counted on you being out there and thinking of me, and I'm sorry for that."

Paul's tense shoulders relax slightly. "I'm sorry, too," he says. "There are a lot of things I wish I'd done differently. I've gotten in the habit over the years of trying to take care of people, but I don't always think about what they really need. I think I did that with you."

"No, Paul, that's not…," protests April before Paul cuts her off.

"I told Gabriel I left Paris because of a family emergency, but I didn't want anyone to know exactly what happened, especially after I screwed it up so badly. I left because my brother Tommy was in a car accident."

"Paul!" gasps April. "Is he okay?"

"Yes, but no thanks to me. I accused him of being drunk when he wasn't, and I tried to fix things when I needed to just sit by his hospital bed and hold his hand," says Paul. April wants nothing more than to gently remove those glasses and kiss his sad, dark eyes, but she knows he has to finish this story. They both need to say everything for once. "Honestly, I left Paris because of Tommy, but I also thought I was doing you a favor. I couldn't help you get your business back once Heart2Heart called everything off, so I might as well just disappear."

"It turns out I'm pretty good at taking care of myself," says April softly. "That doesn't have to be your job. Maybe I could take care of you a little."

"I'd like that," says Paul. He looks at her again like he might finally touch her before hesitating. "Uh, what's in the box?"

April still clutches the precious box, probably way too tightly. She catches a glimpse of mustard yellow through a doorway behind Paul. Maybe this is the key to showing him how she wants every part of him. She's never opened her heart the way he deserves, the way she truly wants to, and it's time. Paul has to know that he can trust her—flighty, moody, April—with his home and with his precious heart.

"May I?" asks April, glancing at the doorway. Paul looks confused but nods, and April strides through the dining room (beautiful old butternut table covered with papers and a laptop) and into the kitchen. The matching countertops, appliances, and wall color feel familiar from Paul's photos, but the room throbs with life and history. Of course it's old-fashioned, maybe over-the-top even by the standards of its era, but it's also vibrant and unique. April groans with pleasure, sighing "I can't wait to get my hands all over this." She catches herself, watching Paul's ears turn red. Her good design moans are uncomfortably close to her sex moans.

"I know it's bad," says Paul. "I get why it's perfect for the website. But maybe you don't have to change everything? My mother was so proud of this kitchen. Sometimes it's nice to sit in here and remember her."

April sets down her box on the table and faces him. "Paul, your kitchen is beautiful."

Paul looks surprised, maybe even a little amused. "You, the home stager, think my ancient kitchen is beautiful."

"Absolutely. It's definitely vintage, but it's also full of warmth and attention to detail. Like that phone over there." She gestures to a perfectly coordinated mustard yellow phone on the wall. "It's got an extra long cord and everything, so the lady of the house can gossip with her friends while broiling the lamb chops and opening a can of peas."

Paul smiles, as if remembering his mother doing exactly that.

"Of course, it needs some freshening up," says April. "We'll have to upgrade the appliances to some modern, energy efficient styles, and we'll probably have to go stainless steel, since they don't seem to make fridges in the color any more. But I don't want to lose the warmth and sweetness."

Paul's eyes sweep around his kitchen, like he sees it for the first time. Then he looks at April with the same wonder, like she's a familiar sight but also brand new. April looks back, taking in every inch of him—the broad shoulders just made to rest your cheek on when slow dancing, the dark hair that needs a trim, the dark eyes behind the stupid sexy glasses. As she sees him in his own home, April knows Paul, knows him deep and true. She sees his loyalty to his family here in this kitchen, and how he keeps his mother's memory with him. She also sees the loneliness in that as Paul neglects his own needs. She wants to be the one who gives him back as much as he gives to her. For once she isn't frightened to show a man her whole heart and how much she can love.

"I brought you something," says April, setting the box on the kitchen table. She opens it carefully, taking her time now, and sets the turquoise pitcher from the flea market on the counter. "See how the contrast makes both colors more vibrant?" Just that small touch is already bringing the kitchen to life.

Paul starts to reach for the pitcher before he catches himself, retreating back to his earlier stiffness. "So when are the photographers coming?" he asks.

"Photographers?" repeats April. She wants to pull more treasures out of her box, like that framed vintage postcard of the girl with the parasol, but Paul's face is like a door slowly closing.

"Will there be a whole camera crew? And I assume they'll have to go over both times in Paris for background? I just don't want them to talk to my family."

"Oh, Paul," April says. "There aren't any photographers coming. Gabriel's not coming. My business is doing fine, everyone has pretty much moved on. And I'm working on more projects that feel like me, with colors and wallpaper and things I love, and people are really liking it. When I'm done with your house, I'll take some pictures and send them to Gabriel for the Maypole website, but they don't even have to use your name."

Paul finally looks at her the way April has been willing him to all along, with an edge of hope and hunger in his dark eyes. So she does what she does best and keeps talking.

"I should have told you the first moment I saw you—I'm here for you, just you. You've always been there for me, all those years. Something about that time we spent together twenty years ago burned its way into my brain and spoiled me for anyone else. We were just kids, but you showed me so much about what it meant to care for someone, and to put their needs first. I spent the next twenty years telling myself that I was too, well, just too much to be worthy of love, but I always knew deep down that someone had loved me once."

"April," says Paul hoarsely. His hands move nervously, and he picks up the turquoise pitcher from the table and presses it to his chest. April watches his careful hands holding her offering against his heart, and any last trace of hesitation melts away.

"When I saw you again in Paris, all the same feelings came flooding back," says April, trying to keep her voice steady. "And it wrecked me, to remember how I hurt you by disappearing like that, and to think about why I always push people away. When you left, it felt like poetic justice, like I was getting what I deserved all along. But now I'm done with thinking that way." She takes a step towards Paul and gently puts her hand over the pitcher. It's already warm from his body.

"Paul, I love your kitchen. It's solid and warm. I don't want to change it, but I thought maybe I could bring a little fun and pops of color." She takes a deep breath, her body tingling with nerves. "I love you. I've loved you since I was twenty-one, and I don't want us to lose any more time. Do you think there's some way—any way—for us to try?"

Paul holds himself very still, looking down at the pitcher. April doesn't even dare to breathe as she wills Paul to accept her offering and *her* right along with it. Finally, she feels his hand one cover hers with perfect warmth over the pitcher. "April, my April," he says, "I love you. It's painfully obvious that I've always loved you from far away. But that's not enough anymore."

Paul sets the pitcher on the table and brushes his fingers against April's cheek. "I need you by my side, in this kitchen or out of it. I need you, I want you, I love you." His other hand wraps around her waist as he presses forward and kisses her, all so perfectly warm and solid and steady. Her Paul. His kiss has all the excitement and passion of the first time on the Eiffel Tower at sunset, but with a luxuriant slowness of knowing they have time. April lets herself have this perfect moment, kissing and being kissed while all the tension melts from her body, and she grips his soft t-shirt to keep from melting to the floor.

April feels something tickling around her feet and startles. The prim little dog sniffs her ankles, looking a bit skeptical of this PDA. Paul is dazed and happy. He takes April's hand and brushes his lips along her fingers. "I want to sweep you off your feet and carry you upstairs."

April imagines how she must look: flushed, lips swollen from kisses, eyes flashing with growing desire deep in her belly. She bats her eyelashes innocently. "Oh, so you want some decorating advice for your bedroom? I have one word for you: throw pillows." She trails a finger across Paul's solid chest as his eyes widen.

"That's two words." He wraps her in his arms again and kisses her until her knees give out. "You look good in this kitchen. The yellow stove brings out the highlights in your hair."

"I'd look even better in this mythical bedroom you keep going on and on about."

Paul laughs, more loose and free than April has ever heard. "You home stagers are all the same," he says. "Worming your way into a poor man's home and talking seductively about throw pillows until he has no choice but to take you to bed."

April takes Paul's hand and leads him towards the stairs, attempting a seductive wink that's more like a grimace but totally worth it to hear Paul's laugh again. She pulls him up the stairs, not entirely sure where she's going but pretty sure they're heading in the right direction. Paul is content to follow, confident in April to find their way.

First door on the right. A neatly made bed with a navy blue duvet and not a throw pillow in sight. A bureau, a single framed photo taken in front of this same house of an unmistakable young Paul with mother, father, sister, brother. Another space of Paul's where April feels immediately at home. She leans back and sprawls on the bed, her skin, her entire body buzzing with electricity to be with Paul. It all feels so new, yet at the same time so natural.

Paul stands next to the bed, staring down at her with fond eyes, and April wriggles and preens for him.

"You should kiss me," says April. "You should kiss me a lot. Why aren't you kissing me?"

"Because I need to look at you first." His voice is deep and gravelly, and April shivers. His husky voice and the way he runs his thumb over his bottom lip is too much. She unbuttons her jeans.

"Then look," she says.

Strange to feel so wanton, and so safe. She remembers this—Paul's intense focus, his parted lips, his taut stillness as he watches the movements of her hand and listens to her panting breath. His arousal is hers, her building pleasure is his. April can't believe how fast it's happening, how high she is already flying. What if she crashes? What if this breaks her into a million little pieces that can't come back together? But Paul is there, sliding onto the bed beside her, holding her so tight so she can completely let go.

"I need…" hisses April. Paul presses into her side, warm and solid and as crazy turned on as she is, but it's not enough. April wants his skin on hers, his moans in her ear. She tries again, a tangle of words trying to form a thought while her other hand strokes him over his shorts. "I want…now…damn glasses…please."

Paul presses into her hand and gives a groan that makes April's growing need twice as urgent. She needs every part of him, and to give him every bit of her.

"Yes," he murmurs. "Oh, April."

He pulls away to open the nightstand drawer while April mutters in protest at the loss of his touch. She forces herself to slow her movements, her fingers now tormenting her slick wetness, while she waits for Paul.

"Jesus," he says, pulling out a comically endless line of condoms.

"And I thought you weren't expecting me," says April, her breath still ragged.

"My sister…"

"What's with you always talking about your sister instead of taking off my pants?"

Paul grins. The glasses finally come off. April wants to protest but Clark Kent is turning into Superman, and Paul pulls his shirt over his head and gets to work on April's jeans. His hot mouth finds her hip bone, her breasts, her neck, while their clothes disappear. April moves her hand to help but Paul covers it with his. "Don't stop," he says. "I love to watch you."

"Yes," sighs April. "Yes, but… I need you, too." She's greedy for everything: his touch, his mouth, her own fingers. She wants it all and all at once. She wants so much, but she knows it's not too much for Paul. She feels his smile against her neck, hears the crinkle of the condom wrapper, and then she feels…oh my God, she feels. Paul moves with her, pressing against her fingers with each thrust while his hands trace her breasts and tangle in her hair.

April's pleasure builds and builds, but she isn't scared anymore. She can ride this wave forever, their bodies moving together, their breath and their moans in joyful conversation. When April finally comes she doesn't hold back her cries and shudders because Paul holds her, keeping her from flying off the spinning planet.

Afterwards she keeps shaking, and Paul covers her body with his.

"Don't let go," she says.

"Never. I love you." He presses her into the mattress while her body grows loose and lazy, like warm honey in her veins.

"I just need to ask you something," says Paul, gently brushing his lips to April's ear while his body melts over hers.

"Hmm?" sighs April, tracing her fingers along his ribs.

Paul props himself up on one arm, his eyes dark and serious. "Any decorating tips for the bedroom?" She feels the laughter rising in his body before she hears it. Paul's joy is a precious gift that she wants to earn every day.

"Well," says April, as seriously as she can while a grin tugs at her mouth, "Maybe some white linen curtains, a framed art poster above the bureau...and my clothes look pretty fucking good on your floor."

Paul nips her neck. "You're the expert. But your clothes would look good on any floor. Especially with my gift for tossing them there."

April sighs happily and pulls Paul close. They've missed those years, but there's still so much ahead of them. Paris was just the prologue.

Epilogue

From the air, it is the Arc de Triomphe that appears as the heart of Paris, a hub with roads jutting out like spokes of a wheel. But as stately as it is, no one spends their life longing to return to l'Arc de Triomphe. It is the Tour Eiffel, hovering off to the side, that inhabits our dreams. Sometimes at night, sparkling with lights, sometimes a ghost in the fog, sometimes a thrilling surprise when you round a corner and it springs seemingly out of nowhere. Sometimes a picture on a postcard.

Just about everyone has seen the Eiffel Tower in some form, but only a very few have taken in the view from the top. And sometimes you meet the right person at the wrong time (or the right person at the right time but you're just too dumb to know it.) So not to hit you over the head with a metaphor, but maybe it's not all about the view *from* the Eiffel Tower, but the view *of* the Eiffel Tower. Sometimes you need a little distance to appreciate true beauty.

Here's the thing—people fall in love all over the world, not just in Paris. They fall in love in office buildings, in prisons, at the grocery store, in dance clubs where you can't even hear each other talk, and even in the hellscape of high school. So maybe we shouldn't be surprised that it took a dated kitchen in Winnipeg, Manitoba for dark-eyed Paul and long-limbed April to finally realize that not only did they love the other person, but that same other person loved them back.

Six Months Later

"I vote for the striped one," says Paul. He's lying on April's bed—well, *their* bed—with April next to him, paging through a book of wallpaper samples. They're burrowed under the covers at noon on a Sunday, April taking advantage of hearty Paul's bed warming skills against the December chill.

"Really?" says April. "I was leaning towards the one with the animals. It reminds me of a medieval tapestry." They're making plans to decorate the bedroom. Paul likes the nine yellow paint stripes on the wall, but April says she's ready to move on. And instead of settling on one of the yellows, she's called in a different direction.

"Exactly. I don't want a bunch of deer looking at us." He slides the book off of April's lap and rolls on his side, stroking her cheek and enjoying her cool gray eyes. "When is Danny dropping off Liza?"

"Soon," says April. "She texted me that she has big plans for a *Drag Race* marathon this afternoon."

Danny is startlingly friendly to Paul, asking him to play tennis and even inviting him to a Red Sox game, but Paul is trying to tread as lightly as possible on Danny and April's co-parenting. Liza was quiet around him at first, but she started chatting when he asked about her favorite queens on *Rupaul's Drag Race* and then never really stopped. She's even watched a few hockey games with him in return.

"Why are they fighting?" Liza asks during a particularly rough match up with Winnipeg and Montreal.

April looks up from editing photos on her laptop. "Number 24 cross-checked our right wing, so he needs to be taught a lesson, sweetie. That's when the enforcer steps in. It's his unofficial job to fight so the pretty boy forwards don't

300

get hurt or get penalties. But really they fight so they don't accidentally start kissing." She winks at Paul and returns to her photos, and Paul remembers for the hundredth time that life with April means getting his world view skewed a little sideways.

Like here, now, in *their* bed, as he strokes April's hair and realizes deer in the wallpaper might be kind of neat after all.

"Teresa is so excited we're coming for Christmas," he says. "I'm supposed to tell you that she misses you, and she can't wait to meet Liza."

"Aww, I can't wait to see her. Are you sure Matty will like that Bruins jersey?"

"He'll love it."

They'd had four blissful days back in late June where April made various small changes to his house that somehow brought it to life. Paul was her assistant, unpacking the Maypole boxes, moving furniture around, and patiently holding picture frames while she decided if they were straight. Plus frequent breaks to tear each other's clothes off and get pushed down on the new couch, or hoist April on the kitchen counter, or even a few times to toss aside all the new throw pillows on his bed.

At the end of four days, two things were absolutely clear: they had to be together, and April needed to stay near Liza and Danny. So this time it was Paul packing a suitcase and heading off for the unknown. Sid agreed to keep Muffin until he got settled, and Tommy and Simone moved into the house when Tommy's lease was up, to keep the pipes from freezing as autumn moved in. Simone loves the retro kitchen, and Tommy promises to keep the bushes trimmed with Sid's supervision. Paul still does the Stone Dry Cleaning taxes and accounting from his new home office (well, a corner of the guest room) in Massachusetts, but he's thinking for the first time in his life about what he really wants to do. He's surprised to realize he wants to be a teacher, and registered for a program that focuses on training mid-career adults to transition their skills and experience to the classroom.

For the first time in his life, Paul isn't trying to be happy. He just…is. He misses Tommy, and Teresa, and Matty, and Sid, but he talks to them a lot and hopes to have Matty visit over the summer. Life with April is, well, a total joy. Every morning that he wakes up to her hair wild from sleep, he can't believe that he's gone from the man who tried not to make waves to the man who gets to wake up with April Andersen every morning.

"Are you still up for New Year's Eve in New York with Gabriel and Selma? Selma promises that her dogs won't try to sleep with us, but they probably will. And Gabriel's so hyperfocused on his party. He texted me yesterday telling me not to even think of wearing a hat. And I wasn't even going to wear a hat, just that little fascinator with the white feathers!" April is so indignant that Paul doesn't ask what on earth was a fascinator. "Selma and I have a theory that he's desperately trying to impress someone."

"Really?" said Paul. "Do you think he's overdoing it?"

April gives him that little look, the one that says *Remember, other people don't need you to manage their lives.* Paul kisses her pretty fingers. "Maybe he's throwing us a surprise wedding." He and April know they're getting married someday and that at some point visa issues will make it urgent, but for Liza's sake it seems better to take it slow.

April cackles. "Can you imagine the look on his face, if I show up to his party in a wedding dress? I think it might actually kill him—but of course he'd kill me first."

"Is he dating anyone?"

"I wish," says April. "He's looking for someone like him. A fellow inner core of sweetness surrounded by neurotic miasma, but that's a recipe for disaster."

"Give him twenty years or so to figure it out." Paul gets out of bed, stretches, and checks out the window overlooking the street, keeping an eye out for Danny delivering Liza. "Hey, it's snowing." He holds out an arm for April to slip by his side.

"The first snow is always magic," says April. "The world becomes so sparkling and quiet."

"I've never seen you in the snow," says Paul. "I've never seen you decorate the Christmas tree, or kissed you on New Year's Eve, or shoveled your sidewalk. Our sidewalk. And I can't wait to do all those things."

"Me, too," says April.

December in New England. Early sunsets. Long dark nights made joyful by holiday decorations—April loves the ones with colorful flashing lights. Life here is just as lovely as Paris in June, with its tower and its bridges and elegant women in sleeveless dresses. It doesn't matter where Paul goes, everywhere is beautiful with April by his side.

THE END

Acknowledgements

Warmest thanks to the family and community that supported me while writing this book. First, of course, is my husband Jim, who has always been my rock and my cheerleader. Our children Charlie and Sonia impress and delight me every day.

Ellen Shershow, I could write ten books about our 1990s European tour. Thanks for your generosity for letting me raid your memories and for many years of friendship.

Pia Owens made this book better. She cheerfully read endless drafts with astonishing speed, making all kinds of insightful comments along the way. I might still be figuring out the ending if not for our Friday morning writing group of two.

Kristin Caulfield's love of Paris is contagious, and I hope we can still talk about all things French after this. Her eye for design and color elevated my website and marketing materials. Thank you!.

My Sunday morning walking group enthusiastically listened to me talk about this project for so many laps around Fresh Pond. I'm thankful for each and every one of you.

My brother Nicholas and my parents Ann and Geoff have provided a lifetime of love and support.

My mother especially always saw me as a writer, even before I did. Thank you for believing in me, and for your contagious enthusiasm in welcoming April and Paul to the world.

About the Author

Jessica Clem Barnard lives and writes outside of Boston. *April in Paris in June* is her first novel. For writing news and general thoughts on life, you can find her on Instagram at @jessicaclembarnard.

Want to learn how Gabriel goes from broke and jobless after Paris to starring on a dating show? Sign up for Jessica's newsletter at <u>www.jessicajbarnard.com</u> for updates on *Becoming Mr. Right.*